LITTLE BLUE BOX

AUSTRALIAN AT HEART BOOK 1

FRANCES DALL'ALBA

Poinsettia
Publishing

ALSO BY FRANCES DALL'ALBA

<u>Australian At Heart Series</u>
Little Blue Box – Book 1
The Stone In The Road – Book 2
The Silk Scarf – Book 3
Rustic Denim Love – Book 4

<u>Sway of The Stars Series</u>
The Shooting Star – Book 1
The Glittering Star – Book 2
The Giving Star - Book 3
The Priceless Star – Book 4

<u>Standalones</u>
Eight Seconds
Jack & Eva

LITTLE BLUE BOX

Print ISBN: 978-0-6451162-0-5

For my family, David, Julia, Emma and Sarah, for all your generous support.

And for Lisa — my critique partner and friend. We started this journey not knowing where it would lead us, and look at us now!

Chapter 1

Ella Harvey dialled her mother's number and slipped the phone into the pocket of her work pants. She adjusted the bluetooth earpiece before tugging at a jammed shopping trolley.

She made her way inside as her mother answered. "Hey, Mum," Ella announced first.

"Ella, darling. How are you?"

"I'm fine, just buying some groceries."

"What do you mean? Aren't you at work?"

Ella directed the trolley to the meat section. "I'm taking the rest of the day off."

"You feeling okay?"

"Yeah, sure. I wanted to be close in case you or Victoria needed me. Has she started chemo yet?"

"They're a little behind and your sister didn't think it was worth driving all the way back home. So, we'll wait it out here at the hospital."

Ella swore.

"What's wrong?"

"You'd think I could control a shopping trolley, wouldn't you? I swear the damn wheels on this thing are designed to move in different directions. God help us, why hasn't an engineer designed something that works?"

Her mother's laughter filtered through the speaker. It was good to hear her laugh. Her natural cheerfulness had been lost in all the turmoil lately.

"That's because you prefer to design bridges, culverts and sewerage systems."

"Okay, point taken." Ella chuckled. Her mother was spot-on. As a civil engineer, Ella fell in love with bridges more often than men.

"Thanks for thinking of your sister today. She'll get through this."

Ella swallowed. She loved her mother and siblings, more so since Victoria's diagnosis. "I'm going to put dinner on early and then do some house cleaning for you."

"I'll appreciate a nice hot meal but don't overdo it. Some days there are more important things to worry about, like that report you have to finish."

Ella jerked the trolley to a stop in the next aisle. "Yeah, nearly done. I'll work on it this afternoon from home." Ella selected a couple of avocados before moving the reluctant trolley towards the ingredients for a salad. "Ring me when Vic's started her chemo."

"I will. Now not too much cleaning, okay? Catch up on your report. I know how important your work is to you."

Ella's chest swelled with pride. She *did* love her job. She often bounced ideas off her mother. Sometimes she got so caught up in numbers and calculations she missed the common-sense things. Her mother was the perfect sounding-board.

"I will."

"And thanks, Ella. Drive carefully."

"Nah, where's the fun in that?"

"Ella!" her mother admonished.

"Relax, mum. As if." They both laughed as Ella tapped her bluetooth earpiece to end the call.

Ella teetered on the ladder shoved against the top shelf of her mother's wardrobe. She sneezed hard. Years of accumulated dust tickled her eyes and clogged her throat as she tossed woollen blankets, dresses and shoe boxes into a pile on the floor. Having put dinner in the slow cooker, she was determined to give her mother's room a thorough clean, then freshen the bed with the new quilt cover she'd purchased last-minute, after finishing her grocery shopping.

It was hard to believe her twenty-two-year-old sister, who was four years younger than her, had been diagnosed with lymphoma. The news had rocked their family again. Only six months ago her stepfather's death had shattered their lives. Her mother deserved something nice for a change.

She swiped the wet rag in the shadowed corner one last time and something slid across the shelf. She pulled it closer and spied a small cardboard box, yellowed and stained, obviously long forgotten. She shook it gently and something rattled inside.

Curious, Ella climbed down and placed the box on the worn bedspread. She bit her lip and fingered the cracked tape that had curled away from the edges of the lid. What was inside? Old love letters from her dad or forgotten mementos of her mother's youth?

Ella blinked back tears. *Damn it. If only Dad was here now.*

As much as she itched to look inside, she knew she should wait. She gave it another gentle shake then put it down again. But it taunted her. What was in there?

She groaned before picking up the box and heading for the kitchen. A glass of water to clear her throat was in order. What harm was there in having a quick peek inside, anyway?

The afternoon sun streamed in through the kitchen window, starting to make a show. The lawn needed to be mowed; she considered pull-starting the old mower and doing the job. It wouldn't take her more than half an hour.

She poured water into a chipped mug that had been her father's favourite and sat down on a stool in the kitchen. She took a sip and eyed the box, ran a finger over the top and removed a thick layer of dust. Technically, she wasn't breaking into it. The tape, once used to keep it closed, had dried and no longer stuck. She could have a quick peek and return it safely to its spot. No harm done.

Gently, she pried at the lid, disturbing more dust. At first it was reluctant to come off, but with a bit more encouragement, she levered it off, taking care not to damage it and give herself away.

When she peered inside, she frowned. On top sat a photo of her mother. She looked young and stunning, most likely in her early twenties. Her light honey-coloured shoulder-length hair and make-up had been expertly done.

"Mum, a blonde?"

Ella had only known her mother with chestnut-brown hair. Which was her natural colour? She peered closer. Who was the exotic dark-haired woman beside her? It wasn't someone Ella recognised.

She put the photo aside and reached in for a little blue box. She cradled it on her palm and lifted the lid. Inside was a delicate gold baby's bracelet nestled on top of a square of white silk. Noticing an inscription, she held it up to the light. *Isabella, 16 May 1990.*

She gasped and dropped the bracelet back into the box. That was her date of birth. But Isabella? Her birth certificate clearly stated her name was Ella. Who was Isabella?

Her hand shook as she picked the bracelet up again. Her fingers tangled around the chain, a thousand questions running around her head. Did she have a twin born on the same day? Surely her mother wouldn't have kept something that significant a secret?

She gazed intently at the bracelet, unable to break the connection. She had no recollection of ever wearing it, but then again, she'd have been a baby. But Isabella? What the ...? Was it a coincidence her name was a shortened version of Isabella?

Her vision blurred. The longer she stared, the harder it was to make sense of anything.

She shook her head to clear the fuzziness and put the bracelet back. Not sure what to think, she picked up the last item in the box. It was a photo of a baby clipped from a newspaper. No details were offered. It appeared as though someone had cut around other figures in the picture, and any words that may have been written below the baby had also been lopped off.

She frowned and placed everything back the way she'd found it. A sickening sensation swirled in her stomach.

And there it was, the problem she'd faced. The identity of her biological father. The only thing she couldn't discuss with her mother. From as far back as she could remember, every time Ella broached the subject her mother tensed, quickly grew upset and ended up in tears. Ella had learned from her early teen years to keep her mouth shut, but the need to discover his identity *never* left her.

She promised herself that one day she would find him. How she expected to do so without a single clue had kept her awake at night. Did this small box finally present some clues?

Her initial reaction was that the baby in the newspaper photo was her. It was hard to be certain, because one baby looked like another. And the oldest photos Ella had seen of herself had been taken when she was aged three. Her mother's excuse over the years that she hadn't owned a camera before then sounded reasonable. So why had she kept this one hidden? If the baby wasn't her, who was it? Not her half-siblings, because she'd seen heaps of those.

What if the woman beside her mother in the photo could help her? Who was she? How could Ella find out without asking her mother? She had nowhere to start. No name, no family, nothing. She cursed under her breath and fisted her hands in her hair. The contents of this box stirred up something deeply emotional in her and left her with no choice but to find an answer to the question once and for all.

Ella jumped when the phone shrilled behind her. She stumbled back but caught the stool before it crashed to the tiled floor.

"H-hello," she stammered when the handpiece was close enough.

"Darling, it's Mum."

Startled, Ella dropped the handpiece, saving it at the last minute with her foot. "Mum, I'm still here," she called out as she bent down to pick it up.

"Is everything okay?"

With the phone against her ear again, Ella's heart pounded. She was sure someone had caught her out. "Yes, Mum, everything's fine. Sorry, I dropped the phone."

"Okay. We're a couple of hours from getting home. Victoria's chemo just started."

"Are you in the same room?" Ella asked.

"No, I've gone in search of a toilet and a coffee. I told Vic I'd be back in a few minutes."

Ella didn't respond immediately.

"Ella?"

"I'm here, Mum."

"I was confident earlier today, but now I'm really scared for her," her mum said, sounding tired.

Ella slid to the floor, her face resting on her raised knees. "Oh, Mum."

"I know. It'll be difficult for her."

Ella rocked back and forth and closed her eyes. What was she supposed to say? Now that the reality of Victoria's second session of chemo had begun, new worries crept in. She'd been so sick after the last round. This time she would lose her beautiful hair. No doubt Ella's mother was just as worried.

She lent strength to her mother by being there. Most days it was enough. She'd always been able to communicate with her mother, without excess words—except, of course, on that one subject.

Ella rose and stretched. She sat on the kitchen stool again and rested her elbows on the bench. The phone was still pressed against her ear. "I better let you get back to Victoria."

"Okay, we'll talk later. And thanks, Ella. Thanks for being there."

"No worries, Mum. Bye."

Ella put the handpiece down but continued to sit, dazed. She cradled her head and roughly massaged her scalp. Her thoughts were scattered. With her family in such a fragile state, she didn't want anything new to upset it.

She loved living with her mother and siblings in their Brisbane home. The laughter, the fun, and all things family. With her much-loved stepfather no longer around, it was more important that she remain close.

Did she really want to learn what her mother was hiding? Would her mother resent her if she unearthed secrets better left buried?

She didn't doubt her mother would confiscate the little box and the clues it contained if Ella told her she'd discovered it. Her heart-wrenching fear of never finding her father forced her decision to go it alone. Better for everyone if her mother didn't know she was looking.

She dragged the cardboard box closer. She turned it in circles, the cogs in her mind clicking over. Maybe she should search for the woman in the photo first. See if that led anywhere.

❦

Zane Peden looked up when his grey-haired boss poked his head around the office door.

"Don't forget you have a client in fifteen minutes. Sorry to do this to you, but I'm on grandad duty this afternoon. I have to collect the grandkids from school and I'm running late. Thanks for holding the fort."

Zane scraped his chair back and stood. "But I've organised coffee with friends. I thought I'd said something to Joanne."

"Son, I leave all the appointment scheduling to Joanne. She's the best office manager I've ever had, so I don't interfere. Apparently, you're the only one left on the floor."

There's no point in being irritated.

"Gotta go, bye."

Zane ran his hand through his hair and sighed. It was time to let go of his irritation at the change of plans. It wasn't a big deal and he couldn't afford not to work. Mr Wilson was flexible with Zane's criminology studies, allowing him to fit in his lectures when needed. With six months to go before he graduated, Zane had no choice but to work as many hours as possible.

He wheeled his chair back under the desk and picked up the phone. Disguising his annoyance, he connected with the front office and asked, "Joanne, what can you tell me about my next client?"

"The only details I have is that it's a woman searching for her father."

"Thanks. Send her in when she arrives." He replaced the handset and, taking his mobile phone from his jacket, sent a message to his mate, Dave.

Sorry, can't do coffee. Boss has me tied up. Can we try again next week?

Dave had been trying for weeks to set up a date. According to him, his new housemate was the answer to ending Zane's single days.

Zane pressed send and frowned. It had been a while, but life was hectic. Between studying, working part-time for an investigative company and spending time with his bustling and busy family, his days were full. He shrugged and ignored Dave's warnings that he was missing out on all the action.

There'd be time enough when he finished his degree, he thought, quickly tidying his desk in preparation for the next interview. He hoped like hell the case was an easy one. Something he could do with his eyes shut, which was possible as long as the client gave him all the necessary clues. This scenario was pretty common. A woman in her early fifties and divorced, her kids out of her hair physically but not financially, and there'd be a good chance she was going through a mid-life crisis. Finding her father would be the cure ...

Yeah, right.

He rose and made for the water cooler. He'd been in this game for too long and couldn't wait to get a new job. His few years as a police officer didn't count. As much as he respected the work, it wasn't for him.

Ten minutes later a knock sounded on his door.

"Come in." Zane rose when the door opened. His eyes widened. He'd severely misjudged the client's age bracket.

He walked around his desk and extended a hand. "Zane Peden."

At the touch of her soft skin, he forgot to shake. His gaze connected with her blue eyes, the same shade as the Ulysses butterfly. Something about her had him wondering if they'd crossed paths before. He rarely forgot a face.

Her attempts at a handshake jolted him out of his daze. Tactfully, she untangled her fingers from his and took a step back. He coughed to give his hand something to do. Plus, to give his head time to cooperate before he said something dumb. "Ah, Miss—?"

"Ella Harvey."

He pointed to the chair opposite his desk. "Please take a seat." *Nice work, mate. You definitely need to get back in the game.*

Zane tried not to stare too intently at her face, and yet his gaze was dragged back to her incredible eyes. She settled in the chair and crossed one leg gracefully over the other. He dropped his gaze to follow her movement.

Eyes back up—fast.

He gathered a notepad and pen from his drawer. Then counted to three as he shuffled papers on his desk and instructed his head to bloody sort itself out. Hers wasn't the first pretty face he'd dealt with over the years. At twenty-six, why the fuss now? He forced his arms to stop their nervous movement and took a deep breath. "So, Miss Harvey. How can I help you?"

Her hands lay on a small package that was resting on her lap against her smart magenta blouse. "I want to find my father."

While she unwrapped the package, he used the opportunity to take in her delicate features. A frown marred her pretty oval face as she concentrated on the task. Zane followed her small nose, which sat between high cheekbones, down to her soft chin. It *had* been a long time since he'd cupped a chin that alluring in his palm.

When she placed the small cardboard box on his desk it shook him out of his reverie.

"Miss Harvey, we'll do some housekeeping first. I have some basic questions we require you to answer and then you can tell us what information you have."

She nodded, her light honey hair framing her face. "Please, call me Ella."

With the package off her lap, she appeared more relaxed. Dimples emerged out of nowhere, either side of her smile.

He reached for their standard interview form used for first visits. "Okay, Ella, we'll start off with some basic stuff."

Zane wrote her name, checked for spelling, then asked for her address, contact phone numbers and email address. He snuck a peek when he asked if she was married or living in a de facto relationship. When she shook her head, his hand momentarily froze. He forced it back into action and ticked the 'no' box before turning to the next page.

"Now, we're going to run through a list of questions relating to your mother."

As she leaned closer to his desk, a waft of lemon and eucalyptus came his way. He inhaled its freshness before beginning on the next questions.

They ranged from where her mother had been born, to where she'd grown up and gone to school, to whether her parents were still alive.

He turned the page and asked Ella questions about her mother's career, where she may have worked, what age she'd conceived, where Ella had been born and where she'd grown up. By page four, Zane realised there were few questions Ella could answer. Her mother's early years, before she'd married, appeared to be a mystery.

He put the pen down and smothered a sigh. It was futile to ask questions about her father. Instead, he said, "Tell me what you know."

Ella exhaled and sat back. "I no longer accept my mother's explanation. She lived her life in and out of foster homes and admitted to doing a lot of crazy stuff in her early twenties. She told me she'd gone camping with a friend and some people she didn't know. That night she got drunk and doesn't remember much. She was five months along when she discovered she was pregnant but was reluctant to search for the father. It wasn't until she met my stepfather that she got her life on track. She's never wavered from this story but I feel like she's hiding something. Every time I broach the subject she gets upset."

"So why do you want to search for him now?"

Her fingers knotted in her lap as her gaze wandered towards the window. "I've always belonged to my family in every sense. I have three half-siblings, Victoria, Luke and Lily, but I need to know who *my* blood ties are," she admitted, turning back to him.

He let her take her time to get her thoughts together as he feasted on her face. When she started talking again, he berated his inattentive mind and switched his focus back to her words.

"My stepfather was everything I needed in a dad. I loved him, and I know he loved me no less than my half-siblings. Six months ago, he died in a workplace accident. If that wasn't bad enough, Victoria has since been diagnosed with lymphoma."

Zane nodded and let her talk without interruption. This kind of information helped put the whole picture into perspective.

"There's no history of cancer on either side of the family, but I want to find out what genes, good or bad, I carry from my biological father. A simple genetics test would be sufficient, but I want more. I know I've let it ride for years, but the other day I came across this small box hidden in my mother's wardrobe." She pointed to the box on his desk. "I hope the items inside might hold some clues. My mother doesn't know I have it because I don't want to cause further stress for her. With Victoria in and out of hospital, my coming to you won't go down well. Anything you uncover, I'd like it kept confidential."

Drawn in by her gaze, he nodded. "The information you have on your mother is limited. Sometimes it can be difficult to track the history of fostered kids, and not knowing your father's name will make things tricky. Is there any way you could find out where your mother was living when she went on that camping trip? What about a copy of her birth certificate and your own?"

She bit her bottom lip as her hand twisted the lapel of her blouse. "I'll glean what I can, but it's always a battle. As for her birth certificate, I'll have to scout around for it in her drawers. It'll be somewhere. I have a copy of mine I can get for you."

"Great. Now do you want to show me what's in the box?"

She handled the box carefully. After she'd removed the lid, she plucked out a small blue box. "Inside this is a baby bracelet. It's engraved with my date of birth and the name Isabella."

He frowned for the first time during the meeting. This wouldn't be a cut and dry investigation. His examination of the newspaper clipping, and her insistence it was a picture of her, further fuelled his growing unease.

"Are you concerned about what your mother hasn't told you?"

She looked down at her lap. "I love her. She's more than my mother, she's also my best friend. But something doesn't feel right, and I can't seem to let it go." She lifted her chin and added, "I want to find my father without having to ask her. Maybe later, once I have some answers, I can discuss it with her."

Zane wrote notes as he nodded. "Is there anything else in the box that might help?"

"Oh, there's this photo of my mother and a woman I don't recognise. I have no idea where to start searching for clues about who the woman might be."

She handed him the photo.

He froze. Stared at it until his vision blurred.

"Is everything okay?" she asked.

He leaned forward, wanting to ask her where the hell the photo had come from, but he unintentionally swept his chair backwards and it bumped into the wall, making enough noise that Ella yelped and jumped up with a worried crease on her face.

His fingers clenched the photo, though he was careful not to damage it. Wheeling himself back under the desk, he placed the photo on top.

Ella sat down again.

Zane wiped a sweaty palm against his pants while his heart thumped uncomfortably. He needed to come up with an explanation.

He looked at Ella and placated her with a shamed face. "My apologies. I accidentally kicked at the castor on my chair. I'll take some copies and photos of the items in a moment and then see you out."

He tried to compose himself, but his beating heart refused to slow down. Ella would notice something was amiss if he didn't get it together.

He handled the photo again and took a closer look. Ella was a clone of her mother. Now he understood why he thought he might have seen Ella before. This photo was a replica of the one sitting in his mother's china cabinet. For as long as his memory served, that photo had sat shoved towards the back, nestled between champagne glasses and judo trophies. Despite not having seen the photo for years, it was definitely the same one. His mother had told him years ago that the friend beside her in the photo had died shortly after it had been taken, in a car accident.

Except Ella's mother was very much alive.

Chapter 2

Half a block away from the investigator's office, Ella scrounged in her handbag for her car keys. The spring sun had some bite, and the full force of its heat pounded on her already tired head. She should be relieved that she'd taken the first step, but it only highlighted what little information she had.

"Where the hell are they?" In the busy street Ella shuffled things aside in her bag. They normally rattled enough to make finding them easy, but all she came across was her wallet, phone, lipstick, hand cream, receipts and some loose change. She frowned, holding the bag open to the light, to better see where they were.

I used them to lock the damn car.

With dismay and a rising sense of panic she realised the keys weren't in her bag.

Where did I drop them?

Had she left them at the reception desk?

She retraced her steps keeping her eyes to the pavement in case she'd dropped them on the way.

When she returned to the office, Ella expected to find the kindly middle-aged lady who'd taken care of her earlier, but she came up short when she found Mr Peden leaning over the front counter, handing paperwork to the receptionist. They both turned at her entrance.

"Miss Harvey?" Mr Peden spoke first. "Is everything okay?"

She looked up and took in all six feet of him. She'd have to admit her blunder sooner or later. *Damn*. Her face heated up—it wouldn't take long before her embarrassment became apparent.

"Did I leave my car keys here? I've misplaced them."

Mr Peden turned and shifted things on the front counter. "Joanne, have you come across any keys?"

Joanne shook her head.

"I'll take a look in my office."

When Mr Peden left, Joanne rose and did a scout of the reception area. She lifted cushions in the waiting room and tidied magazines on the coffee table. Ella's keys were nowhere to be found.

"Do you have a spare key at home?" Joanne asked.

Ella ran a hand through her hair. "I do."

"Can I offer to ring someone or organise a cab?"

Joanne was being thoughtful and kind. "Thank you, but I should be able to manage that." She looked at her watch and sighed.

Mr Peden returned and shook his head. "Sorry, no keys in my office. Did I hear you say you have a spare set at home? You don't live too far away. How about I give you a lift there and back?"

She looked up into chestnut-brown eyes. Her heart picked up pace the longer she stared. Of course. He knew all her personal information from her date of birth to phone numbers and address. With so much transparency, her tongue was reluctant to move.

"I'm going to be late getting back to work anyway," she managed. "I'll organise a cab."

"My car is parked in the basement. We can do the drive quickly enough."

Her feet remained frozen. This was awkward. Throw good looks into the mix and the last thing she wanted was to start their working relationship on the wrong foot. Was accepting a ride from him crossing the line and getting too personal?

Joanne came to the rescue as only a woman with intuition could. "Miss Harvey, I would trust my only daughter with Zane. Go on, you'll be back in a jiffy."

Huh. Had she really come across as being concerned about getting a lift with a stranger? To be honest, she was more worried about making a fool of herself. Put a gorgeous man in front of her and anything was possible. She might be proud of her ability to be a strong woman in the real world, but there were some instances in her past when a good-looking man had been her occasional downfall.

Zane turned to Joanne. "I'll lock up my office when I get back. See you soon."

Ella followed his tall and rugged form to the lifts. She reminded herself they had a business relationship. Ethically, any move made by either one of them would be wrong and distasteful. They didn't speak as the lift made its way to the ground floor, but she snuck a peek at his dark brown hair and olive complexion. What a shame, he looked damn good in his long-sleeved shirt and tie. She barely remembered her last boyfriend, though it was unlikely this man was unattached. Pity. Weren't all the good ones taken?

Stubble had already begun to show on his cheeks, though it was still early in the afternoon, and for some absurd reason, she wanted to rest her cheek against his to know what it felt like.

Okay, now this was beyond normal. Despite reacting as if she desperately needed a man, she'd learned to live without their constant presence. It certainly made life a lot less complicated. Well, it had in the past.

The doors slid open. He lifted an arm to keep them from closing and waited for her to leave first.

For a fraction of a second, she hesitated. "Thank you," she uttered, grateful he couldn't read her mind or see the way she blushed in the dim underground car park.

She gave him directions for the quickest way to her home then sat back. She was normally confident and a little bossy around men, constantly competing with her male peers for the right to work on different projects. She couldn't understand her discomposure with this one. *Maybe it's because he knows so much about me.* Should she strike up a conversation or sit back? Usually, she made an effort to be friendly with everyone around her. Why was she shy all of a sudden?

Impatient, she plunged in with the first thought that came into her head. "Have you always worked as an investigator?"

He flicked a glance her way as a red stoplight turned green. "I did a few years as a police officer first."

"Oh." That was unexpected. "What made you change?"

He chuckled as he shifted gears, slowing the vehicle as they approached another set of lights. "A bullet inside my rib cage helped."

She turned in her seat. "You were shot?"

He shrugged and took off again. "A domestic incident turned ugly. A few weeks in hospital was enough to convince me to try something new. I've nearly finished a degree in criminology and I'm looking forward to a job behind a desk."

Cripes. It always amazed her how a person could surprise you.

He talked a little more about what sort of work he wanted to do and before long turned into her street.

"Where do you work?" he asked, stopping the car in front of her modest family home.

She swung the door open, and put one foot out. "I'm a civil engineer with Cardillo & Hancock." She stepped out. "I won't be a minute."

"Nice," she heard him say.

⁂

Parked behind her white Mazda, she thanked him and awkwardly offered to pay him for his time.

He shook his head. "Don't be silly."

Ella stepped out of his car and watched him idle back into the traffic. He turned back for a split second and, to her embarrassment, caught her staring. He waved before disappearing into the traffic.

She groaned. Where had her confidence gone? *You're losing it girl. Once upon a time men shook in their boots around you. Now, not only do you shake but you stumble over your words, too.*

Time to push him to the back of her mind. Unless ... oh hell, she knew she would succumb. A bit of cyberstalking didn't hurt anyone. Five minutes on the Internet later that night and she would learn if he was attached or not. If he had a girlfriend, there'd surely be a photo to prove it.

She frowned as she stepped into her car. Maybe she *had* lost it. Sure, she'd had her share of boyfriends, but she hated that she was always in control around them. Just once, oh holy loving saint, she would love for the man to take control or make the first move. This wasn't easy to find in the engineering world she worked in, where she had to be tougher, stronger and more capable than the men around her, just to prove herself. This made them mean and she didn't want that. How would she ever find what was right for her?

⌘

Zane reached his floor and was met by a smiling Joanne.

"Guess what?"

His brows rose at her question. She could be referring to a million things.

She lifted a set of keys off her desk. They jingled as she placed them on the front counter. "They were beside the pot plant near your door."

He reached for them and then rattled them in his palm. They belonged to Ella—a decorative leather name tag with her name on it said so.

"If you ask me, it's a great excuse to meet up for a coffee."

Zane looked up and smiled. Joanne was acting more like his mother every day. He pointed his finger accusingly at her. "I'd organised to have a coffee with Dave's new housemate this afternoon, but you scheduled Ella's appointment in its place."

Joanne's laughter bubbled around the small reception area. "Zane, my dear, there's a reason for everything. Get her to bring the birth certificates with her instead of dropping them here." With a cheeky smile, she added, "Now you have two reasons to ask her out for a coffee."

And lose my credibility as a principled investigator. "What about the rules, huh?"

Joanne waved him off. "Puh. Nothing should stand in the way of getting to know a gorgeous girl." As she switched off her computer and prepared to leave for the day, she added, "It never used to in my day."

Zane saw her out and then headed for his office. While the rules said he should transfer this case to someone else, hell would freeze over before he took himself off it. He had business to attend to. Like finding out why his mother lied about what happened to her friend in the photo. Again, that sickening swirly knot cramped his stomach. What hornet's nest was he walking into?

Chapter 3

Zane gave up trying to sleep and heaped a few pillows behind his head. Another restless night. He picked up his phone and noted the time with disgust. He groaned. *Six a.m.* Saturday morning was the only day of the week he was able to sleep in. By the time Sunday morning rolled around, he'd be on his Ducati, tearing up the kilometres for the hour ride to his parents' home on the Sunshine Coast. His mum would have breakfast ready and they would catch up on all the family news. If his dad wasn't busy, he'd join him for a ride. Zane recalled the many rides they'd shared and his early morning scowl disappeared. From the day he'd purchased his own bike, riding had always been his favourite thing to do with his dad.

He yanked open the curtain behind the bedhead, allowing the morning sun to stream into his room, then he reached across to his bedside table for the photos he'd studied the previous night. The colour copy of the picture featuring his mum and Ella's sat on top.

No clues here.

His opinion hadn't changed. It was the same photo he'd grown up with, regardless of how long he looked at it. His frown deepened. He couldn't understand why his mother would claim the friend had died. Whether it was his policing years or his criminology knowledge coming into play, he couldn't ignore the sense of unease that settled in the pit of his stomach.

This wasn't something he wanted to push to the back of his mind. It would rumble and tumble inside his head forever, forcing him to look closer. Except the last thing he wanted was to cause any unrest with his family. They meant everything to him. His mother and father had a great relationship—the kind he hoped to have for himself one day.

He slid the picture to the side and sighed. The next photo was a recent one his mother had given him of 'her boys'. His dad, himself and his two younger brothers, Alex and Trent. It was a good shot.

Growing up he'd idolised his father. Loved him with an intensity he was only now beginning to understand. But something intangible hovered in a deep corner of his mind. He never acknowledged it, never understood it and always left it alone. He couldn't attribute it to anything his father had done, because as a father, he was the best. He was always there for Zane, willing to share advice and as dead-keen on riding motorbikes as he was. They had so much in common that Zane's weird thoughts didn't make sense. They were absurd, except they wouldn't go away. Over the years he'd learned to suppress them, until Ella handed over the photo of their two mothers. Then that imaginary thing he'd kept at bay for so many years started to grow and expand inside him, disrupting everything connected to his everyday life, including his sleep. And he was only up to day two since he'd viewed it.

Zane had spent most of the night trying to pick similarities between himself and his dad. Told many times over that he looked like his mother, he wanted one feature, one solitary thing he could confidently say was the same as his dad's. As he compared their features, he couldn't find a single one. When he inspected his brothers' faces, he could see his father's eyes and nose on Alex. Trent had inherited his hair and cheeks. The obvious genetics were there. In him, they were missing.

After Ella had handed him the photo, his reaction—sending his chair hurtling backwards—was the catalyst in acknowledging the blurred thoughts in his head. Hell, he had no idea what to call it or how to describe it. Sometimes it reared its ugly head and made him question things. Like whether his father was really his father. There, he'd finally labelled the hazy thought.

For one instant, he even debated whether he and Ella shared the same father but dismissed it immediately. There was something dark and ethnic in his genes that was completely missing in Ella.

He laid the two photos side by side and grimaced. It bothered him that his mother had lied about her friend in the photo. Had the few years in his job made him suspicious by nature? How could he find out the truth without upsetting anyone? He didn't want to create an issue that might not be there. Except he knew, with a sinking feeling, there was something to be found. It wasn't going away and was somehow connected to Ella.

With the evidence spread over his lap, he picked up the next item—the copy of the newspaper article that had been printed on the back of the baby's photo. The photo itself had given him no clues at all. Except that Ella was certain it was of her. He hoped the article on the reverse side would lend some clues. But if there were any, he was missing them. The edges of the article had been lopped off, but it mentioned a gala concert being held as a fundraiser. No place, no time, no details. Only words cut short and sentences stopped in their tracks. But something about it sent an electric pulse through his body. A clue was there for the taking and it was staring him in the face. He just had to grasp it.

He strained to come up with an answer. Frustrated that he couldn't, he picked up the final photo. It was of the little blue box and the bracelet, the only item with a very concise clue. For whatever reason, Ella's name had been changed from Isabella. He hoped her birth certificate would help. It wouldn't be the first fraudulent one he'd come across.

Zane let the photos slip across his navy-blue quilt as his shoulders sagged against the pillows. He closed his eyes. The chances of finding Ella's father were slim. Confidentiality laws in Australia were tight; even looking into electoral rolls was off limits. The phone directory and the Internet were the biggest windows of opportunity, but without a name, it would be near impossible. If neither Ella's birth certificate nor her mother's gave any further clues, he would be at a dead end. Her only other course of action would be to approach the Salvation Army. They were an organisation authorised to look for missing persons.

Finding a person with a name was easy. It'd been a long time since he'd had a case with so few clues. For any success, it would be up to Ella's mother to fill in the gaps. Unless he asked *his* mother. But was he ready for that? Hell no. Not until he upended every stone there was to lift. This was his family's reputation at stake. He didn't want to be responsible for wedging apart his parents' relationship. He'd seen firsthand over the years how secrets, once exposed, could tear a family to shreds. No, he wasn't ready. Not yet, anyway.

He envisioned having to tell Ella the news and grimaced. It was clear she didn't want to cause her mother stress, but he saw no other way. A quick glance at the birth certificates and he'd be able to tell her whether he could help.

His eyes fluttered open. Dust particles floated in the strip of sun dancing across his bed. A smile tugged at the corners of his mouth. Reluctant as he was to be awake so early, the thought of seeing Ella again helped clear his grumpiness. They were meeting for lunch so he could return her keys and study the birth certificates. He felt a shameless urgency to see her again, to touch her. Fleetingly would be enough.

Consorting with her outside the office wasn't strictly forbidden, but it would be frowned upon. Except his heart tripped a beat as he pictured her lovely face, and he let other thoughts invade his mind: his hand touching her cheek, her body drawn up against his on his bike ...

He needed to take himself off the case so he could see her without the guilt trip.

Suddenly drowsy again, he closed his eyes and without meaning to fell asleep.

"That's it." Zane jerked upright in bed, groggy and still half asleep. He rubbed his eyes, scarcely able to believe he'd dreamt it. The vital clue. *My God.*

He scrounged around for the photos left on his quilt and reached for the one of the newspaper article. *Could it be for real?* With his heart thumping, he re-read the article for the umpteenth time and the first word he was looking for slapped him fair in the face. Color. Not spelled the Australian way. He read further and the second word also smacked him hard. Glamor. Another word with American spelling. Towards the end of the article, he found another. Bejeweled. A fundraiser held not in Australia but in America. *Yes.* Ella had been born in America and she had no idea. *Holy shoot.*

In a trance, he re-read the article again, falling back against his pillows. *Now what?* America was a big place. Way bigger than Australia. Where the hell did he start?

He jerked upright again. *Christ.* He fumbled for his phone and yelped when he noticed it was eleven thirty. *How the heck did I sleep so long?* He had one hour to get ready and be in the city to meet Ella.

Zane rounded the corner of the street and slowed to a walk. Dressed in knee-length denim shorts and a cream polo shirt, he paused to get his breathing under control. He checked Ella's keys were in his pocket and they rattled against his hand. He was a few minutes late and inhaled a lungful of air to calm his racing heart. With the café only a hundred metres away, he ran a quick hand through his hair and affected a casual stroll, exhaling slowly. He wanted to walk the final stretch calmly.

Why was he so nervous?

He spotted Ella. She leaned against a pillar with the afternoon sun streaming over her golden hair. His breath caught in his throat as he stared at her.

Was my dream a rambling nightmare? Was she really born in America? What does my mother know?

It went against every ethical rule in the book to keep information from a client, but this had now become personal. Somehow, his mother was involved. The more he tried to deny it, the more his head refused to back down. He and Ella were only weeks apart in age. Was there a chance he'd been born overseas?

He wished he could pull out his birth certificate right now and have a look at it. He knew where his mother kept documents of that nature, but he couldn't remember ever handling it. His mother had taken care of the paperwork when he'd applied for his driver's licence, passport and tax file number. Not something a grown man wanted to admit, but he honestly hadn't needed to use his birth certificate in a long while.

With twenty metres to go, he made a silent vow as Ella waved. Until he had a chance to sneak a look at his birth certificate, he would keep his thoughts to himself. After all, he would have to provide evidence to substantiate his claims.

He clenched his hand around her keys in his pocket and their sharp edges dug into his palm. If the clues he had were not enough to trace her father, he would take himself off the case. In his private time, he would follow every lead he could to learn why their mothers had once had their photo taken together and why *his* mother had lied.

What then? He still needed reasons to see Ella. Her smile alone caused his heart to beat hard and all he'd done was touch her hand once, in a quick handshake. This lunch was a deal-breaker. He'd play his cards close to his chest, so this job didn't blow up in his face and prevent him from seeing Ella again.

Chapter 4

Ella recognised Zane straight away. Though she was hiding behind her sunglasses, she didn't want to appear too eager and only turned her head slightly to watch his approach. It was hard to miss the way his denim shorts hugged his legs, the muscles on his thighs stretching them with each step. She imagined running her hands over his strong thighs. *Ugh. Stop it.* The day before she'd imagined her hand against his stubble, today his legs.

When he was only a pace away, she straightened and wiped her palms against her black yoga pants. His dark European complexion didn't make it any easier to ignore his good looks. A surge of adrenalin zapped through her, and the decision to wear a fitted jogging shirt started to worry her. She was sure her pulse, jumping erratically under her skin, would be obvious.

When he smiled, she melted. Her hand quivered by her side. *Why? Damn it. He's probably married.*

"Ella." He reached for her hand and engulfed it in his warmth. "Sorry, I'm a little late."

What's a couple of minutes in the whole scheme of things? Stupidly, she wanted to swoon. She claimed her hand back and cleared her throat. "I only just arrived myself."

He did a cursory glance over her casual attire. She made every effort not to squirm under his gaze. When his gaze levelled with hers again, he asked, "Did I forget something?"

She frowned, not understanding.

His mouth tilted. "Are we having lunch or are we working out?"

A smile claimed her face. "I'm meeting a friend after lunch. We're taking a Zumba class."

His eyebrows rose. "Zumba class? Sounds interesting. I don't think I've ever heard of that."

Ella chuckled as she headed for an empty table. "You haven't lived then."

"Is that so?" he challenged. "I bet it's a girly thing."

She laughed—she liked his humour—and pulled out a chair. The ocean-blue sails above provided enough shade, so she removed her sunglasses and placed them in her bag. Zane sat, and his chestnut eyes continued to sweep over her face.

"You're right. It's a class full of females," she admitted.

"So, I'm not likely to want to go?"

"Not unless you like the idea of being in a room full of sweaty women moving to fast music."

He perched his elbow on the table and rested his face on his hand, appearing to seriously contemplate his response. But the gleam in his eyes gave him away. "I'm not sure I could handle all of that."

She contained her laughter but blurted, "This is ridiculous." Why was she so relaxed in his company all of a sudden? She shook her head. *Go figure.*

His hands rose in defence. "Sorry if I'm offending you, but *you* started it."

Ella smiled, certain he wasn't sorry one bit. "I suppose we should get this over and done with."

He sat back. "What? Lunch?"

She groaned. That had come out all wrong. "No, sorry, I meant ... um ... did you bring my keys?"

"Oh that. I thought, like most women, you might have wanted all the initial questions out of the road. You know hobbies, sports, do I have a nickname and am I married?"

"Hey," she said, acting offended, "I'm not the investigator. That's your job."

It was his turn to laugh, and the sound of it surrounded her like a safety net. "How did we get from Zumba to that?"

In their own intimate space, they flirted—she knew the signs—and the rest of the world faded into the background. She was enjoying this, and the purpose of their lunch was relegated to the side.

"So, um, did you bring my keys?"

His eyebrows rose. His hand delved into the depths of his shorts pocket, and she heard the familiar tinkle of the tiny bell attached to her keyring.

He reached across the table, captured her hand and placed the set of keys on her palm. Using both hands, he wrapped her fingers around the keys, lingering for a fraction of a second before withdrawing.

She gulped when their eyes met across the table. She had her keys back, so why were her hands trembling?

"Thanks."

He was the first to stumble back to normality. "So, will I get it over and done with?"

She reached for her bag and put her keys away. Any excuse to look away. But her gaze was dragged back to his hands, sinewy fingers and all, lightly tapping the tabletop.

When she looked up, he leaned forward, his chestnut eyes fixed on her. "I don't smoke, my nicknames are too embarrassing, I jog or go to the gym when I feel like it, I eat junk food sometimes, I'm neither married nor rich, and I have one passion I might share with you."

Passion. She wished he hadn't used that word. It was enough to burn—her skin flamed up. Heck. Had she really started this stupid conversation? If so, she deserved everything she got. "Er, should we order lunch?"

Seconds marched on with her breath caught in her throat. This was the step after flirting, and she was damn certain he felt something, too. Or was it her imagination?

"Did you bring the birth certificates?" he asked, slowly picking up the menu.

She nodded, doing the same. She had located her mother's only minutes before Victoria and her mother had arrived home the day before, and this morning, she'd made copies to leave with Zane, hoping to return her mother's by the end of the day. She reached into her bag and handed them across the table.

He smiled, "Great. Let's order and get this investigation under way."

After they'd ordered, Ella witnessed a fleeting moment of uncertainty on Zane's face. He held the original birth certificates in his hand and caught his bottom lip in his teeth.

"Did you find out where your mother went camping?" Zane asked.

She recalled the stilted conversation she'd started the previous night. Her mother, as expected, was agitated when Ella had brought the subject up. She was concerned about how sick Victoria was, they all were, but Ella had gently persisted.

"She told me it was in Mount Isa. I know that's where she met my step-dad. He was a newly appointed engineer straight out of university, and she worked in administration."

He nodded but didn't ask anything further.

She'd been relieved her mother had conceded that small piece of information. It'd been the hardest father-related conversation she'd had with her mother, but the pressure to uncover a clue before today's lunch meeting had reached an impossible level, and she felt she'd had no choice.

Her mother had shown all the usual signs of agitation and nervousness—which was starting to make sense to Ella if her mother was hiding something.

Zane avoided eye contact with Ella and pretended to study the birth certificates. He didn't need to any further. Frauds. Both of them. Her mother was no sooner born in Sydney than Ella was born in Mount Isa. So where were they born? He would have to establish that first. In a lot of cases, a birthplace provided the answers for everything else. Was Ella's mother under a witness protection programme? Was she running away from a crime? Someone had helped her with the fraudulent certificates, which would've required a lot of money, especially a quarter of a century ago.

He mulled over the documents, not surprised to see 'unknown' next to 'father's details', and his expert eye picked out the fraudulent pointers he'd learned to recognise from his early days at the investigative company—those finer details a cursory glance would easily miss.

But the facts remained unchanged. Ella was paying their firm to find her father, only without a name they couldn't progress. She needed to know this. He might officially close the case, but that didn't mean he would stop looking for answers—unofficially.

Their lunch arrived. Distractedly, he picked up one half of his toasted sandwich and took a bite, studying the certificates. *Okay, so where to start?* After today, where did he search for information? It was a safe bet to concentrate his search on the period between Ella's birth and her third birthday, when her mother married. Except where did he begin? Which city in America? Hell, which state?

He looked up. Ella concentrated on her lunch, her body tense.

He put his sandwich down. "Ella?"

Her face whipped up.

"Is there any chance your mother knows more about who might have fathered you?"

Her shoulders sagged when she placed her fork down. "It always upsets her to talk about it. She's never changed her story, and ... and I have this feeling she's keeping a secret."

Tell me about it. My mother too.

Dejectedly, she leaned forward on her elbows and cradled her chin. "I mean, she must have some idea of who it was, even if she narrowed it down to three or four men." Moisture glazed those amazing blue eyes when she flicked her gaze up. "But she won't say a word and I haven't got the heart to upset her at the moment."

Zane placed the birth certificates down. He finished his sandwich and let her eat more of her lunch before he said, "The fact remains that without a name our search becomes impossible. Even if you try the Salvation Army, they'll have the same problem." He ran his hand through his hair. "I'll discuss it with my boss, but we had a similar case a year ago and our hands were tied. Eventually, the client's mother confessed, making our search a lot easier."

She toyed with her fork, spinning it in circles on the tablecloth. She sat hunched over her plate and must've decided she'd had enough to eat.

"The truth is I'm a little scared of what I might uncover." She glanced up again, a sad lilt to her mouth. "I told myself I'd make an attempt and if I found nothing, I'd give it up. Maybe later, once we know Victoria has pulled through, I might try talking to Mum again. I'll tell her about the little box I discovered, and she'll have to come up with some answers for that. Maybe you can help then."

"What?" Suddenly fearful that he'd have no reason to see her beautiful smile again, he lifted his hands in defeat and asked, "Do I have to wait that long before I see you again?"

Her dejected look transformed into a smile that speared him through the chest. "Did you have something in mind?"

He leaned back and rested his hands behind his head. "As a matter of fact, I do. How would you like to come for a bike ride tomorrow morning?" This was the make-or-break scenario he'd thought of earlier.

Her eyes widened.

He would have to cancel his usual visit home and would ride in the opposite direction. No way would he bring Ella anywhere near his mother. Not yet. The photo proved she was the clone of an old friend—his mother would see it straight away. He was not going to be responsible for shattering his family's tight-knit unit. Not until he had concrete proof of … something.

"On a motorbike?"

He nodded and rested his hands on his thighs.

Guarded, she said, "Can't say I've done that before."

He caught her wary expression. "Well, then, you haven't lived."

It took her a moment to catch on. When she did, she fell into irresistible laughter. Her smile transformed her face in unimaginable ways. It left his head spinning with possibilities.

"Is this the passion you spoke of?"

"Yes."

As her laughter subsided, the thought of sitting close together ran riot through his mind.

"Is that a yes?"

She nodded. "If you let me pay for lunch today."

He narrowed his eyes and frowned. "What? You think I made the offer so you could fix up the bill?"

She leaned back. Was his scowl scaring her? "No, it's … it's just that I don't expect you to pay."

He rose a little hastily and pushed his chair in. "Yeah, I know, these days everything has to be equal rights. But today I'm paying *and* I'm inviting you for a ride."

Hell, that hadn't come out right. *Take it easy boy, you don't want to scare her away.*

He made an effort to soften his glare. "Well, you know what sort of ride I mean."

Geez, why couldn't a man pick up the tab without a fuss? He'd been accused before of being too old-fashioned. Had he upset her? She worked in an environment where she was up against a man every turn she took, with no love lost between them as they jostled their way up the corporate ladder. His offer to pay all the costs of their lunch was as foreign to her as him speaking in Mandarin.

She reached for her handbag and rose, and his stomach dropped with dread.

"Was that a yes?" He hoped she hadn't changed her mind. Why was he so desperate for her to come?

He thought he witnessed relief crossing her face, he couldn't be sure, but her nod of agreement was music to his ears. Well, some sort of music whistled around his head.

"What do I wear?"

He tried to breathe normally, not sure if it was her acceptance of his invitation or her tight-fitting outfit now back in view. "Jeans and closed-in shoes. I have a spare leather jacket and helmet."

She moved a step closer. "Where will I—?"

"Meet me at my place."

She looked up, worry lining her face. "Thanks. I'd like to avoid home for a while. I don't want to seem like I'm having a great time when things aren't fantastic for my family."

He nodded. "Okay." *Definitely the best move. What if her mother recognises me? Let me do some serious digging around first. The longer we can avoid meeting each other's family the more time I have.*

As he led the way to the cashier, the pulse on the tips of his fingers tingled as they rested on her shoulder. *Now to get to the bottom of this mystery.*

Chapter 5

At a loose end after parting with Ella, Zane sent a message to Mr Wilson.

Are you in the office?

Before Zane had reached his car, his phone pinged with a message.

For the next hour.

His boss often worked the Saturday afternoon shift. It was his way of catching up without the interference of phones ringing and client interviews. Zane was a ten-minute drive away and wanted to air his concerns about the case.

When the elevator doors opened, Joanne sat in her usual spot.

"Hey, what are *you* doing here?" Zane asked.

She smiled in her motherly way as her fingers flew across the keyboard. "I'm taking Monday off, so I want to clear my desk before more is added to it."

He leaned against the counter. "Do you think Mr Wilson has a few minutes free?"

Her hands stopped mid-air. She flapped one and dismissed his question. "You didn't seriously just ask that?" She made a point of sighing heavily before she started tapping at the keyboard again. "We *are* talking about you, aren't we? An almost favourite son."

Zane smiled at her theatrics. "I have a conflict of interest in a case, not to mention zero vital pieces of information."

Joanne paged Mr Wilson then waved Zane away. "Go on in. Would you like a hot drink? I'm making the boss a coffee."

He nodded. "The usual, thanks."

⁘

"Zane, son, what brings you here on the weekend?"

Zane liked the way Mr Wilson treated him as if he were family. It always made him smile. "Got a few minutes?"

His boss nodded. Zane sat, opened the A4 yellow envelope and took out the evidence on Ella's case. He moved files on Mr Wilson's desk and spread out the four photos and the copies of the birth certificates.

"Is this regarding the young client searching for her father?"

Zane nodded and leaned back in his chair. "Her mother told her she was too drunk on the night Ella was conceived to remember who the father was, so we don't have a name."

Mr Wilson cocked his head to the side. "That's tricky. What have you told the client?"

Zane rubbed at his cheek. "I told her that without her father's name, it's virtually impossible to proceed."

Mr Wilson tapped the end of his pen on his notepad. "So why haven't you closed the case?"

Zane wheeled his chair closer and leaned over the desk. "I sighted the original copies of these birth certificates today." He pointed to them. "They're frauds."

Mr Wilson nodded. "And?"

"See this photograph." Zane pinned it to the desk with his finger and slid it in front of Mr Wilson. "The blonde lady is our client's mother. The other lady happens to be my mother."

Mr Wilson whistled long and low. "Fraudulent birth certificates don't bode well. There could be a hundred reasons why they have them, and another hundred why the mother doesn't want to be identified."

"Exactly."

When Joanne entered with hot drinks, they both looked up, and Zane shifted the photos so Joanne could place the mugs on the office desk.

"There you go, boys. Enjoy." She moved the photo of the little blue box and put down a plate of biscuits. "Oh, look. A Tiffany jewellery box."

Zane's shoulders stiffened. "A what?"

"A box from Tiffany's jewellery store. It's missing the white ribbon, but I can pretty much bet whatever's inside came from one of their stores. Here," she said, making her way to Mr Wilson's side of the desk before sliding his keyboard towards her.

Mr Wilson picked up his coffee and took a sip. Zane sat frozen to the spot as Joanne's fingers tapped in the silent office.

"Here we go, I'll read what it says. *'Tiffany has one thing in stock that you cannot buy, no matter how much money you may offer. He will only give it to you. And that is one of his boxes. Glimpsed on a busy street or resting in the palm of a hand, Tiffany Blue Boxes make hearts beat faster and epitomize Tiffany's great heritage of elegance, exclusivity and flawless craftsmanship.'*"

Zane's jaw dropped. "Thanks, Joanne. You've confirmed one clue for me."

"My pleasure." She left them to it.

"You were saying?" Mr Wilson wrapped his hands around his mug and leaned back, resting his leg over his thigh.

Zane reached for his coffee and took a sip. "Our client found a hidden box in her mother's wardrobe. It contained these items." Zane pointed to the photograph of each item and explained what they were and Ella's reaction to them. "I recognised this photo. I've neither met our client nor her mother before, but a copy of that photo has sat in my mother's china cabinet for as long as I can remember."

"Interesting."

"This morning I nutted something else out. The newspaper clipping on the reverse of the baby photo contains American spelling. So, I think our client was born in America. When I discovered the birth certificates were frauds, it further cemented my thinking. Joanne recognising the little blue box as coming from Tiffany's makes it even harder to ignore. I'll have to check when Tiffany's came to Australia, but I bet they weren't here twenty-something years ago."

"So, where does your mother fit in?"

Zane took another sip of his coffee and gulped it down noisily. "No idea." A few drops of hot liquid spilled on his hand. He hastily put the cup down and wiped them away. "Lately, and I'm not sure why, I've been questioning whether my father is my biological father. All my life I've been led to believe he is."

Mr Wilson nodded, his lips puckering like they always did when he churned over evidence. He reached up and plucked at his mouth with his fingers. Clearly, he was thinking things through.

"So, do you want out?"

Zane rested his elbows on the desk. "Officially, yes."

Mr Wilson's eyebrows rose. "And unofficially?"

Zane rubbed at his jaw, his mind whirring over the evidence so far. "I have to find out why my mother is in this photo. I'm going to look closely at my birth certificate and my parents' next time I go home. If they're frauds, this investigation will become personal. It's not something I'll be able to let rest."

Mr Wilson sat back and formed a steeple with his fingers. "How will the client take the news?"

Zane rolled his shoulders back and took a deep breath. "Her stepfather was killed six months ago, and her sister's battling lymphoma. She doesn't plan to give up, but now isn't the right time to pepper her mother with more questions. She believes her mother's hiding something and can't understand why she won't provide more information as to who might have fathered her. At the very least she'll be looking for answers about the items she found hidden."

"Okay, son." Mr Wilson leaned further back in his chair and put his hands behind his head. "Close the case with the client for now. But take care with what you do on a personal level." He wheeled his chair in and placed his elbows on the desk. "I've met your dad and he's a good soul. Whatever you unearth I want you to be strong about it. If I've learned anything in this business it's that the reasons people change their identities, if not for criminal purposes, are usually for the best."

Zane reached for the evidence and began putting it all back in the envelope. He tried to push back the lump in his throat. This was exactly what concerned him. Should he leave it be? Would he unearth secrets better left untouched? His parents loved each other, and it showed every day. If they weren't so cute, it'd be sickeningly embarrassing. It had been during his teenage years, but he'd gotten over it when he realised how special their marriage was.

If they never discussed something from their past, why should *he* be the one to bring it into the light? Except it would never leave him. Not now, not in two years' time, and quite possibly not in ten years' time.

He rose and reached for his coffee cup. "I'll tread warily, don't worry. To be honest, I'm not sure where to start. It'll be another week before I make it home to visit the folks. I'll also need to look at those certificates without Mum knowing." He gave his boss a smile. "I'll have to get her out of the house for that." He shook his head and chuckled. "Not as easy as it sounds."

Mr Wilson joined in. "Joanne tells me you had lunch with the client today. Did you return her keys?"

At just the mention of Ella, Zane's heart threw out an extra beat. "I did."

"And?"

Zane stood at the office door, ready to leave. "And I'm taking her for a bike ride in the morning."

Mr Wilson's chuckle and, "Fast work," followed Zane as he walked down the hall towards reception.

If Joanne noticed his smile was different, she didn't say. But it felt different and he left the building counting down the hours until the morning. It was stupid to be this excited. He had to give Ella bad news and that should be enough to create a few hiccups whenever he thought of her. Throw into the mix the connection between their mothers and he should be wary as all hell. Add to the cauldron that he had no intention of telling Ella about that connection and stupidity took on a whole new meaning.

He was absolutely certain that to tell Ella too soon would be a mistake, and *not* to tell Ella was the death of anything that might happen between them. He was caught between a rock and a hard place, and he didn't like it one bit.

Chapter 6

Ella drove to Zane's suburb. Trees shaded both sides of the street and the morning sun left the bitumen road dappled with light and shade. When she found his house, she parked across the road.

She'd brought the barest of essentials, a few dollars in cash and her sunglasses. She would ask to leave her car keys inside, along with some snacks for when they returned.

Ella locked the car and made her way across the street, inhaling the crisp early morning air. Dew droplets, visible in the morning rays, clung to the leaves. Her shoulder rubbed against them on the low-lying branches as she walked past.

She spotted Zane in his front courtyard working with the bike. He looked up and waved. *Oh hell*. Her heart quickened. She smoothed down her lightweight denim jacket and clumsily buttoned it up, needing something for her fingers to do. Then she forced her legs to keep moving.

What was she nervous about? The ride? Or was it something else? She cringed, not liking that he knew so much about her private life, and she so little about his.

After their lunch the previous day she'd been out of sorts. Unable to confide in her best friend like she usually did, she hadn't enjoyed her Zumba class at all. The thought of again broaching the subject of her father with her mother as soon as Victoria was well enough didn't help. It would mean upsetting her mother, which was the only thing holding her back.

But damn it, this is my father we're talking about.

She shook her head and wished she'd slept better. When she'd flopped onto her bed last night, her mind had refused to shut down. Memories of those chestnut-brown eyes and disarming smile had kept her awake, her restless night one continuous weird dream. Her cheek would rest against his; her hands would travel over his muscled thighs. Over and over. She would have to watch herself. She was more likely to say something stupid when she was tired.

On reaching his courtyard, she tried to quell the quiver that worked its way around her body. She was losing the battle; it was not something she could envisage going away any time soon.

She couldn't remember ever being under the spell of a man before. Why would the extra stress about finding her father make it different this time? In all her past relationship experiences, she wore the pants, and as much as she was determined to follow in her own footsteps, she couldn't seem to convey it this time.

"Good morning," Zane greeted, still busy doing something on his bike.

Ella took a deep breath and tightened her grip on the bag she carried. "Hi."

He balanced the bike on its stand and straightened, then stretched his arms above his head and made some sort of waking up noise before dropping his arms again.

"Ready to go?" he asked with his million-dollar smile.

Ugh. How could the simple act of watching him stretch send her pulse in a whirl? She wanted to beg him to stop, but he was matching all the right actions with all the right sounds. Every cell of his body screamed out masculinity. So where was the problem?

"Um ... could I leave my keys and some snacks inside for later?"

"Sure. Come this way." He led her inside, speaking over his shoulder. "Does the food need to be kept in the fridge?"

She followed a few steps behind, unable to keep her eyes above his waist. His black riding boots finished her off completely; she had to concentrate solely on breathing in and breathing out.

"Er ... some of it," she managed to answer.

"I'll grab a small icepack so we can take it with us. I have some food too."

Once inside, Ella looked around the small, tidy living space. She smiled when his back was turned. Did he have a massive clean-up last night, or was his place usually like this? The only man she knew who lived alone was her brother, and *he* had a long way to go in learning housekeeping skills.

Zane took her shopping bag and commandeered her keys. "I'll put these in here." He opened the bottom drawer in his kitchen and placed the keys inside. "We don't need someone breaking in and finding them on the table." His eyes twinkled in her direction before he turned to the freezer and reached for a gel icepack.

"Okay, you hold this." He handed her a small esky and the shopping bag. "I'll grab the helmets, gloves and jacket."

Her mouth was seriously dry as he walked off. His black leather jacket hugged his broad shoulders and tapered down to his waist. With her bottom lip caught between her teeth, she tightened her grip on the goods and turned. She hoped in the next few minutes she might revert to her usual self and start a conversation.

She found her way to the courtyard, and in no time at all, Zane had joined her and had the water and snacks stored in the bike's side packs and his leather jacket secured to the throat.

If he was nervous, it didn't show. Meanwhile, like an imbecile, she could barely get a single word out, and her replies to his chirpy chatter consisted of one-word answers.

"I'll run through a few pointers you should know about riding doubles."

She nodded.

He made last-minute adjustments to the bike, then said, "Okay, the first thing you shouldn't do is make sudden movements while we're riding.

Move with me, especially when we turn a corner. In other words, don't lean the opposite way to the bike. You'll have to sit up close and put your arms around my waist."

She swallowed as he handed her a pair of gloves. "I think I can manage that."

He raised an eyebrow and smirked.

She blustered. "I mean ... you know ... leaning in and ..." Oh, shit. *Of course, I'll do whatever you want.*

"All good?"

When she didn't respond, he frowned. He reached out, sat his hand on her shoulder, sending a charge to her rib cage, and gave it a quick squeeze. "Hey, you okay? There's still time to change your mind. We don't have to do this."

She shook her head, took a deep breath and proceeded to put the gloves on. "No. No, I'm good to go."

Then he did the weirdest thing. He leaned in and brushed his lips against hers. Heck, wasn't she usually the first to make a move? Even weirder was that she felt as if she were floating, inches above the ground, until he moved back and pierced her with his gaze.

He coughed, clearing his throat. "Ah ... it's hard to do that with a helmet on."

Finally, thank God, his words were enough to snap her out of her trance and she laughed. He laughed too and looked relieved.

She reached for the helmet he held. "Okay, show me how to secure this thing and let's get going."

He chuckled, put his arm around her and squeezed her by his side, before concentrating on the task.

She wrapped her hands around his waist when they were both seated on the bike. The tangy smell of leather coated with orange oil was strong, even with all the head gear. She shuffled up against him and held her breath as he kick-started the bike and headed towards the road.

A whoosh of air, a little cool, brushed against her body, buffeting her jacket. She sat perfectly still. Adrenalin coursed through her veins as a smile struggled to fit in the confines of her helmet.

Why had she never tried this before? The sense of freedom and danger, unparalleled, when you put your fate in someone else's hands. He had promised to take it easy and stop if she felt uncomfortable. He told her to press three times against his stomach if she was nervous and wanted him to pull over.

But she neither pressed nor became agitated, only hugged Zane tighter as he wound his way out of Brisbane towards the national parks in a north-westerly direction.

Zane was sometimes a little reckless when he took to the open roads, but now he reined in his need for speed, very conscious of his passenger. Acutely aware of her arms around his waist, he was unable to nudge the bulge in his jeans to a comfortable position for riding.

He smiled at the turn his thoughts had taken. Being this close to her did all the right things to his body. It had been a bloody long time. He would have to tell Dave to stop hassling him now. If Ella agreed he wanted her to hang around. What surprised him the most was the speed at which things were moving—and he wasn't referring to the odometer reading on his bike.

He'd always been the kid who barrelled headfirst into everything, but this thing between them was at a stage where he needed to rein things in. How could they be sitting this close and only on their second date?

But man, it felt good. He'd never doubled with any girl before and couldn't understand why it'd taken him so long. But selfishly, riding was *his* time away from the world and the stresses of work. It wasn't something he wanted to share with anyone, so having Ella join him for a ride within days of meeting her spelled out a lot. Whether that was good or bad he couldn't tell yet.

The longer they rode, the more he sensed her relax. He was conscious of her, waiting for her signal to stop, but he noticed her arms were not wound as tight as they had been, and he could have sworn he heard her singing.

His destination was a lookout he knew well in the D'Aguilar National Park. It boasted toilet and picnic facilities and a memorable view. He wanted to make the morning as unforgettable as possible, and he had a few ideas. He still had to tell her about his concerns regarding the case and his reasons for backing down. If that upset her and she hated the view, the morning was doomed.

With that in mind, he kicked down the gears on the ascending road. She sat up behind him, her helmet touching his with a quick tap. When he turned off the main highway, she remained still, allowing him to brake to a stop and rest the bike on its stand.

He slid off the bike, balancing it so Ella could do the same. When he removed his helmet and gloves, she did likewise and turned to stare at the view.

The blue summits in the distance, covered in sheltered pockets of subtropical rainforest, curtained the panoramic vision on the valley floor. Scribbly gum and vast expanses of eucalypt woodland roofed the remainder. A river wound its way north, and with the brilliant green of the trees hugging the waterway, it resembled a jade python. The sun dropped its morning rays on the meandering water, and it glimmered from their vantage point.

Zane took Ella's helmet and gloves and rested them on the seat alongside his. Without asking for permission, he unzipped the heavy leather jacket she wore and laid it over the handles, then did the same with his own.

"What do you think?" he asked, nodding his head at the view.

"It's amazing. I've never been here before."

Phew, one tick for me.

He moved behind her and placed his hand on her shoulder. She swung around, and in two seconds flat he was trapped in her gaze. Zane wanted to kiss her, but this was too fast by his standards.

"Are you okay?" Concern creased her face.

He savoured the strong smell of eucalyptus, not sure if it was coming from the trees or her. He didn't want to bring up the case, not yet. That would sour everything. Now was his moment to ask, to kick into action what he'd been thinking of doing all night. Without another second's thought the words tumbled out of his mouth.

"I'm going to kiss you—again—properly."

Oh, shit, no asking like a gentleman, just demanding like some barbarian. If she refused, who would blame her?

She turned back to the view, a smile on her face. Stunned, his brain told him it wasn't a 'no'. Was a smile a consent to kiss? Or was this a mysterious trait women had where you had to read their mind?

He forgot about glory and everything it entailed—it was do or die. He nuzzled past her hair and touched her neck, giving him precious seconds to rethink his next move.

Come on, brain. Kick into action if I need to stop.

He ignored his own plea and turned Ella away from the view. He let his breathing return to normal as he gazed into her depths. The memory of this morning's fleeting kiss still seared his lips. No stopping now. He tilted her face towards his and groaned. He wanted more than a quick touch this time, so he pressed firmly, and her mouth came alive under his.

He was happy for it to go on and on. Time fogged his headspace and was quickly forgotten. They ignored passing motorists. The distant wolf whistles and gleeful calls were dampened by the pounding of his heart.

Her arms wound around his neck and he held her closer.

He knew they had both felt something at lunch the day before, though they'd done their best to ignore it. Their flirting had been fun and contagious, but he didn't want to resist it any longer.

When he needed to breathe, when oxygen was more important than the potent rush of blood flowing through his veins, he released her, nervous about scaring her off. This was too fast. First date or second, it didn't matter. He had to slow down.

But as her warm breath brushed across his cheeks, and as he fixed his stare on her blue eyes, the importance of slowing down became irrelevant. In true Zane style, just how he loved to ride his bike, he leaned forward for more. He forgot his resolve and traced a path down her cheek. His mouth sought solace in the spot where her neck joined her shoulder. As a reward she sighed contentedly, which only encouraged his greedy need to have more.

Help, someone. But there was no help to be found and, the longer he stayed connected to her soft and fragrant skin, he seriously didn't seek any.

When he finally pulled back, he took her hand in his and took his fill of her beautiful face. "Did you enjoy the ride?" He asked as he rubbed small circles over her knuckles. His need to constantly touch her verged on desperate.

"Yes." Her smile transformed her face and enchanted him with those dimples that came from nowhere.

When a car sped past, breaking their reverie, Zane let go of her hand. "I brought a picnic blanket, so how about we find a quiet spot in the shade and have something to eat? Do you need to be back by a certain time?"

He carried the small esky and handed her the water bottles as they walked away from the lookout and car park. "I promised my sister I'd spend some time with her researching cancer help groups in the area. It'd be helpful if I could be back by ten."

Zane spread the blanket beside a tree and sat down. He leaned against it, opened his arms and beckoned her towards him. "Easy. We can stay another hour before heading back."

She settled against his chest and he didn't hesitate to wind his arms around her. He also didn't waste another second. He moved her hair aside, wanting to taste her again. Her silken hair brushed against his cheek as she leaned back, allowing him easy access.

"Ella?" He moaned near her neck.

"Hmm?"

"We shouldn't be doing this."

"I know. Ethics. It's a tricky situation but ..."

He chuckled and raised his face. She wasn't silly. "What snacks did you bring?"

She reached for the cooler beside them. "Delicious hummus and crackers."

"Really?" That didn't sound like food.

She twisted around and eyed him warily. "Well, what did *you* bring?"

Had he made it that obvious what he thought of hummus? "Triple choc-chip biscuits."

"Really?" She burst out laughing.

He joined her, and they finally relaxed together. He needed this. Actually, he needed a lot of things—answers as to why their mothers shared a photo, reassurance that it was for the best that she didn't know about this connection yet, and diplomacy when he told her about being unable to search for her father. For now, he wanted to concentrate on the sexual pull he was certain they were both feeling and were reluctant to avoid.

Even if it meant eating something so sickeningly healthy.

Chapter 7

They sat side by side, hips touching and her hand captured in his. The smell of hummus and rich chocolate hung in the air between them. Very little food was left bar a few biscuits they'd saved for later. Ella couldn't believe how much she'd eaten. Trying to keep up with Zane, she'd consumed way more than she normally would. In between mouthfuls and scraping hummus onto crackers, they'd talked about their work, what the future held for them, and how Zane's was about to change.

Taking a breather from that topic, Ella smiled when Zane lifted her hand and nibbled on the ends of her fingers. She twisted to watch him and feasted on his good looks. "Did you bake the biscuits? They're delicious."

His gaze didn't waver far from hers. "No. Mum did."

When he reached across and cupped her neck, desire began its heated throb, leaving her aware of every nerve ending in her body. He leaned in, his warm breath brushing against her skin, his mouth trailing between her chin and shoulder. She flexed her tingling fingers and tried hard not to moan. "She's ... she's a great cook."

It didn't matter what she said after that. When his mouth reached hers, she was gone. Not a vestige of control; not a single desire to find any.

His lips teased. She ran her hands over his chest and the teasing quickly disappeared. The kiss turned intense and dizziness took over. There was no room for anything else, only the sweet taste of the food they'd eaten and the stimulating prickle of his skin against hers.

She hadn't noticed he'd released her until his voice penetrated her senses. Breathless, they stared at each other.

He cleared his throat. "Ella, I need to discuss the case with you."

With a jolt, her back straightened. *Now?* She'd been dreading this but knew it couldn't be avoided. Reluctantly, she nodded. Not because she didn't want the case to proceed, but because of the guilt and pain it would bring her mother when she next asked questions.

Zane leaned back against the tree and raised his knees. His hand rested casually on her thigh. "Yesterday I had a chance to discuss your case with my boss."

She nodded to let him know it was okay to go on.

"We need your father's name in order to proceed."

"I suspected as much."

"When you're ready to talk to your mum about it, we'll be more than happy to continue with the case. A name will make all the difference."

Her stomach tied itself in knots. How long did she wait before talking to her mother? She traced the checked squares on the rug while she contemplated how to approach it at all.

"There's also something else I want to discuss."

She looked up and noted Zane's serious expression. She swallowed, unsure if she should be nervous or not.

He reached for her hand and held it between his. "Sometimes there are good reasons for why a mother keeps this sort of information from her child."

Her frown deepened. "What do you mean?"

He stretched his fingers against her palm. Her hand looked tiny in comparison. "What if you're the result of a rape? That's what I mean. Or perhaps it's worse."

"Worse?" Her heart plummeted. She'd never considered this.

"What if your mother was sexually abused? What if you're the result of incest?"

Incest? She stumbled to her feet. A sick sensation jammed against her chest and she ran an agitated hand through her hair. "Then it's important I find out."

Beside her in seconds, Zane wrapped his arms around her. "It might not be any of that. She might've been drunk on the night you were conceived, just as she claims."

Ella wrenched away from him and ground her teeth. "Why put those stupid thoughts into my head? Next you'll be telling me we could be siblings."

Arms hanging loosely by his sides, his shoulders dropped. "That's a ridiculous thing to suggest, but it's my responsibility as an investigator to discuss all possible outcomes with you. You have a choice not to take it any further. In some cases, the results of an investigation have caused untold damage and hurt to the client. They were better off not knowing."

"But ... but a person has to learn this sort of thing eventually. You can't live a full life and not know that your father could also be your grandfather, or uncle."

"Your father could also be a criminal. He might be in prison." He reached for her hand again. "Then again, he might be a nice man, happily married now. You might have half-siblings you don't know about." He attempted a smile and drew her close, resting his mouth against her forehead. "I don't want to hurt you, but I have to paint the picture for you. If you manage to elicit a name from your mother, you have to be prepared for what we find."

Everything Zane said made sense, but the gut feeling that her mother was hiding something was still there. How drunk did you need to be to have no recollection of who you had sex with? Unless she had used the hardcore drugs available in her day.

She should come right out and ask her mother if she was the product of rape or incest. As much as the thought was abhorrent, now that the seed had been planted, she'd get no rest until she knew. She almost cursed Zane for opening her mind to these possibilities, but she was a big girl now. It would hurt, but she'd be strong enough to cope.

She squeezed his hands and stared boldly at him. "Will you look at me any differently if I'm the result of rape or incest?"

Zane swore. "Come here, *now*, girl." He wrapped his arms around her and pressed her so hard against his chest she struggled to get enough air into her lungs. Just when she thought he would never release her, he let go. He grabbed hold of a shoulder with each hand and jerked her away. His chestnut-brown eyes blazed with possessiveness. Something she'd never seen in a man before. "I'm going to pretend I didn't hear that, but just so you know, the answer is no."

Before she could get her thoughts in order, his mouth claimed hers again. She swayed against his tall frame and was glad his arms wound securely around her and held her upright. She had a lot to take in and wanted his strength. Not something she usually asked for from a man. Always proud of her independence. But Zane's advice rocked her core and she needed him close.

It would take time for her to sift through it all. Of all the scenarios she'd imagined over the years, at no time had she considered anything so sordid. Not once had she associated finding her biological father with something as horrific as what Zane suggested. None of it might apply to her situation, but the thought of it sent a weight hurtling down to her feet. For now, she would hold these horrid possibilities close to her chest and nurse any impending pain. Maybe it was a good idea to put the search aside for now—well, at least until Victoria pulled through this round of chemo and Ella had the strength to talk to her mother again.

A droplet of water landed on her nose. Followed by another few. The cool liquid trickled down her cheek as Zane stepped back and looked up. The mist had thickened around them.

Zane flashed a smile and spread his arms wide. He looked heavenward and spoke loudly. "If the message here is for me to stop kissing this beautiful woman, it's not going to work."

Ella laughed, lightly shoving at his chest. "This looks like it's setting in. Maybe we should head back."

His shoulders slumped. He looked up again and shouted this time. "Okay, you win. We're stopping."

With no one else around, they were free to make as much noise as they wanted. His words to some otherworldly god warmed her from the inside, but the heavier the drops of water fell, the colder she became.

When an involuntary shiver shook her body, Zane took her hand and they raced over towards the parked bike for their jackets and helmets. Under a tree, where they were saved from the worst of the drizzle, he asked, "Can I see you again?"

Ella's teeth chattered while Zane did up the last of her buttons. "What time do you have lunch at work?" she asked.

"One o'clock." He handed over her gloves.

"Meet me at the entrance gate to the Botanical gardens tomorrow."

He hesitated for a moment, poised with his helmet above his head. "No way. How about you meet *me* at the entrance gate to the Botanical gardens?"

"What?"

He reached across and gave her a peck on the cheek, then indicated that she should put her helmet on. His smile disappeared behind his helmet, while she swore behind hers.

Christ, did I really wish for a man who wants all the control? She was going to miss not being in charge, but for once she might enjoy it.

The ride back was mostly downhill, but she could tell he was taking it easy on the wet road. She stayed relaxed with her arms around his waist until a thought came to mind and she couldn't resist. She pressed against his stomach three times. Zane slowed down and pulled over. Without hesitating, he stopped the engine and climbed off.

With the rain easing, he ripped off his helmet and helped her remove hers. "Hey, what's up? Are you okay?"

She'd planned on staying serious as long as possible, but now she burst out laughing.

His eyebrows arched and confusion covered his face. "What the hell is going on?"

She hung her helmet over the handlebars and said, "I'm going to kiss you—again—properly."

"You're kidding me?" He looked skyward again, "She's joking, of course." Rain dripped off his dark hair. He flicked a hand through it and sent droplets in her direction.

When his gaze fell back to hers, they latched onto her face, his Adam's apple moving when he swallowed. Then he reached out and rested his hand on her neck, claiming her mouth and blasting heat to her toes.

But all too soon, he pushed back. "Please, put your helmet on."

Without another word, they left the lonely stretch of road. The rain got steadily heavier, but although her jeans became sodden, she concentrated only on the way her blood rushed through her veins, the way her heart crashed against her ribs and the way heat pooled at the spot that rested against his back.

But a duel had begun. God, how she craved a man who took some control, but hell, it was going to take some getting used to.

⸎

Zane watched Ella's vehicle disappear around the corner. It wasn't until his neighbour sent a cheery hello from the other side of the fence that his trance broke and he realised he was staring at an empty street. He waved back and made his way inside.

He missed her company already. It was a pity she was running late and had needed to leave the moment they'd returned. He smiled when he remembered how she stopped their ride for a kiss. *God, she has a cheek.* But he wasn't complaining. He liked a strong woman who wasn't afraid to have her way. Or at least try to have her way. He chuckled and decided he might relent and let her. Sometimes.

He thought of the photo and what he hadn't told her yet, and grimaced. Despite the sensational morning they'd shared, he sensed a long and painful road ahead. He would never be able to deny knowing about it from their first meeting. She was clever and not a person to be walked over. He was banking on being able to fully explain his reasons and give her some answers at the same time. One right to cancel out one wrong. The theory sounded good, but experience told him these types of cases rarely panned out that way.

Feeling lazy and lethargic, and thinking he'd much rather be lying in bed with the gorgeous Ella beside him, he took out a bowl and prepared another serve of cereal as an early lunch. He had a job to do—make a list of all the Tiffany stores in America that had traded approximately twenty-six years ago—and now was the time to start. He hoped another idea might come to him. Apart from searching missing persons files and cold cases there was little else he could do. As it stood, if there were more than a dozen Tiffany stores the process could take weeks.

He groaned and took his first spoonful of cereal. In the meantime, he wanted to spend as much time with Ella as was humanly possible without alerting his mother. Any inkling of a girlfriend and he'd be awash with invitations to bring her home. This was one girl his mother wasn't going to meet in a hurry.

Thinking of his mother reminded him of his birth certificate. He made a mental note to visit home the following Sunday morning. Then he'd be back by the afternoon to share the rest of the day with Ella. Already he couldn't imagine not seeing her every day.

Zane rested his chin in his hand and continued to eat. He spilled a spoonful when the realisation of his situation hit him: he was a lost cause—and to a woman!

Somehow, Ella had snuck up on him and he didn't mind one bit.

Chapter 8

"I'd better go. I promised Victoria, I'd take her to a cancer group meeting tonight."

Ella languished in his apartment with her legs stretched along his as they lay comfortably on his couch facing each other.

"How has she been?"

"Rotten."

Zane pushed her hair off her face as she turned away and looked out into his courtyard. He could tell when Victoria was on her mind.

"I feel guilty for being so healthy and ..." She turned back, and Zane connected with her blue depths.

Something lodged in his throat, and he coughed to clear it, "And?"

"And ... and happy." Tears brimmed behind her eyelashes. She blinked to clear them; misery etched on her usually smiling face.

He settled beneath her and cupped her face. "Do you mean that?"

She smiled, hesitantly at first, before she dropped down beside him and latched her mouth onto his earlobe. It only took a few nibbles to render him weak and useless. He didn't let on though.

Near his ear, she said, "Thanks for being a good listener." She groaned before adding, "I can't believe what a crazy week it's been. My lunch hour will never be the same again."

He could tell she smiled against his cheek, regardless of how worried she was about her sister. No doubt she was thinking the same things he was.

On their first meeting at the Botanical Gardens, they'd found a secluded grove housing the perfect bench. Their bottoms had barely touched the seat when their mouths had fused and their hands had explored—as much as his business suit and her smart work outfit had allowed. As bad as it sounded, lust counted for everything. With scarcely five minutes to spare, Zane had raced back to the office while shoving down his sandwich.

"It's starting to get serious. My indigestion that is."

She laughed and he joined her. It was a relief to take her mind off the seriousness of Victoria's illness, even for a few minutes.

"I ended up sneaking into the office with about thirty seconds to spare, then hid my lunch in the top drawer and took small bites when no one was near." Ella confessed.

At her revelation, he shook with mirth. The same scenario in the park was repeated on Tuesday, Wednesday and Thursday. He was beyond help, now. He didn't think he could cope without seeing her every day. Not seeing her beautiful face and hungry mouth on Friday had nearly killed him.

When their laughter died down, he prepared himself for her departure. He was glad she was able to sneak in these few hours with him, but her guilt for not spending more time with Victoria was evident. Victoria was suffering the worst possible effects of her latest chemo treatment, so Zane understood where Ella's priorities were. He had to let her go without making a fuss.

Ella's reluctance to introduce him to her family was a good thing. She kept apologising, and promised she would do so once Victoria got over this bout of sickness. But Zane didn't push the issue. The last person he wanted to meet was Ella's mother. He had an inkling she would recognise his name and face, and he wanted to be better prepared before they met. He wasn't any further advanced with his search, though he'd compiled a long list of Tiffany stores that had been trading when Ella was born.

He gently kneaded her back. It stilled when she sighed. "You okay?"

"Victoria is starting to lose her beautiful hair. It's coming out in clumps, and it's so awful to watch. Chemo has so many side effects."

He tightened his hold around her and squeezed. "You often hear of cancer patients cutting their hair short before it falls out."

"I know. We talked about it, but I think she was trying to delay it for as long as possible. This morning she was in tears and threatened to do something soon. To make matters worse, she won't go out because she's too scared of catching something and doesn't want friends to visit in case they have a cold. Being stuck indoors is depressing her."

He found her forehead and pressed lightly, and her heart beat a rapid blip against his own. It hurt his chest to know the pain she and her family were experiencing, but he didn't know what else to do. Apart from distracting her when she was able to spend time with him and provide comfort when she was feeling down, he was at a loss. He wanted to be her safe haven, a place she could come to when she needed time out.

Zane let her lay quietly while he drank in her eucalyptus scent, the heady smell doing a good job of relaxing all his muscles. He closed his eyes and savoured the image of their bodies entwined on the couch. Being with this woman lent him a sense of everything falling into place.

She stirred and muttered something.

He opened his eyes. "I know you have to go, and that you're sad and not in the mood, but would you like me to take your mind off things? I promise I won't keep you longer than ten minutes."

He could feel her smile against his neck. "You have to ask?"

"Hey, that was me asking nicely." He feigned shock, finding and hungrily biting *her* earlobe this time.

She moaned and writhed. It sent all the right messages to different parts of his body.

"You're right," she said. "I am feeling down. I could use another ten minutes of your attention to get me through the rest of the day. How about we roll onto the floor so we have more space?"

He gripped either side of her hips and aligned her squirming body over his. "I say my bed has plenty of room and is comfier."

She chuckled as she found his mouth and grabbed his bottom lip between her teeth. When she freed him, she whispered in a throaty voice, "I can't. That'll take longer than ten minutes."

Zane laughed and slid off the couch, taking her with him. She must have grabbed the cushions on the way down, because he felt their softness beneath his head. He shifted her shirt and unsnapped her bra so it now hung loosely under her shirt. His gaze found hers and held it.

The battle between them had begun. That's what he loved about her; she gave as good as she got. When her mouth slammed onto his, they each raced to take what they could. The scrape of her teeth, wherever they touched, had his veins throbbing, his heart ready to explode. It left his body on fire, a pile of ashes dumped on the ground, whenever she drew away. Already, Sunday afternoon was a lifetime away.

He pushed her shirt up, determined to have his share. He found a nipple and closed around it, enjoying its softness. Her breathing was rushed and ragged near his ear. He held back, trying to be gentle. She obviously didn't want gentle. She clung to his hair and pulled down hard, her fingers twisting around his short strands.

He took a risk and closed his teeth around her nipple. It was enough for a groan from Ella to reverberate around his head. Enough for his heart to crash like a drum. Too much for his rock-hard appendage begging to be released.

She pulled away suddenly, leaving him dizzy. "You're dangerous. Has it been ten minutes yet?"

He sat up, shaking and with his chest aching. She pulled her shirt down leaving her bra loose. She appeared as breathless as he was, though his lungs slowly started to function again. "I think it was only eight."

She laughed and gathered herself up before reaching under her shirt to fasten her bra. When she was done, she rose and looked down at him. Her smile slipped away as she chewed on her bottom lip. "I really need to go."

Zane stood up and reached for her.

"No, no, don't." She took a step back. "If you touch me, I'll never leave."

He understood. This thing between them had come about with lightning speed and had left his head reeling. No matter what happened, his life was never going to be the same again.

"Okay. I'll let you walk out. I'm riding up to visit the folks tomorrow and I'll be back after lunch. Can I see you then?"

She bunched up her hair neatly and retied the ponytail. "I'd like that."

A whoosh of air left his lungs as he sighed with relief. Relaxing against the wall, he shoved his hands in his pockets. "Deal," then he let her go home without any further fuss.

◈

His knees shook, then he landed on the floor in his mum's office with a thump.

Shit.

A quick glance was all he'd needed. His father's and brothers' birth certificates were legitimate—his mother's and his own were not.

Luck had sided with him that morning when he'd arrived in time for his mother's usual delicious breakfast. His mother had a Tupperware party to attend and his father had given his word to help an old mate repair his mower. Zane wished them a good day, waved them off, and promised to lock up the house when he left. He could stay as long as he wanted, but the rush to get back in time to see Ella drove all other thoughts from his head. Check the birth certificates then get the hell back home. Fast.

Only now his legs wouldn't move. He didn't know what he'd expected to find. He sure as heck hadn't wanted to find fraudulent documents. They even smelled suspiciously like the paper Ella's certificate and her mother's were printed on, even though he knew that would be impossible after all these years. But the fraudulent details were clearly there. He couldn't pretend he hadn't seen them.

Now what?

What sort of secret was his mother keeping? Did his father know about any of this? Zane was close to leaving deep gouge marks on his scalp if he didn't stop scratching. He stretched his legs instead, hoping it might send the images in his head away.

It didn't.

Discovering fraudulent certificates only made him more confused, unrested and lost. Made him feel as if he didn't belong anywhere. Yet all his life he'd been led to believe they were a family. They weren't. He and his mother had come from a different place. He didn't doubt the link he had to her. He just didn't know what it was.

His thoughts returned to the warning he'd given Ella. Except his advice meant jack-all, because he knew deep down, he could never have prepared himself for this news. There must be a reason his mother had gone to all this trouble to hide her past. Finding it would open a big wound he wasn't sure he wanted.

Find it, though, he would. Where to start? He had no idea.

He held up his birth certificate again. It hurt like blazes to read 'Father, unknown.'

Damn. How had he lived all his life never once setting eyes on this sheet of paper? No wonder his mother guarded it fiercely.

He bit hard on his bottom lip as moisture crowded his eyes. He'd be damned if he allowed a single tear to trickle down his cheeks. Hell, he hadn't cried in years. There'd been no need. His life was good. He was happy and healthy. Had a great family. Now had the attentions of a gorgeous woman. What more did a man need?

The truth.

Zane blinked back the moisture and rolled his shoulders. He stared into space, not seeing anything except for the 'Father, unknown' line tattooed behind his eyelids.

How long he sat like that, he had no idea.

The laugh of a kookaburra outside the window broke his trance. He rose, his legs still shaking, and sighed.

Treat this like another investigation.

Yeah, sure.

Zane wasn't stupid. He knew whatever he unearthed could tear his life and his family apart. It was possible that he might not share DNA with his father, but he loved him with every fibre of his being.

Turning to the printer, he scanned copies to take with him. Another chat with his boss was necessary after this discovery. What advice would Mr Wilson give him? Like with Ella's situation, there wasn't a single clue Zane could draw on, except for the photo of their mothers.

Zane placed the certificates back where he'd found them—in the office, with every pen and paperclip in its exact position. After he locked the door of his parents' home, he stood wistfully on the front porch, nervous about the weeks ahead. He let his gaze wander to the distant mountain peaks. Now he would need Ella to keep *his* mind distracted.

He knew the pitfalls of unearthing long-buried secrets. He fully understood the risks and the one hundred or so reasons to leave things alone. This was what his training had taught him, except it didn't apply to him. Not anymore.

He donned his leather jacket and gloves, and made his way to the garage where he'd left his bike. Hunched over, helplessness dragged him down.

He would need to approach his parents. He was in the same scenario as Ella, and the same advice applied—he needed a name. Right now, he had nothing. Not even the suggestion that his dad wasn't his biological father.

As he hoisted himself onto his bike, he was certain of one thing. There had to be a connection between him and Ella. But what? The photo of his mother and Ella's burned a hole in his side.

He gasped, whipping his face up. "Shit." *His mother's photo*. He'd forgotten to look at it.

Zane left his gloves on the bike seat and took long strides back to the house. Unlocking the kitchen door, he flung it back in his haste to reach the lounge room. He knelt in front of the china cabinet and glimpsed the photo shoved towards the back. Sliding the glass door open, his hand reached over trophies long ago positioned in pride of place until he held the frame. He knocked a couple of trophies over as he snaked his arm back to where he sat, the photo firmly in his hand. As he stared at it, his vision glazed over. He wished for all the world he'd made a mistake. But he hadn't. It was a duplicate of the one Ella had shown him. Now there was no disputing it. A real connection existed between their mothers.

Zane righted the fallen trophies and placed the framed photo directly behind the glass door before sliding it closed. He fell to his backside in the carpeted room with his hands fisted by his side, and contemplated his next move. Minutes ticked by, but no solution came. Surely with all his experience in policing and investigating, he'd be able to think of something? There had to be a way to go forward. He hoped like blazes his boss had some ideas because *he* didn't.

Okay, time to leave. He would go home first and phone Mr Wilson.

But he thought of the afternoon he'd planned to spend with Ella and his shoulders lost their tension.

He rose. Tomorrow would be soon enough to speak to his boss. To call off the afternoon with Ella wasn't an option. But he did have to constantly push aside the niggle of guilt rearing its ugly head. He needed to tell Ella about the connection between their mothers, but he wanted to learn more first. He was always one for doing his research thoroughly.

She would understand when he told her. Right?

He locked the house again and made his way back to his bike. Climbing on and kick-starting it, he wheeled it onto the road, considering the evidence he'd gathered from Ella as he took off down the street.

Re-thinking any missed clue he might've overlooked. He would need to use Ella's clues to solve his own mystery.

An idea came to him as he gathered speed. Should he use this time alone at his parents' home to search cupboards and hidden spaces? The temptation was there, along with the fear lodging itself in his chest. What if he didn't like what he found? Did the advice he'd given Ella not apply to him? *Shit.* It wasn't like he could sit back and do nothing. If only the possibility of damaging his family could be forgotten. He would barrel his way forward and find the answers. Confront his parents.

No, he wasn't up for that this afternoon, and the lure of seeing Ella was too strong. But he would return soon and conduct a search. There had to be something, somewhere—something only obvious when you needed to find it. No doubt it had been staring him in the face all along, if only he'd known to look for it. He was desperate enough to find any clue that would give him answers as to why his father was unknown.

At the intersection that led onto the highway, about two kilometres from his family's home, it struck him. *My God, the newspaper clipping.* He'd read it countless times, never making the connection. He'd read and re-read the list of Tiffany stores, but the place names had meant nothing. Until now; it all came together with one almighty bang and made perfect sense.

One of the lines in the article ended with 'Bo'. Another line started with 'setts'. The list of Tiffany stores was seared onto his brain. Why hadn't he seen it before? It now seemed too easy. The city the newspaper clipping was written about was Boston, Massachusetts. This was where he needed to concentrate his search.

He shook his helmeted head and reprimanded himself for not seeing the clue earlier. God knew how many times he'd read the article. This was the kind of thing that set apart a good investigator from an exceptional one. With dismay, he realised an exceptional one would have picked it up a lot sooner. Thank goodness this job was only a fill-in leading onto the next. He had never felt so incompetent and lacking in skills.

The blare of a horn startled him.

In his periphery, he glimpsed a black utility, only metres away. Too late, he realised he hadn't given way at the intersection. He swerved, but the vehicle collided with his bike, ramming into the rear end. It sent him and the bike hurtling and skidding on its side along the bitumen. Near the edge of the road, the bike rolled over Zane's hurting body and he groaned with pain. Then his head struck a signpost and everything went dark.

Chapter 9

Ella tried Zane's number for the umpteenth time, frustration driving her nuts. *What the hell is this? Some freaking control game?* Why wasn't he returning her messages?

She paced her bedroom. The last thing she wanted was to alert anyone in her family to how agitated she was. They didn't know about Zane. *She* barely knew him, but he had become so vital to her. Had he struck her clean from his life, without even one lousy phone call? It was eating away at her, one chunk at a time.

She didn't want to declare she was desperate yet, but the hold she had on her sanity was fast slipping away. She *had* to see him again. Was she so distasteful that in a matter of twenty-four hours he'd changed his mind about wanting to be with her?

She flopped onto her bed and flung the phone to the floor. What excuse could she use to see him again? With her arms stretched out wide on the bold yellow quilt, she clenched fistfuls of it, knowing the answer. But she steadfastly refused to acknowledge it.

The minutes ticked by and still no beep from her phone. It was nearly dinnertime. Victoria had been okay today, surprisingly. She hadn't thrown up once and had managed to eat a little food. Ella's thoughts churned from one cog to the next. The moment was wrong. She had to control her impatience, which was always a struggle when she was wound up. She made an effort most times, but common sense wasn't anything she was interested in that afternoon.

She'd sworn she wouldn't ask any more questions until Victoria finished this round of chemo treatment. She vowed not to cause any angst for a while, but Zane had promised to spend the afternoon with her. *He'd* broken a promise, and she was acting like a spoilt teenage brat. *If he doesn't want you, get over it.*

She *had* to see him again. Any excuse would do. Ella couldn't believe she was thinking it—to confront her mother again so soon. But if she could glean some information, anything, she would have a reason to visit Zane at work tomorrow.

Ella dragged her feet towards the kitchen. She took a moment, leaning against the doorway, listening to her mother whistle as she prepared dinner.

Of course, she's happy. Today is a good day for Victoria.

Her mother's back was to her as she stepped into the kitchen and made her way to the fridge. She secured a lettuce, a capsicum and a carrot before shutting the door and turning towards the sink to make a salad.

"Oh hello, darling. I was wondering when you were going to show up. Are you feeling okay?"

Don't say another kind word, Mum. For God's sake, don't.

Her mind twirled with the weight of her question. It tortured her and caused a sick sensation to swirl around her stomach.

Ella had no clue she'd spoken her thought aloud— "Am I the result of rape or incest?"—until she saw the stunned look on her mother's face.

The oven door slammed shut as her mother let go of it and straightened. "My God, Ella. No, and that's the truth."

Ella threw the salad items into the empty sink and spun around. "Then why the hell can't you tell me who my father is?"

Oh, this wasn't what she'd planned.

She tried to control her anger, caused by Zane's silence but directed at her mother, except her voice rose of its own accord. Her sisters would hear everything, but she couldn't stop.

"How much alcohol could you have possibly drunk that you can't remember at least a couple of the guys you were with that night?"

She felt like a heel shouting at her mother, so it only made her feel worse when her mother's shoulders drooped.

"I told you the truth, Ella."

Ella gritted her teeth. "Don't give me that bullshit. Spiked drinks were rare in those days. You're keeping something from me, and you know it."

Lily strode into the kitchen, Victoria a few steps behind. "Why are you shouting, Ella?"

Ella was on the verge of blubbering. To upset her mother was the last thing she wanted, but she only sought the truth.

She bit harder on her bottom lip, trying to hold it together, refusing to break down in front of her mother and sisters. But it hurt, not knowing who her father was. It miffed her more that she wasn't going to glean any further information, giving her the much-needed excuse to see Zane tomorrow.

"Ella, what's wrong?" Victoria prodded, putting an arm around her waist.

Ella couldn't talk, not with her emotions bubbling below the surface.

Her mother hadn't moved an inch. Even the pot of boiling water hissing on the stove wasn't enough to break her frozen state.

"Ella?" Victoria insisted.

Ella took a step back, not wanting to infect Victoria with her foul mood. The poor kid; it wasn't her fault she was sick.

With rigid shoulders, Ella turned away, the pounding in her ears deafening, but she couldn't hold back one final dig to her mother.

"I will find out who Isabella is," she choked out, a sob escaping as tears began to pour down her face.

Ella grabbed her car keys with every intention of driving to Zane's home. It was irresponsible to drive in this condition, but she was beyond caring. Right now, she wasn't the practical and smart engineer, changing the world with her innovative ideas. She was a nobody, cursed with uncontrollable anger. She was one of *those* people, unable to handle rejection in a mature way. Never had she wanted to rely on someone else to make her happy, but there it was. She was that person. Adding to the mix was that she'd hurt everyone she cared about. How much worse could her day get?

Barely able to make out the road, she used her sleeve to wipe at her face and drove one-handed.

With dusk approaching, she let everything out, shouting and hiccupping. "I'm sick and tired of being kept in the dark." She changed gears and kept up her solo conversation. "Sick and tired of being dumped and not even face to face."

Ella had done a great job of upsetting everyone at home. Why not continue with Zane and tell him exactly what she thought of how he'd given her the flick? She pushed away the small voice at the back of her head reminding her that he was only supposed to have called her at lunchtime. But nothing would sway her.

"Sick and tired. Period." She growled and thumped the steering wheel.

Driving past Zane's apartment, she registered through her bleary eyes that the lights inside were off. *Is he hiding from me on purpose? Is he keeping a low profile knowing I'm bound to come around?* Parking the car, she slammed the door on her way out. *We'll see about that.*

She stretched her stride to match her mood, swung his gate open and walked to the back porch. Knocked and rang the bell over and over again. When she realised no one was going to answer the door, she fell against it. Big, salty tears began to fall again, this time combined with almighty sobs racking her torso. She was helpless. How the heck had she let one man have a single ounce of control, leaving her so wretched after so short a time? Had she gone completely mad?

"Hello. Can I help you?"

The voice startled her, and straightening, she took a step back. A middle-aged man leaned over the dividing fence.

"Are you looking for Zane? He's not home. He took off this morning on his bike, and I haven't heard him come back."

She attempted a lop-sided smile, the man's concern clearly genuine. "Sorry. I ... I didn't mean to disturb you." A heated flush crept up her neck. She shuffled her feet and fought the urge to cover her face with her hands. It would be a ghastly sight. "I ... I was looking for Zane." She mumbled and cleared her throat. "I guess he had more important things to do today."

The man's fingers tapped the top of the rail. What was he thinking? That Zane was getting rid of another girlfriend? She'd put her last one hundred dollars on it.

"Would you like me to tell him you dropped by?"

Ella swiped her face again, her sleeve well and truly saturated. "Thanks, but that won't be necessary." *What sort of message could I leave?* Turning away, she attempted a half-hearted wave before thanking him and saying goodbye.

Ella sat for a few minutes in her car and contemplated her life. She didn't think it was possible to feel more miserable than she did watching Victoria go through her chemo treatment. But heck, here she was, more down in the dumps than ever.

Hell, her mother wouldn't want to talk to her after she'd shouted at her. Zane wasn't talking to her for whatever reason and her sisters would be mad that she'd upset their mother.

No one would be talking to her for a good while.

True to her prediction, when Ella arrived home last night, exhausted and hungry, she'd gone to her room unopposed. It hurt that no one attempted to check up on her. And this morning she'd left without bumping into anyone and had bought breakfast on the way.

Now, she was taking an early lunch, with every intention of beating Zane at his own game. A practiced conversation ran through her head as her shoes clicked staccato-fashion on the street leading to his office. She wasn't so stupid as to arrive when he was likely to be out, and every swearword she knew sat on the tip of her tongue, ready to be used if needed.

Ella roughly tapped the elevator button for the fifth floor and pasted a smile on her face. She was prepared to greet the receptionist without a snarl, even though a smile was the last thing she wanted to display. Her head ached, her stomach grumbled and her heart hurt too, damn it. Regardless, she'd be super sweet to the receptionist, though she had every intention of speaking to Zane. If her request was denied, she would ignore the woman and walk through to his office. Yes. She was in control now and no bastard was going to have his way with her again. Ever.

When the doors slid open, Ella rounded the corner to find the receptionist busy typing. She remembered Zane calling her Joanne.

Joanne's typing halted as she looked up, a worried frown etched across her brow. "Hello, dear. Can I help you?"

Ella squeezed her keys. She'd forgotten to put them in her handbag and for a moment she wished it were Zane's neck she was squeezing. She held on to her fake smile and asked, "Is Zane available for a few minutes?"

Joanne's eyebrows drew together. "Ella, isn't it?"

Ella nodded.

"Oh dear. You haven't heard?"

Cymbals crashed in Ella's chest; her heart was speeding up recklessly.

"Heard what?" she managed to ask, despite her tongue doing a good job of forgetting its role in her mouth.

Joanne rose and walked around her desk. She put her arm around Ella's shoulder and steered her towards the sofa in the waiting room, indicating she should sit down.

"Heard what?" Ella persisted, panic flowing through her veins.

Joanne sighed. "He's okay now, but he came off his bike yesterday when a utility struck him. His head hit a signpost, so they're keeping an eye on him for one more night. His dad told me that he should be able to leave hospital tomorrow. He'll stay with his parents for a couple more days."

Heat flushed Ella's body. She swayed backwards, dizziness attacking her senses. Her hand held her stomach, not sure why she suddenly felt nauseous.

"The great news is there's no broken bones."

Ella tried to make sense of what Joanne said, but shame engulfed her. Not once. Not for one teeny second had she even considered something might have happened to him. That he might have been on his way to her. Instead, she'd subjected him to scorn, hate, contempt and anger, ready to hurl every vile word under the sun his way. And what about her mother? Her heart crushed further. How much hurt had she created in one lousy day? Why couldn't she have curbed her fury for once? Oh Lord! She'd left a trail of pain so long it would take the rest of her life to mop up. Her impatience was something she *had* to control.

Joanne had left her but returned with one of Zane's business cards. "Here, love. This is his parents' phone number on the back. Ring them. They'll tell you how he is."

Somehow, Ella mumbled a thank you and clasped the card tightly. When she left the office, tears fell. They'd been waiting patiently behind her eyelids for the slightest trigger.

She was such a sham. She wasn't worthy of being around anyone. How would she ever get past the carnage of her behaviour during the last twenty-four hours? She didn't merit the loving family she had, and she didn't deserve Zane.

Early days or not, they'd clicked with alarming speed so that her entire universe centred on him. But for one crummy afternoon she'd doubted him and had left a trail of destruction so long in its wake, she would never be able to repair it.

Oh Zane. You deserve better than me. Would she ever have the guts to tell him how badly she'd treated him and her family?

Chapter 10

Ella crunched the gears, her concentration level sitting around zero. The road that led to the Sunshine Coast was congested as usual. She hoped when she reached the motorway in a few kilometres the traffic would clear up a bit.

She'd requested the afternoon off work. When she'd spoken to Zane's dad last night, he told her Zane was a lot better and was more than keen to leave hospital. By the time she would arrive at the address Zane's father had given her, Zane would be there resting.

It didn't help that she felt like the worst person in the world; her guilt was doing a fantastic job of riddling her mind. She decided to make amends all round. Her treatment of Zane, though he had no idea of it, left a sour taste in her mouth. She would do anything to help his recovery.

More guilt twisted around every organ in Ella's body, knowing that Victoria had experienced a bad turn after Ella's outburst. She'd been rushed to hospital. Her mother, more flustered and upset than Ella had ever seen, ignored her when she arrived home from work that afternoon. Ella had been ready to apologise and make amends, prepared to admit she knew of the hidden box in her mother's wardrobe. But dinner had been a sombre affair with little conversation. It hurt, punching her in the guts, but she deserved no better.

Later that night Lily had questioned Ella, but Ella had kept her mouth shut.

To lessen the guilt, she'd made a pact to ask nothing further of her mother until Victoria recovered. If one short outburst could cause this much disruption in their household, Ella would move cautiously from now on. She loved her family and, with all her heart, wanted her baby sister to get better. The loss of their dad still hurt everyone. The loss of Victoria would shatter them completely. She didn't want to be responsible for that.

An hour later she turned into the Peden's street and was met with a row of homes with well-established gardens. Greys and browns were the predominant colour of houses in this neighbourhood, with roof pitches and gables of all variations. Lawns out front were neat, small and a healthy green.

Did Zane know she was coming? Had he told his parents about her? She shrugged. She could claim to know him from work. He could fill in the gaps later.

She rang the bell once and waited. The door opened and a man smiled a welcome. "Hello. Are you the lass who phoned last night?"

She returned his smile and stretched out her hand. "Yes. I'm Ella."

"Come in, come in." The man opened the door wider and indicated that she should follow. "I'm Jonathan, Zane's dad."

She walked into a front sitting room that had large windows overlooking the side gardens. "How is he?"

Jonathan ran a hand through his hair, which was dark but flecked with grey. "Much better. We're grateful he came out of this with only a bump to the head. The doctors assure us it will heal with no lasting effects. I've been thanking my lucky stars every day."

Ella smiled, relieved. The dark circles beneath his eyes were evidence of how worried he'd been over the past couple of days.

"He's got some mates coming over tonight, so I'm glad you could make it today. The more the merrier."

"Thanks. I need to be back in the city by five, so I'll try not to tire him."

His father chuckled. "He hasn't mentioned you to us. Do you work together?"

She paused before answering. "Ah ... yes, we do. I'm only new."

"That's great. Look, I'll be out the back tinkering on an old mower." He pointed to his left. "His room is the second door on the right. If you want something to eat or drink"—he turned in the opposite direction—"the kitchen is that way. Zane's mother couldn't find a replacement for work today, so I volunteered to stay home and keep an eye on him."

"Thanks, Mr Peden. If I need you, I'll come looking."

He clasped her shoulder and squeezed it. "Thanks. If you can cheer him up, I won't argue. He was a bit down in the dumps this morning and not saying much. I can only hope it's the damage to his bike that's upset him. But as I told him, it can all be fixed. Anyway," he indicated she should make her own way to Zane's room, "I better not hold you up." He turned towards the kitchen with a wave.

She removed her heels and left them near the door. She took in the modern furniture dotted around the large sitting room. The occasional dated piece somehow fit in with the room's ambience. Intrigued by a couple of photos, she gingerly walked on stockinged feet towards them. A smile blossomed when she recognised Zane.

Then she took a deep breath and made her way towards the hallway, tapping her fingers along the maple top of an old china cabinet in the lounge room.

Something in her periphery jerked her to a stop. She backtracked and dropped to her knees, baffled. She closed her eyes, certain *she* was the one who'd received a bump to the head.

Slowly opening her eyes again, she came face to face with the photo of her mother and her mysterious friend—the same one Zane had taken a copy of to help with the investigation. She slid the glass door aside with shaking fingers and reached for the photo, trying to make sense of what she saw. Why the hell would Zane have framed his copy? But on closer inspection, it looked like an original and one that had been in its frame for many years. A photo Zane would've recognised when she'd first shown him.

Heat rushed over her skin and her heart palpitated in angry bursts. He'd nearly fallen off his chair that day! *My God*. Had he lied to her ever since?

She clutched the frame to her chest and rose on shaky legs. *What the hell's going on?* Why was a photo of *her* mother in *his* parents' home? She barrelled down the hallway and burst into his room without knocking.

His eyes snapped open. The smile on his face lasted two seconds before it melted away faster than ice cream on a scorching day. "Ella, what's wrong?"

If his reaction was anything to go by, her face must have looked like thunder. "This is what's wrong." She held the framed photo towards him and witnessed his shoulders sag against the pillow.

"Oh. Please calm down, Ella, I can explain."

Her elbow fused at the joint. There was no way she was going to drop her arm or the frame. "What?" she demanded. "What can you explain? How much you've lied to me?"

He exhaled. She should've been worried about the state of his health, his bump to the head, but she couldn't get past the discovery of the framed photo to give a damn. Controlling her anger? Well, that went out the window too.

He raised his hand in a helpless gesture before he let it flop by his side. "I'm investigating. You have to give me more time."

Through clenched teeth, she barked, "It doesn't excuse you for not telling me."

"I'm aware of that." He tore his gaze away, his face falling. "Technically, your case has been put aside, so I'm not required to say anything."

What? Her breathing sounded noisy by her own standards. She worried her protruding eyes would pop out, the muscles around them straining with the shock of it. "*Technically!*" she shrieked. "You can kiss me and do all sorts of things with me, but *technically*, you can keep this sort of information from me?"

He sat up straighter, his hands clenching in his lap. "Do you want to hear me out, or not?"

She bared her teeth and hissed, "Not anymore." She flung the frame at him, hitting a pillow instead. Storming towards the door, she stopped short at his next words.

"Don't you dare tell a soul about this."

She turned back and snarled, "Don't *you* dare threaten me."

She slammed the door and raced out of the house. Kilometres down the road she remembered her shoes near the front door. Too late, tears stampeded down her face. She had no intention of returning for them and regretted her impulsive bout of anger. She *did* want to listen to what he had to say, but now the opportunity was lost. Oh, good Lord, when would she ever learn?

Was it less than forty-eight hours when she'd last driven with tears coursing down her face? She needed to grow up and strengthen her backbone. How the heck would she cement her place in a man's world if she was prone to crying every five minutes? This had to stop. Now!

While stopped at a red light, she reached across to her handbag on the passenger seat and snatched a couple of tissues from it. She needed all her wits about her to figure out what finding that photo meant. With her crying reduced to the occasional sniffle, callous thoughts snaked their way around her head. What was the connection? Who was the friend? Zane's mother? Aunt?

She swept away the last bit of moisture from her cheeks as a strong resolve began to grow. She could find another investigator and fast-track her plans to find her father. Already she had an extra clue, and wasn't their work meant to be done with the utmost discretion? Zane would never need to find out she'd gone elsewhere.

But her heart did a loop and her shoulders sagged against the seat. For once, she didn't care how congested the traffic was going to be getting back into the city. She didn't curse the snail-paced cars that jammed the freeway. All she could concentrate on was the fact that Zane had lied to her, from their very first day.

All that time together and he'd known about the photo, had proceeded with the investigation without her authority—without her knowing. *Damn it*, without trusting her. That hurt. It hurt in places she'd never known existed. That small voice she'd pushed to the furthermost reaches of her mind, turned around and came back screaming, reminding her it was what she deserved. For hurting her mother, her family and, without his knowledge, Zane.

Her face dropped as the traffic came to a standstill. An accident ahead would mean she'd stay this way for hours. Ella was past caring because it was unlikely, she'd find a way forward after this latest fiasco. She spiralled downwards into a messy depressive state and would need all the help she could get if she was ever to make it back on top.

Chapter 11

⧢

"Mum, thanks for all this." Zane placed the esky near the fridge then reached for the kettle.

His mother emptied the esky, lifting containers of ready-made meals from it and putting them in his freezer. "Don't overdo it next week, okay."

He nodded, finding mugs and spoons. "Did we remember the milk?"

She set it on the kitchen table. "Yep."

Zane smiled. His over-organised mother was at her best when she could fuss over any of her children.

His father had insisted Zane stay until the weekend, and as his head hurt for a few days, he'd appreciated the extra attention. There'd been moments when his mother had sat by his bed chatting and he'd wanted to ask about the fraudulent birth certificates. Each time something had held him back. Once he'd uttered the first word, he could never take it back. His discovery would change his family forever, and he wasn't ready for that yet.

As for Ella, the only way to win her back was to come up with answers. Find her father.

Luckily, the accident hadn't obliterated from his mind the vital clue he'd worked out only seconds before impact. Authorised to access registered sites at work, he couldn't wait to begin his search.

One bike accident and one week later, he was ready to start. Each clue he'd discovered so far had moved him one step closer to working out the mystery connection between his mother and Ella's. He was determined to work it all out, but at what cost? He wasn't sure.

"How do you want it? With milk and sugar?"

"Here, let me. You've done enough this week." Zane nudged her towards a chair then took over the tea-making duties.

"That's what mothers are for. A mother will always do what's best for her child. She would give up her life for them."

Her statement, said matter-of-factly, slammed against his chest.

Ask her.

Not in a million years could he get his tongue to work as he placed her mug down.

Sitting across from him, she took her first sip. He looked into her dark eyes. There was a message hidden in their depths he couldn't fathom. What exactly had she done? Had she given up a previous life to ensure his safety?

When she reached for the Anzac biscuits, it was as if shutters had closed over her secret.

Oh, Mum, was it that bad?

He didn't want to open old wounds, but he had a right to know who his biological father was. Only once he'd followed every lead without success, would he confront her for answers.

"I left your friend's shoes in the car. I suppose she'll be chasing you for them."

Zane shrugged and smiled casually. He pictured Ella's face, full of fury. She was even more beautiful when she was furious. Life with her would never be boring.

"She's always forgetting things at work," he said. "I'll bring them in on Monday. She'll be wondering where she left them." There was no reason his mother should question the story he'd made up.

He tried to sound nonchalant about getting Ella's shoes back to her, but with too much time on his hands during the past few days, he'd decided returning her shoes would be a very big deal.

He got that she was angry with him, but he didn't appreciate how she'd thrown the photo frame towards his head. Thank goodness it'd landed on the soft pillow and cushioned the sound of the impact. The last thing he'd needed was his father racing inside from the garage. Zane had risen from bed and returned it to the china cabinet. No one was the wiser to what Ella had discovered.

Now, he cursed his stupidity for not pushing it back behind all the trophies and glassware where he'd originally found it. But it was too late now for self-recriminations.

He took another sip of his drink and frowned. Yes, getting Ella's shoes back to her was going to be a very big deal. Whether she liked it or not.

⌘

Showered and with a mug of hot chocolate, Zane settled in bed and rested against a heap of pillows. He took another sip as the computer booted up.

Okay, here goes. We have a starting place.

Excitement buzzed in his chest. He had a concrete starting point and a place from which to build. He'd re-read the newspaper clipping and it seemed there were other instances where the words Boston and Massachusetts had been lopped off. With certainty, he knew this was the city to start his search.

He accessed the missing persons and cold case files and started searching thirty years earlier to make certain he didn't miss a thing. He trolled and crosschecked over and over, often coming across the same unsolved mysteries.

Two hours later, his hand jerked to a stop on the mouse, his breath coming in short and shallow bursts. There she was. A small photo. Tiny compared to others. Grainy, too, as though the image was handed over as a last resort, not wanting to believe she was missing, or possibly murdered. He zoomed in on the short article attached to the image of Ella's mother.

Police are seeking the whereabouts of Catherine Van Der Meeliko, last seen with her one-year-old daughter, Isabella, on May 22, 1991 at her Boston home ...

The write-up mentioned an address in Boston and how Catherine's husband, Thomas Van Der Meeliko, was worried about the child and the unstable nature of his wife's health.

Unstable?

He pushed the laptop aside and threw off the covers. Scrambling from the bed, he rummaged through his briefcase until he found a notepad and pen.

Okay, as much info as you can.

Zane wrote down details—names, dates and places—and scrolled through other search engines, gathering as much information on Ella's father as he could. Always hopeful that something, anything, would turn up about his mother. Where the hell was the connection?

Zane flicked a glance at his bedside clock and registered it was close to midnight. He rubbed his tired eyes and whistled long and low. He let his head fall back and pushed his laptop aside. *Holy shit.* How did he tell Ella her father was one of Boston's most influential men, with old money dating back generations? He lived in Louisburg Square, Beacon Hill, for goodness' sake, only the most expensive residential neighbourhood in all of the USA.

Zane shook his head and stretched his numb arms. There was scant information on Thomas's next marriage but enough to know that Ella had a half-brother and sister. Zane couldn't quite work out what had happened to the wife. It wasn't clear if she and Thomas had divorced or she'd died. As for Thomas, he worked in his family's investment business and had a stronghold in politics.

So, what had made Ella's mother leave? Where did his own mother come into it? If she was raised in America, how the hell could he not detect even the slightest American accent or inflection in her voice? Had she schooled herself so well that no one had ever considered she'd been raised in the States? What about his dad? Was he in the loop or had she lied to him all these years too?

He closed his eyes and, doubting he'd get much sleep, planned how to tell Ella what he knew. Well, he'd thought he would until he woke to a new day.

Ella twirled her pen around her finger. She was owed holiday time, so maybe she should take time off. With misery eating away at her, her productivity was at an all-time low. Her senior manager hadn't said too much yet, only asking if she was okay. She'd nodded, loosely holding onto her emotions, tears never far away. Which wasn't like her at all.

Tensions at home were getting worse. Her mother was silent, and everybody could sense something was afoot. *God, if only I knew what.*

Ella was keeping her pact, staying quiet until Victoria was completely in the clear. Except she wanted her mother to say something—anything. Didn't she want to know how Ella had come across the name Isabella? Apparently not. Instead, her mother's frown etched deeper into her forehead and her worry lines became more pronounced. Had Ella caused them, or was her constant anxiety about Victoria to blame? As much as Ella hoped it was Victoria's illness, gut instinct told her otherwise.

She shelved any plans to find a new investigator. It wasn't worth it. It was bad enough not having her dad around; not being able to talk to her mother was killing her. Slowly, painfully, with each passing day. With Zane no longer in the picture everything felt grim. There didn't seem to be a reason to get out of bed and she couldn't hide the horrible and drawn look on her face. She was barely coping at work, so she would probably lose her job next.

She picked up her coffee cup and took a sip. She screwed up her face as cold liquid trickled down her throat. *Yuck.* She rose from her cubicle to get a refill and stopped in her tracks. There was a commotion at the reception desk—someone was arguing with Samantha.

No one got past Samantha without an appointment or a phoned confirmation. She manned entry to their floor with a battleaxe in her hand, and God help anyone unauthorised who stepped on her territory.

Other colleagues rose from their seats to get a better look at the disturbance.

Ella froze when she recognised Zane heading her way. A bad-tempered Samantha tailed him. She pulled on his sleeve, trying to halt all six foot of him.

Ella put her coffee down with shaking hands. She would need all her wits and limbs on hand.

"Ella, he told me he had to see you *now*. That it was a matter of life or death. I tried to stop him and phone you first."

Ella glanced from Samantha's apologetic face to Zane's scowl.

"Is she always such a dragon?"

For a fleeting second, Ella wanted to laugh—God, he was gorgeous, and anyone who could outwit Samantha deserved a medallion—until she realised what he held in his hands.

"Is this your desk?" His chestnut-brown eyes pierced hers.

She didn't say a word, but someone else answered for her.

"I believe you left these behind." Zane plonked her heeled shoes in the middle of her desk.

When titters and laughter rose up from those close enough to see and hear the exchange—which by this stage appeared to be everyone on the floor—shame engulfed her. She didn't doubt her skin was awash with colour as heat consumed her face and neck.

"I need to see you after work at my place. And, yes, it is a matter of life or death."

With that, he turned and walked out, broad shoulders tucked neatly in his work suit. His face covered in half-day stubble, something she wanted to rub her cheek against—if she didn't kill him first.

I'll give him *life or death.*

Chapter 12

Ella drove to Zane's home with every swearword she knew on the tip of her tongue, ready to lash out. Until she reached his street and the tension in her shoulders drained away. *Is it really a matter of life or death? Remember the last time you wrote him off?*

She remembered all too well.

His little episode with her shoes was a mean trick to play. In front of all her colleagues he'd made her look a fool.

She parked her car, letting it idle a few moments before switching it off and bringing forth all those swearwords again, just in case.

Zane waited on the back porch. She wasn't surprised he'd heard her arrival seeing as she'd slammed his side gate harder than necessary. His eyes were broody, his suit long since discarded for casual knee-length shorts. A navy cotton tee stretched over his broad chest.

Determined to have the upper hand, Ella pressed her shoulders back and ground her teeth, but then her eyes were drawn to his bare feet. For a moment she weakened, willing to do anything to have those feet rub against her legs. Inwardly, she groaned, realising how much she missed him.

She gave her head a quick shake, sucked in a ragged breath and ignored her pounding heart. With a straight back, she gave him a glare worthy of an Olympic gold medal. "You wanted to see me?"

He beckoned for her to come inside. When the door closed behind her, she held her ground for a moment before lashing out. "That was *not* a nice thing to do to me at work."

Zane's eyebrow rose sharply. "Neither was throwing a frame at my head."

She'd regretted throwing the frame the second it had left her hand. "I know, and I'm sorry, but you've been lying to me since the day we met."

Zane took a step back. "I could've lost an eye because of your temper."

She clamped her jaw, trying to keep said temper in check. "I said I was sorry."

Zane turned away and headed for the kitchen. "I didn't want anyone to think I owned those heels."

"Nice change of subject," she muttered, reluctantly following and hating every step she took. "You could have thrown them away. I don't want them back."

He stopped and spun around, only a breath between them. "Well, you have them now."

Deadlocked. Neither gave an inch. Neither looked away.

Heat flushed her neck. With anger or something else? "So, who's dying?"

"No one." His warm breath reached her cheeks and made her dizzy.

She quirked an eyebrow. "More lies?"

"Christ!" It was the first sign of a crack in his armour. "I needed you here today."

"Why?"

His gaze dropped. "Truce first."

"Like hell."

Before she could grasp together her next words in this slinging match, he'd reached out and gently tucked his hand behind her neck. In an instant, she was brushed up against his chest. His mouth lowered and proclaimed her as his. And yep, this was where she wanted to be. This was where she belonged, and she didn't shy back. Her tongue slashed across his, satisfied she was the cause of his groan reverberating around them.

When she pulled back, cool air on her wet lips caused her to shiver, and she released the fistful of his shirt. She gasped, taking in all the air she could and swayed. He caught her and tightened his grip around her waist.

"I'm here now. What did you want?"

His hand dropped and she instantly missed its warmth.

"Do you want to stay for dinner? I have a freezer full of precooked meals."

Aaaarggghh! He was impossible and this was no longer a joke.

"Zane," she yelled when he turned away and walked towards the small kitchen. "I have better things I could be doing." *Did she?* She hissed between drawn lips. "Don't you dare walk away from me or I'm leaving."

He disappeared through a doorway. "Come and have dinner, and I'll tell you who your father is."

Ella froze, her world tilting on its axis. Seconds ticked by as she stood paralysed, unable to move. When her vision clouded, she reached up and touched her flushed skin. She blew out a series of short breaths and, when a tingling increased in her limbs, recognised the signs of hyperventilation. She made it to the couch just as her legs buckled.

He can't know. I haven't given him a name. She rocked from side to side. Her insides refused to stop quivering. If he was lying, she was certain she was capable of harm—or worse.

She burst into tears. She covered her face, trying to hold back the wave washing down her cheeks. Why was Zane doing this? Remorse washed over her. She hadn't meant to hurl the frame at him. Was she going to pay for that mistake for the rest of her life? And why was she crying again? She'd never cried as much as she had in the past few weeks. She was growing tired of her inability to control her emotions. Where was the strong, fierce and independent girl she used to be? The one her parents had been delighted with as far back as she could remember.

She curled up, unable to give a damn where that girl was. She would give up looking for her, too.

◦◦◦

Zane heard a sob, dropped the takeaway container onto the kitchen bench and legged it back to the lounge room.

Jeez, she's crying? He hadn't meant for this to happen.

He was ashamed of his antics earlier that day; he hadn't once considered how highly strung she was and how he shouldn't have pushed it. Damn it, would he ever stop to think about his actions before barrelling ahead?

"Hey, hey, it's okay." He slipped her heels off and picked her up. Her tears continued unabated, washing over his arms and dripping onto his shirt. Instead of slowing, sobs heaved from her throat, compounding his guilt. His good-guy meter dived to an all-time low. "Shh, hey, I didn't mean to upset you."

In his bedroom, he pulled back the covers of his bed and laid her down. Lying beside her, he swept her hair back while he pressed light kisses on her forehead, giving her time to calm down.

When only the occasional hiccup escaped her soft lips, he lifted his shirt and used it to wipe her face. She looked everywhere but at him.

"Do you want to talk about it?"

She shrugged, using his sheet to mop up further. "From the day I thought you'd dumped me, when you were in fact in hospital, everyone's been mad at me. I thought you were, too, until I learned of the accident. But first I screwed things up at home, which I did royally."

Zane listened to her recount her sorry tale with regret on his part. *Shoot.* She really was mixed up and hurting a lot, and her family's pain was taking its toll. He shouldn't have been so hard on her. Though his anger at her for throwing a tantrum with the frame was justified, he could see how everything had built up around her.

And he'd missed her. *Badly*. He tucked her face under his chin and tightened his hold, absorbing as much of her pain and hurt as he could. He needed something to tide him through the uncertain days ahead. No doubt a lot was about to unfold. When he filled her in on what he now knew, he couldn't guarantee it wouldn't bring more shocks the more clues they unravelled. He had a sense of what waited for her in Boston after reading countless articles. There was no telling how the meeting with her father would go. It could go either way. Good or bad.

She pushed away, piercing him with her watery, red-rimmed eyes. "Do you really know who my father is?"

He nodded. "But I insist we have dinner first. Then I'll go through everything I've learned and how I came to find him." He held her gaze and willed her to agree to his condition.

She dropped back, nestling into the pillow. "The mysterious friend in the photo is your mother, isn't it?"

"Yes, but I don't know how they're connected yet."

She rolled to face him and clutched his hand. Squeezing tightly, she asked, "Will you give me one tiny detail before we have dinner? Then I promise to wait."

Zane debated what to tell her—as part of their truce, she deserved something for his unnecessary behaviour. He lowered his head until his lips touched hers, trying to lose himself in her presence. Her lemon and eucalyptus scent swamped his senses, and the urge to savour every single moment with her was strong. He pulled back a fraction and pinned his gaze on her. "I'm pretty certain you were born in the States. Boston, Massachusetts, in fact."

Ella gasped, her eyes widening in surprise. "No way. My mother doesn't have an American accent."

"Neither does mine, but I think I was born there too. I'll let you be the judge when I tell you everything. Now," he made to get up, "do you need to be home any time soon?"

She groaned and covered her face with his pillow, her voice muffled. "Like I said, everyone's mad at me."

He tugged on her hand, encouraging her sit up. "I'll feel better if you send a message telling them you'll be late. Let's not make them madder. Also, please don't say a word to your mother about me. I have a hunch she'll recognise my name, and I want to uncover all the facts I can first. I'm not sure about you but I want to be absolutely certain about how my mother is connected before I say anything to her. I'm not sure how far back my father fits in, but the last thing I want to do is destroy what I've always considered my parents' perfect marriage."

Ella discarded the pillow she was hugging and sighed.

"They mean everything to me," Zane added as he took her hand and helped her off the bed.

She nodded, and he saw complete comprehension on her face. "I get it, Zane, I really do."

"I'm glad." He drew her in close. Relief surged through his body as he kissed her closed eyelids. This discussion between them could've gone a couple of ways at this point, but so far, it was going okay. "I'll finish getting dinner ready while you let your family know you'll be home late."

Zane trailed his thumb down her arm, leaving goosebumps as she turned and left the bedroom in search of her handbag and phone. While he'd been nervous about how she would react to the news of her father, he was even more anxious to know whether she would forgive him. He didn't blame her for being distrustful. He'd be the same in her situation. Zane had known all along that he had to tell her about the photo, sooner rather than later, but he'd never imagined she would stumble across the second one in his mother's house. It'd come as a shock that his plan to keep her away from his mother for as long as was needed had so easily unravelled.

Chapter 13

"Could I borrow a change of clothes? I really want to get out of these." Ella wiped her hands on a tea towel, satisfied the kitchen was clean and tidy, and pointed to her restrictive pencil skirt and blouse.

Zane disappeared for a minute. When he returned, he said, "I've put some choices on my bed." He squeezed her shoulder. "Go on, I'll get the laptop up and running."

She struggled to keep her nerves at bay. Over dinner, which she'd barely eaten, Zane had stressed how important it was for her to weigh up her options after he told her what he knew.

What the heck?

She unbuttoned her blouse and let it fall to the floor, then unzipped her skirt and let it fall, too. She could choose to forget all about her father and instead spend precious time with Zane, right here in his bedroom. God, she'd missed him so much. The days since she'd discovered the second photo had been excruciating. During that time, she'd changed into another person—one she wasn't proud of, her actions ruled by her heart and not her head.

She picked up her clothes and placed them on the bed. Taking one of Zane's shirts, she slipped it on. As it covered enough, she ignored his shorts and removed her stockings instead.

She took a deep breath. Her senses were on high alert. The more Zane pushed for her to consider her next move carefully, the more concerned she became.

What has he found? Her gut instincts were rarely wrong—he was nervous, but why? How much would her life change in the next hour? Suddenly, the food she'd eaten wasn't sitting so well and so she swallowed hard to keep it down. *I can do this.*

She squared her shoulders, lifted her chin and left the room.

She found Zane at the table with his laptop and a folder beside it. He looked up and gave her a lop-sided smile. "Ready?"

She pushed a chair up against his and nodded. He put his arm around her and pressed her against him. When he leaned closer to kiss her forehead, she drew strength from his warmth.

"Okay. Firstly, I want to point out that your mother must've had a good reason for leaving her old life behind. Our discovery might do more harm than good."

She nodded, for once lost for words.

He opened the folder. "Birth certificates. All frauds. Yours, your mother's, my mother's and mine. But not my dad's or brothers'."

Her heart jolted. *Frauds?*

He spread them out in front of the laptop. "Can you believe it? I'd never once laid eyes on mine. My mother always took care of official paperwork. Look at this."

He picked up his copy and pointed to the line stating his father was unknown.

Ella gasped. "You had no idea?"

"Nope. None at all. Until a week ago I'd always believed my dad was my father. I never had any reason to question it. Why should I? We were your average happy family. He certainly didn't treat me any differently to my brothers."

"Oh, Zane." She rubbed her hand on his arm. His statement was a brave one and was sure to be affecting him more than he was letting on. To learn that piece of information would've been hard. She stretched her arms around his broad shoulders and placed light kisses on his neck, needing to find a way to comfort him. "I'm so sorry. This was supposed to be about me. I didn't mean to mess up your life, too."

He chuckled wryly. "Let's keep going. Your news is still to come." He pulled out the photos of the items Ella had discovered in her mother's wardrobe.

He held up the photo of the little blue box. "The baby bracelet was purchased at a Tiffany's store. Joanne in my office recognised the box as one given with any jewellery purchase. Tiffany didn't exist in Australia twenty-six years ago."

She leaned over his arm, wanting a closer look. She never would've guessed the box was a clue.

"So, we have fraudulent birth certificates, jewellery purchased in the States, a version of your name and your date of birth on the bracelet, and"—he picked up the photograph of the baby but instead showed her the reverse side of it—"a newspaper article."

He slid it to her side of the table and tapped the edge of it. "Took me a while, but some words are spelled the American way."

Dumbstruck at all the clues he'd worked out, Ella could only nod.

"Well, last week, after I'd compiled a list of all the Tiffany stores in existence twenty-something years ago, I was riding home from my parents' when the final clue came to me."

He swivelled in his seat and brushed his lips against hers for a fleeting moment before adding, "It came to me when I was supposed to stop at an intersection. When I didn't, the utility hit me. You could say this clue was the cause of the accident."

"What clue?" she asked, fingering the spot his mouth had just touched.

"One of the cities on my list is Boston, Massachusetts. Look here." He pointed out and explained the partial words.

Her mouth dropped open, then she uttered, "The newspaper was published in Boston. So, I really was born there?"

"Precisely."

"But ... but how did you find my father?"

He straightened the laptop and clicked the mouse. "I searched registered websites for missing persons and cold cases, which I have access to. Let me show you what I found."

She ran her tongue over her suddenly dry lips, curling her fingers in her palms. "Is he alive?"

"Yes. Very much so." Zane swung the laptop in her direction.

Ella yelped when the image of her mother, looking about the same age as she did in the photograph Ella had found, stared back at her. Ella squinted at it, getting as close as she could to the words attached to it. She read silently, absorbing and memorising every word, reading it over and over.

When she finished, she sat back, a chill raising goosebumps along her arms. Her vision blurred, the words of the article filtering past her eyes. "What did my father mean about being worried for her sanity? He couldn't have been referring to Mum?"

Zane rested his hand on her exposed thigh, and the sudden warmth, compared to the cold streak sliding across her chest, burned. "I've researched Thomas Van Der Meeliko, your father. When you read some more, details might become more apparent. I'm pretty sure you have a half-brother and sister."

"Really?" She gasped.

He took command of the laptop again and coordinated more mouse clicks. "Here we are." He turned the screen in her direction again and she was confronted with an image of her father. His eyes were a dead giveaway; they were the exact same shade of blue as hers. Even the shape of his cheekbones matched hers.

She devoured every word of the article attached to the photo. Isabella Van Der Meeliko was a long, long way from Ella Harvey. Her father was rich, powerful and lived in an expensive suburb. His great-great-great-whatever-father had made his fortune and then passed it on from one generation to the next.

When she'd had her fill of that article, Zane opened the next page. Here, she was confronted with her half-siblings and the news that their mother had died. No exact details were given, only speculation by the journalist.

Ella sat in a trance, the words swimming across her vision. She'd spent years wanting to know who her father was, but she'd never imagined this. Why had her mother left? She was a grounded, sensible and down-to-earth person. She would've had it all. But had she?

How had she maintained her secret for all these years and how the heck had she lost her accent? That was what really baffled Ella. She'd never once suspected it. Never had her mother uttered a single word that Ella might've laughed over because it had come out wrong.

Ella shook her head as the impact of the truth hit her. Her mother had lived an entirely different life, in a different country, with a husband of such magnitude. But for some reason she'd walked away from it all.

Zane rose from his chair and stretched his arms above his head. For once in her life, Ella had no words to express her surprise or her anxiety regarding what she should do next.

She tensed when Zane stepped behind her and gently massaged her shoulders. She *was* uptight. About everything. "What do I do now, Zane?"

His pressed against her neck gently rubbing. He kissed the spot beside her ear. "I know this could be dangerous, but do you want to go to Boston?"

She swivelled in her chair. "What?"

"You know, take a well-deserved holiday. A week is enough. Just don't tell your mother you're going."

With a wry chuckle, she said, "So I should lie?"

He crouched beside her and tucked a strand of hair behind her ear. "You could tell your family you're going to Hawaii. It won't be a lie. A lot of flights complete their customs in Hawaii before they land on the continent."

"How can I leave in the middle of Victoria's chemo and before I fix the mess I've created? Anyway, I don't want to go alone."

He leaned in and left the softest of touches along her neck. A delicious shiver ran down the length of her body. "I know this thing between us is new, but would you allow me to come too?"

She let her eyes flutter closed and moaned when his lips reached her eyes. He tilted her face, making his access easier. She sighed with pleasure and asked, "You ... you would come?"

She sensed him draw back abruptly. She flicked her eyes open, missing his closeness.

"I have a stake in this too, remember. I need to look for leads about *my* father and the connection between your mother and mine."

"How are you going to do that?"

He closed the lid of the laptop and tugged at her hand until she rose from her chair. "We'll start at the library." He led her towards his bedroom. "They keep microfiche copies of old newspapers. If we search from the date you disappeared, who knows what we'll find. Then we'll do a tour of all the posh suburbs, which tourists do in Boston, and we'll check out your father's home."

Lifting her, he laid her down on his bed and joined her. "You can decide then if you should approach him or not. Until then, I deserve your undivided attention for at least the next twenty minutes."

Despite all her anxieties, she chuckled. This man had taken control and she was okay with it. Trust him to drag her to the bedroom to take her mind off things. Her head *was* clogged up; she had no idea how to move forward. Should she go to Boston? No one was likely to made a fuss if she left for only a week.

The feel of Zane's hands on her body and the amazing things he was doing with his mouth deserved her undivided attention. So, she pushed the Boston trip to the side for now. If she had her way, she would stretch this interlude for longer than twenty minutes. And yet ...

She shoved him away and rolled over until she straddled him, then paused, half-grinning, as she was too far away for him to kiss her.

He groaned and she relented, convinced she'd made her point.

I'll decide who's in control.

I'll decide who's in control.

Chapter 14

"What's going on, Ella?"

As Ella was packing her suitcase for her departure the next day, she tried to ignore her sister, who was lying on the bed.

Ella glanced up fleetingly, admiring the colourful swirls on Victoria's headscarf. Regardless of how sick she was, and with no hair, Victoria still managed to convey a sense of elegance. Ella was almost envious, which was crazy considering how unwell Victoria was.

Ella zipped the suitcase shut and dragged it onto the floor before flopping onto the bed beside her sister.

"Please don't lie to me. You never have before." Victoria said.

Ella sighed. It'd been the longest two weeks of her life. Since learning of her father's identity, she and Zane had spent every spare moment gathering information before they left for Boston.

Ella wanted to be prepared. She wanted the upper hand. It was her usual way.

Rolling onto her side, she took Victoria's hands in her own. Zane's warning ran riot in her head. *Best we don't tell our mothers we're going to Boston.*

"You're not going to Hawaii, are you?"

Ever so slowly, Ella shook her head.

Victoria gasped. "What are you doing? Is it something illegal?"

"No," Ella yelped, squeezing her hands around Victoria's before releasing them and groaning into her own. She didn't need her mother to race into the room at this crucial point.

"Are you in trouble?" Victoria asked.

Ella opened her arms and beckoned for Victoria to lie against her. Ella tucked her sister's face beneath her chin. "Vic, I'm not in trouble and I'm not doing anything illegal." She squeezed her closer and added, "You have to trust me on this."

Holding Victoria this way, she was reminded of the many nights her sister would sneak into her bed when they were younger. They'd shared a bedroom, and there had been many mornings when Ella would wake to find Victoria's tiny body tucked up against her own.

She slid back and pinned her gaze on Victoria's soft hazel eyes. "I promise I'll tell you everything when I get back. Please don't keep asking me. I made a promise that I wouldn't say anything until I returned."

Victoria's brow creased. "What if there's an emergency? Can't you leave details of where you're going and staying so we can contact you? Put it in an envelope and seal it. I won't open it unless I have no other choice."

Ella sagged back onto the mattress. Victoria had a point, and if she promised not to show anyone, where was the harm?

"I won't say another word, but I know you're keeping something from Mum."

Ella's eyes opened wide.

"I also know this has something to do with finding your father. I've been sick, but not enough to notice the questions you've been asking Mum lately."

Ugh. "No, it's ..."

Victoria put her fingers to Ella's mouth and silenced her words of protest. Not that Ella had any idea what she'd been about to say.

"Shh. Don't say anything. I hope you find him, and that it makes you happy and complete."

Why did she have the best sister in the world? And why was the universe doing everything possible to take her away? She couldn't help the morbid thoughts that followed. She was the one who should be struck down with cancer and made to leave this world early. That old song her mother used to sing, 'Only The Good Die Young,' had never rung so true.

Her chest shook with an involuntary shiver. What was it? Was it the pressure of not being able to share her new discovery? The fear of what she would learn? Or knowing that her sister knew her better than she thought? She tried to hold her emotions together. Clenched her hands into tight balls and worked damn hard to keep it in.

Her sister's concern only hastened the arrival of Ella's tears and they streamed down her face. She risked fracturing the sacred circle of her tight-knit family. She almost didn't want to know the reasons her mother had left her old life but talking to her at this stage would only create more havoc.

Go to Boston, she told herself, *come back and then talk*. If the truth was revealed there'd be no need for any more secrets.

Victoria held her close, muffling the sound of her crying. She always knew what to do, how to help.

Was all this effort to find her father worth it? What about the introduction of her half-siblings to their family?

At least Victoria promised not to ask further questions.

Morbid thoughts returned—*what if Victoria's health declines and we don't get the chance to share this closeness again?*—which brought on a fresh rush of tears. Ella was soon exhausted and couldn't decipher what she was crying about. Her head was a jumbled mess, and fear refused to dislodge itself from her chest. She could very well be the one to destroy her happy family. Zane had given her enough warnings and scenarios.

Her thoughts returned to her father. The frightening volume of information she and Zane had sourced about him alarmed her. It wasn't always good; occasionally words like 'scandal' were used in articles about him, which caused unease to settle close to home. She couldn't understand the problems only the rich were exposed to. Public image was everything, or so it seemed.

She hoped the media had it wrong. Wasn't it normal to prey on the famous and wealthy? A huge percentage of stories the media published were hyped-up untruths, so she was prepared to give her father the benefit of the doubt. She would make up her own mind once she met him.

A tiny voice pushed her to persist and not turn her back on the idea of travelling to Boston. She'd been hoping her father might offer to pay for the best medical team and leave no stone unturned when it came to Victoria's treatment. In the early days, after the diagnosis, Ella had dreamed of winning the lottery and having all the money in the world to treat her sister. Reality though could be a kick in the guts and she hadn't hesitated to help her mother cover some of the medical costs.

The question, though, that kept Ella up at night, twisting and turning, and haunted her into the small hours was would life be the same when she returned in a week's time? It was the unknown territory of Boston that she feared most. She should just talk to her mother. It was the obvious thing to do. But then what? Would her mother continue to lie? Would she tell lies to cover lies so the truth never came out? Would she paint a horrible picture of her father and scare her from ever meeting him?

It was Ella's dream to find her biological father, so it was time for her chin-up and can-do attitude. What was the worst that could happen? If he wanted nothing to do with her, she'd live with it and never look back, but at least she could say she'd tried.

So engrossed with her own thoughts, Ella momentarily forgot where she was until Victoria made to get up. Ella's tears had slowed and she used her shirt to mop up some of the moisture.

"You'll only be gone a week, Sis. You'll be home before we know it, and we'll both lie here on this very bed laughing at what all the fuss was about. He can only be human, right?"

Victoria's practical approach to life never failed to amaze Ella. Considering the awful days she endured, she never missed an opportunity to make others feel better.

Ella gave her a lop-sided smile. She sat up, put her arms around Victoria's shoulders and hugged hard.

"I'm sorry. I promised not to pry, but do you know who he is?" Victoria asked.

Victoria's out-of-the-blue question startled Ella, but without hesitation she nodded.

"Right. I want a full report when you get back." Victoria laughed at her own bossiness. On her way out, she halted at the door. "Don't forget that information for me. Leave the envelope under your pillow. I'll come and get it when you're gone and put it in a safe place." Before she closed the door, she said, "I'll give Mum a hand with dinner. Come down as soon as you look decent."

Ella chuckled. No doubt she had puffy eyes. "Okay, thanks."

Ella flopped onto the bed, her thoughts switching to Zane. It had been hard to find time to spend together during the past two weeks and she suffered because of it. She closed her eyes and wound her arms around her pillow. It was easy to bring his essence to life; she fed off her feelings and thoughts when they were apart. His stubble against her cheek, his legs against hers, his mouth playing over her face. *Ugh*. She didn't want to cope without him.

He said he'd organise their flights and accommodation so she could concentrate on her research. He'd also promised his boss that he'd work overtime in preparation for his absence. It all amounted to less time together.

A shiver of apprehension zapped along her breastbone. They planned on sharing the same room to save costs, and this might be the time to show Zane how she felt about him. Every minute they spent together reaffirmed how much they suited each other. Did he feel the same way? They never spoke of love or the future. Their time was consumed with finding their fathers and unlocking the secret they'd stumbled across. Was it a crazy idea to travel to Boston with a virtual stranger? Maybe. Would she change her mind? Never. They shared a kindred spirit, and any doubts they were siblings had been squashed. One glimpse at Ella's father and they'd known with certainty that he couldn't also be Zane's.

Ella had spent hours trawling the internet and had been able to gather much information on her father. She'd followed his political career, researched the companies he was associated with and learned of other immediate family members. They all seemed to be an integral part of Boston society.

She rolled onto her back, flung the pillow aside and stared at the ceiling. Her mother's reluctance to talk stung. Ever since Ella had uttered the name 'Isabella' a barrier had risen between them. Ella had noticed it straight away. Her sisters hadn't sensed it, but for Ella, her mother may as well have speared her through the chest. The effect was much the same. They warily stepped around each other and their conversations were stilted and awkward. It didn't help that Ella was glued to her laptop for hours on end.

She hadn't dared check if the little box of evidence was still hidden in the wardrobe. Her mother would've guessed where she'd learned the name, but why say nothing? Had she deduced something about this holiday, as Victoria had?

Ella exhaled, pressing her fingers down on her scalp.

This week she would keep her promise—to say nothing to her mother until Victoria finished her round of chemo.

Next week might be different.

Chapter 15

Ella closed her eyes, resting them from eyestrain. Hunched over the burgundy timber tabletop, with her thighs nestled against the ornately sculptured legs dating back to the last century, she massaged her temples and opened her eyes again. She found it hard to believe she was in one of America's greatest libraries and wanted to absorb the room's intensity.

Art pieces and heavy looking tables filled the vast, hushed reading room known as Bates Hall. The space was illuminated by a profusion of green lampshades resembling fireflies. A series of arched windows on the eastern side dwarfed most of the room. Internet and power connections were discreetly placed to ensure modern technology took nothing away from the ambience of the room. Dominated by its domed, coffered ceiling, the room resembled a wide-arched barrel vault.

She inhaled the smell unique to libraries that only a bookworm could appreciate. The strong scent of old leather mingled with the polished fragrance of the tables.

She jumped when Zane whispered, "Want to take a break? Go out to the courtyard?"

As they'd already been given permission to leave the material on the desk when they needed a break, Ella tidied the collection of microfiche plates they were reading and nodded, then waved to the librarian on their way out.

She was met with a blustery autumn wind, a relief from the sterile air indoors. Zane released her hand and they both clutched their jackets a little closer to their chests. It wasn't too cold, but rather a pleasant change while they recharged.

"I'll grab us a snack. You find a seat." Zane gave her a quick kiss and turned towards the café they'd discovered. She followed the arched walkway that enclosed the courtyard, which was square in shape. A similar four-sided pond, with a fountain spraying water into the air, was built at its centre. She reached up to her cheek to brush off the cool droplets that had carried on the breeze.

She smiled and left the cover of the walkway. Her shoes sank into the soft lawn of the courtyard. She sat at an empty table and relaxed, mesmerised by the continual rise and fall of the water as it sprayed upwards from the fountain's base.

With her elbows resting on the concrete table, she yawned and rubbed her face, surprised by how tired she felt. They'd arrived bone-tired at noon the previous day. She'd been relieved to find their motel room comprised two single beds, and she'd slept soundly until morning.

With so much going on, she didn't think she could deal with her feelings for Zane. She wanted to wait until she had more available headspace. A shared bed wasn't on her agenda yet.

"You okay?"

Zane sat beside her and placed his purchases on the table, then seeming to change his mind, swung one leg behind her. He pulled her against his chest and wrapped his arms around her.

Her backside only just fit on the concrete picnic seating and she burst out laughing. "Weirdo."

"You love it," he teased, his mouth ravishing her neck and ears.

And she did. She closed her eyes and rested the back of her head against his cheek, hoping he was holding her properly.

When he eventually stilled his mouth, he asked, "I take it the *Boston Herald* didn't give you any new leads?"

She pushed against his arms and climbed over his thighs to sit beside him. "No." She unscrewed the top off the water bottle and took a sip then reached past him for the sandwiches he'd purchased. "Absolutely nothing."

They'd found one short article in *The Boston Globe*, announcing Thomas Van Der Meeliko and his wife, Catherine, were no longer married. Details were scant and there was no hint of her disappearance. Ella would have been just over two years old when the article was printed. How had her father managed to keep that sort of news out of the papers? Would he have paid for silence back in those days?

Every single newspaper article she read, in some small or big way, exaggerated the importance and impact this family had in Boston. Whether the article related to a donation to a charity, or a political decision made for the benefit of the city, emphasis was always placed on reminding the public that a member of the Van Der Meeliko family was involved. Under different circumstances this could have been her upbringing. Ella shuddered, certain she would've hated it. She preferred privacy and distance from the limelight. But would she have known any different?

Zane insisted they keep searching but her patience had long since run out. The only reason she kept silent was because Zane needed to find clues about his mother. He didn't say much, but the few things he had said spoke volumes. So, she swallowed back her impatience and stuck to the monotonous task of scanning old newspapers.

She unwrapped a sandwich. "The *Herald* barely goes a day when a Van Der Meeliko isn't mentioned. It's tedious reading, the articles covering either political or financial news. I wouldn't mind if I had more time, but when you're after specific information these articles start to sound the same." She took a bite and passed the other half of the sandwich to Zane, then stated, "And no clues on your mother, either." She looked up at the building's roof and shook her head. "Who is she and what is the connection with *my* mother?"

They ate in silence, Ella trying to clear her head of the fuzziness from concentrating all morning. Her ears pricked up when the sound of a flute carried on the breeze. It was the sweetest sound she'd ever heard. She turned towards it and gasped. How had she not seen the neat rows of seats and the crowd gathered in the courtyard? The music mellowed her fractious thoughts when a bride and her father made their entrance. Ella glanced at the other visitors in the courtyard; invited or not, everyone sat transfixed.

The groom and celebrant waited at the front of the crowd. Seeing them transported Ella to her childhood, when Luke had been forced to play that role of groom, and she and Victoria had taken turns as the bride.

Zane sat behind her again and gathered her in his arms. He whispered near her ear. "Is this your kind of wedding venue?"

She hesitated before saying, "I would've said no, because I always imagined a small chapel by the ocean, but this is so appealing and special. The photos will look amazing with the green lawn and the gorgeous building in the background."

"Chapel by the sea, huh? Good choice," he said, as she soaked up the image of the happy couple in the beautiful surroundings.

⸙

Ella and Zane sat holding hands as the small tour coach wound its way around the historic Beacon Hill neighbourhood. With her head resting against Zane's shoulder, Ella inhaled the familiar woody scent of his aftershave. It permeated his shirt and skin and reminded her of how, as a kid, she had lain on the lawn under the trees in their backyard. Being with Zane reminded her of happy times with her family during her childhood. She failed to recall any past boyfriend who brought to mind these carefree memories.

When she glanced outside again, she wasn't surprised to see narrow streets fringed with historic gas lamps. The place had that sort of feel to it. She took in the old colonial-brick row houses with beautiful doors, decorative ironwork and brick sidewalks. Every few minutes the coach stopped and the tour guide named the owner of the property and told them a little of its history. It soon became apparent that the Federal-style houses in this suburb were regarded as the most desirable homes in Boston.

"This is the residence of Thomas Van Der Meeliko and his family." Ella straightened and took in every word the tour guide said. "A pioneering family and one of the first to settle in Boston in its early days, they were prominent banking businessmen and, to this day, are still strong in commerce and finance. In the centre of Boston's CBD, you'll find it difficult to miss the building synonymous with the Van Der Meeliko name. Tonight, if you're in the central business area, look up. The name is lit up on all four sides of one of the tallest high-rises."

Ella absorbed all this information, squeezing Zane's fingers tightly. *Her father owned a high-rise?* Only when Zane gently prised her hand off his did she realise how tight her grip was. Glancing down for a second, she swiftly jerked her head back up, not wanting to miss taking in her father's residence, what could've been her childhood home. What sort of family had that much money?

"This area is known as Louisburg Square, a very desirable residential neighbourhood," the tour guide continued.

"The most expensive residential neighbourhood in all the USA," Zane whispered close to her ear.

She gasped. What reasons did her mother have for leaving? In all the newspaper stories Ella had scanned, not once had she read anywhere that her father was an undesirable husband, including to his second wife. There must have been a good reason for her mother to leave, and why had Thomas been concerned for her sanity?

Ella craned her neck back. She wanted one last glimpse of her father's home before the coach trundled around the corner.

"The next part of our tour takes us to the Massachusetts State House. It's prominently positioned at the top of Beacon Hill and ..."

She switched off, thoughts swirling around her head. They'd spent two days at the library with no success, so Zane had insisted they treat themselves to a day of touristy things. Which they were now enjoying. But tomorrow was Thursday, and by Saturday, they would be on their way back home. There was no more time to waste.

She turned away from the window and faced Zane. He stared at her with an odd look on his face.

"What?" she asked.

He placed his arm around her shoulder and pressed her against his side. "More to the point, what's going on inside your head? The cogs are vibrating through your skin."

She rolled her eyes at him before smiling. His ability to sense certain things was scary. "I'm going to pay my father a visit tomorrow."

"What?" Zane sat up erect, his hand pinching her shoulder. "You need to think about this."

Ella shrugged his arm away and, trying to whisper, instantly rebelled. "What for? Didn't you say it was my decision whether or not to make contact? I'm not coming back to Boston any time soon. It's time to sort this out. What's the worst he can do? Deny my existence? He'll be the one to miss out on my great company for the rest of his life."

A frown burrowed its way along Zane's brow. "You're too impatient. Let's talk about this first before deciding the best way to go about it."

He refused to turn away and kept his gaze pinned on her face.

She shook her head. "I'm not wasting this trip, and we don't have any time left for planning. We know who he is and where to find him."

"What if he won't see you straight away? You probably need to make an appointment a week in advance."

She pushed her shoulders back and turned away from Zane's frown. "Then I'll walk past his secretary and find him myself. After all, didn't you do something similar not so long ago?"

Chapter 16

"I'm coming with you." Zane scrubbed a hand over his face as they sat drinking coffee.

"No, you're not."

He shook his head. "Jesus, woman, you don't have to do everything on your own."

"I have to, okay. It'll be harder for him if someone else is there. Anyway," she dropped her stubborn demeanour, "I always pictured it as just him and me the first time we met."

How could she explain to Zane that she wanted to soften the burden of the shock her father would experience? If her mother had truly vanished without a trace, for whatever reason, it was only fair that Thomas was protected from this life-changing moment with as few people around him to witness his reaction.

At this stage, there was no evidence to prove her mother had been forced to leave. And what role had her stepfather played in all this? As much as she wanted to believe her mother had made the right decision for the right reasons, she was yet to understand why. But she wouldn't take sides. Not until the full facts were presented to her. Tomorrow it was her father's turn to give his side of the story.

Zane splayed his hands out wide. "We didn't get a chance to discuss how to do this. So much can go wrong. I'm worried. You're ... you're holding your emotions so close they'll choke you. You need to know how to handle a bad outcome."

"Talking about it isn't going to change anything. Whatever the outcome, good or bad, I'll have to handle it. We've got precious little time left and this is why we came, right? To find my father?"

This was the closest they'd come to arguing. Since her declaration on the tour coach, Ella had steadfastly refused to discuss the matter further and remained adamant that she would go the next morning alone.

They sat at a trendy outdoor café in downtown Boston where the white neon lights on the Van Der Meeliko building were clearly visible. Zane hoped Ella was sifting through the same doubts he was about what they were doing. If she was, then she'd know how worried he was. He'd seen too many bad endings when separated families were reunited. Ella had no idea how wrong it could all go.

He couldn't hold back his own disappointment at not finding a single clue about his mother's identity. What had he expected? He should've asked his mother for details before he left. Except he knew, only too well, once those first words were uttered, they could never be silenced.

He slid his coffee cup to the side and nursed his head in his hands. They'd eaten a full dinner followed by coffee, but the coffee hadn't satisfied. Not like it usually did. He wanted to suggest they move their single beds together, if only to hold her in his arms all night. But he conceded it wasn't the right time to push their relationship further. She was at her most vulnerable at the moment, so the timing sucked.

"Come on, let's go for a walk." He left money, including a tip, in the bill folder and rose, not giving her a choice.

Their difference of opinion would sour the mood for the rest of the night if he didn't do something about it soon. Wary of her plan, it went against all his training and experience to relent and change his mind. And with her stubborn mindset, neither would she.

Zane couldn't stop her. He knew that much. He worried there'd be no happy outcome and it would sour their relationship. Call him selfish, but his entire focus was on keeping Ella happy. He understood the terms of her agreeing to come to Boston—to keep her by his side, he had to find her father. Which meant he had to allow her this first meeting, regardless of how much it chewed him up inside.

⸎

They strolled side by side. She hadn't missed the way Zane knotted his fingers together before dropping his arms by his side. Despite his agitation Ella was sticking to her decision. She wasn't always proud of her stubbornness. It was hard to budge when cemented in place, especially when that stubbornness was coupled with her impatience and an unholy streak of anger that sometimes showed its ugly head.

Why did she struggle to convey her thoughts to Zane? Every time she opened her mouth to explain, it came out all wrong, which only upset him more.

What didn't he get? In her mind it was simple. How much longer was she going to put it off? For years, she'd dreamed of finding her father. Now, she was in the same city, knew his name and where he lived. In her books it was a case of 'go for it'.

The dream was to become best friends and reunite him with her mother. It'd been a fanciful vision, more so since the death of her stepfather.

Underlying all this was the fact that she had no idea why her parents had initially separated. She wanted to believe time could heal, and held on to this belief, but at the same time she was adult enough to realise there was a good chance her parents could never be reconciled.

Ella looked up from the pavement and sighed. The busy streets buzzed with flashing lights, music and visitors. The mid-week crowds were most dense around the bars, clubs, café's and cinemas. A light sprinkling of rain earlier had roused the dust off the street, and it mingled with the smell of fumes and burnt rubber, drifting off the bitumen with the traffic.

All this only brushed the outer layer of her thoughts. Impatiently she swept her concerns about tomorrow to the back of her mind and concentrated on the man who walked beside her with his hand swinging close. She found his fingers and relished the tingling sensation that ran along the length of her arm when their hands entwined. His touch never failed to make her feel alive. Though they were at odds with each other, he could still twist her in knots, make blood rush through her veins at breakneck speed and ignite a magnetic pull deep within her. When they touched, all she wanted to do was lie naked against his skin and enjoy the heady experience.

They'd been walking for half an hour before it dawned on her. They were on holiday. Sure, it was for a purpose, but her feelings for Zane were real. More real than they'd been for any of her former boyfriends.

This disagreement was leaving a sour taste in her mouth, and she didn't want to spoil the rest of their stay. Regardless of what happened with her father, she wanted Zane to remain a constant in her life. She loved this man.

Her heart jolted. Why had it taken her so long to realise what he meant to her?

Yes, I love him. It felt good to admit it. She let the words tumble freely around her head and press against the seams of her heart.

She stopped in her tracks and bit her bottom lip. He was hurting because of her. If he hurt, so did she. She turned to face him. His eyebrows rose in question.

"I'm sorry," she blurted.

He took both her hands and leaned in, rested his forehead against hers. "I'm sorry too. Look, about tomorrow, I'll wait for you in the foyer when you visit your father. I won't stop you."

She pressed against his fingers. "I wasn't thinking of my father. I was thinking of you. Us."

"Hmm."

She closed her eyes and took a deep breath. "I love you, Zane."

He stiffened against her then cupped her face.

"Ella," he whispered, "my God."

She opened her eyes to a smouldering look before he reached down, leaving no doubt in her mind about how he felt.

Passers-by jostled around them in the busy street. Someone's lewd comment of "find a room" reverberated in her ears, but it didn't diminish the chemistry hammering between her and Zane when their mouths melded. His tongue duelled purposefully with hers, the taste of coffee still strong between them, heady and exciting. She wanted this kiss to go on forever. She'd scale her father's high-rise building if it meant it would never end.

Finally, Zane drew back and nibbled on her lip. Her heart continued to race as she steadied her breathing. She looked into his dark eyes. A beat of silence followed and he seemed to choke with emotion.

"Ella, I … I love you, too." His eyes watered and his shoulders sagged, as if with relief. "I'm so glad you came into my life."

She touched his chin. The prickle of his stubble and his words ignited every nerve ending in her body. "Oh, Zane. I know I'm being impatient, stubborn and annoying, but … but can we go back to our motel and talk about it in the morning?" Then she suggested, "Maybe we could push the beds together?"

His eyes widened in surprise. His smile was adorable and she feasted on it. His posture relaxed and the permanent scowl on his face vanished. His Adam's apple bobbed up and down as he swallowed. When further speech seemed impossible, he nodded and grasped her hand, turning her in the direction of their motel.

❦

Zane shut the motel door, trapping Ella against it. He pinned her with his gaze, his hands flat on the door's surface either side of her face. The intense royal blue of her eyes enhanced in the shadowed entrance to their room. The shock of her declaration left his throat tight and a painful bulge in his jeans.

With hunger, he sought her mouth and forgot she had to breathe. He shrugged off his jacket and let it fall to the floor. With a punishing hold on her mouth, he unbuttoned her jacket, then peeled it from her shoulders. It pooled around her feet, and he used a booted foot to kick it away. He took a step closer and slid his hands over her jean-covered buttocks. He swung her against his hips.

She groaned into his mouth and pressed against him as he lay down in the darkened entry and draped her body as gracefully as he could along his length.

At this change, her fingers turned frantic in her eagerness to unbuckle his belt and undo his buttons, all poise now gone. Zane followed her example. With her jeans loosened, he delved into their depths, his hands finding silken, soft skin.

In their desperate rush, buttons couldn't be undone fast enough and writhing limbs were caught at strange angles. His moans mingled with hers until, frustrated with his arms trapped in his half-removed shirt, he burst out, "Not like this, Ella."

A vein throbbed along her neck and her face fell against his shoulder. "You don't want me?" she muffled against him.

He tightened his hold around her. "Oh, I want you all right." He filled his lungs with much-needed air. "But I don't want our first time to be on the floor of some strange motel."

Ella deserved better and he was prepared to deliver. He'd lost it for a few minutes there, but that was easy to do around Ella. As much as he found self-control difficult, even painful around her, he hoped the magic between them never dissipated.

He connected with her bare skin under her shirt. "While I push the beds together why don't you have a shower and change into something easier for us to get into? No buttons, clips or zips. We don't need those tonight."

He lifted her limp form away from his shoulder, wanting to look into her eyes, desperate to connect with her, except laughter fringed the edges of her mouth and reached into the depths of her eyes. She flopped against his shoulder again while laughter bubbled from her throat and poured over him. Like pure liquid. He was the large scoop of ice-cream and she the chocolate topping. She seeped into the cracks and crevices while the excess coated the surrounding floor. Sweet, delicious and to-die-for. He ran his tongue over his dry lips. How would she taste when he finally got the chance to fill his need?

Her giggling distracted his thoughts. It quickly became contagious and he succumbed to it. She had the ability to draw every emotion out of him in a single day. Today had proved it. She was a variety of flavours and he wanted to taste every single one.

Chapter 17

Wearing a cotton t-shirt pinched out of Zane's luggage, Ella wrapped a spare blanket around her shoulders. The autumn air carried a cool nip to it and brought out the goosebumps on her arms when she first stepped out onto the balcony.

When she'd come out of the shower, she'd found the beds pushed together and a couple of condoms on Zane's dresser. She smiled as her gaze wandered over the array of city lights reaching out into the far corners of the horizon. She was glad Zane hoped for a busy night as she was more than ready. Her declaration of love earlier only heightened her anticipation.

Their room was located on the fifteenth floor, so she'd decided to soak in the view of one of America's greatest cities, while she waited for Zane to finish his shower. She considered joining him but held off. The bed would be the perfect starting point to make a memory that would last forever.

As she leaned against the balcony rails, she looked up into the dark sky. Marred by light pollution, there weren't too many stars to be seen. It made her sad to think she might've grown up never knowing the spectacle of a sky full of dazzling stars. This should've been the city of her youth, but for some reason providence had stepped in and changed the course of her life.

A gentle breeze picked up her light honey strands. Her hands were scrunched tight around the edges of the blanket, so when hair plastered across her mouth and cheeks, she left it there.

Her thoughts returned to Zane and the coming night. It was hard to hold back her euphoria. She'd never slept with any man and loved him at the same time. Heat pooled at the base of her belly and when she tightened her pelvic muscles, tingles shot along her limbs.

She gasped when arms wound around her waist. "Zane," she spluttered, her heart racing a hundred miles an hour. *How did I not hear him come out of the shower?*

"Mmm. Can I join you inside that blanket?"

She held one side open and he stepped into its warmth. When he chuckled, the silk of his bed shorts rubbed against her bare thighs.

"Um ... nice shirt," he said and, moving behind her, took control of the blanket. Holding the corners around them with one hand, he pushed her hair aside and didn't hesitate to kiss her.

She groaned, losing traction on the tiled balcony. "You did say no buttons, clips or zips." She whimpered as she closed her eyes and let desire surge.

"Did I say that? Well, I want my shirt back. Now."

She dropped her head back and chuckled. "Take it."

Zane picked her up, blanket and all, and walked inside where the furniture was lit by only one bedside lamp. He used his foot to slide the glass door closed then laid her down on the bed; the blanket fell to the floor. He must've drawn the bed covers after his shower, because she felt soft sheets beneath her. His gaze never left hers.

He lay beside her, and didn't hesitate to reclaim his shirt. The only piece of clothing she was left wearing was her underwear. He hadn't made a move to remove those yet, though she was desperate for him to do so. She could feel his hardness and was impatient to feel him against her naked skin.

He reached over and brought the covers over them, then snuggled closer. Their legs entwined and she untangled her arms to encircle his neck. She caught his gaze and held it. Words wedged in her throat, but it didn't feel right to talk. Too much was passing between them. With their eyes locked and hands brushing against naked skin, talking seemed sacrilegious.

A slow rhythmic pulse was set in motion when he reached down and took hold of her hips. He pulled her towards his hardened mass and pressed against her, softly at first and then harder. His breathing sounded loud, or was it her own raspy breath? His gaze had a stranglehold on hers and refused to let her go.

"Are you sure about this, Ella?" he whispered, his chest heaving hard against hers.

Was he crazy? Her eyes must've widened in surprise, because his mouth turned up at the edges.

She blinked, breaking the link. "Do you have any idea what you're doing to me?"

His hands stilled before sliding up her bare back. "I still have to ask. I'll stop if you say so."

"Would you cope?"

He sank back and feigned death, making it sound painful. "I might die, but eventually I'd come back to life."

Ella chuckled and brought her hand up, tightening her hold around his neck. She was enjoying this banter as much as the anticipation of what was to come; she smiled into the crevice of his shoulder. She wanted it to take all night.

But Zane had other ideas. He expertly removed her underwear along with his boxer shorts. The time for talking was over.

Every muscle tightened when his hand moved south of her belly button and his palm pressed against her. His fingers disentangled the crisscross of hair and she gasped when they found entry and slid in. She sank into the softness of the mattress and closed her eyes. Her eyelids flickered open for a moment when he gently kissed one. Then her nose, cheeks, down, down, down to her neck, his fingers never letting up with the slow, rhythmic action deep inside.

She ached with the need to touch him. She reached down and, enfolding him in her hand, rubbed up and down.

"Don't," Zane said in a gruff voice, "not yet."

She released him and let her hands explore his chest instead, touching the scar she knew was the bullet wound he carried. When she came across the small buds of his nipples, she tweaked them, raising them to their fullest before licking and rolling the buds with her tongue. Clamping her teeth around one, she gave a gentle bite.

Zane groaned and pushed his fingers further inside her.

Zane had to back off, or he was going all the way—without her. He yanked her away from his chest and forced his mouth on hers. Anything to distract his body from what she was doing to him. He wanted to slow things down, enjoy the ride for as long as possible.

Except he didn't know how much longer he could hold out. He rolled on top and stopped for the beat of a second. He was searching her face when her legs opened in invitation. He wanted skin on skin, the feel of sliding in and out of her moisture, but that would be irresponsible. As excruciating and painful as it was to deny himself, he gritted his teeth and held back from slamming into her.

With every muscle in his body strung taut, he panicked when light-headedness threatened to lose him completely. He backed off and hung over her in the push-up position, his shoulders trembling. Unsteadily, he sat back on his knees. His penis rested on her stomach and throbbed with a life of its own. She reached for him and enfolded her hand around him, gently massaging.

He reached for a condom and ripped the packet in his haste to put it on. She tenderly swatted his hands away and took hold of the condom, preparing to do the job herself.

God help him. She was going to take all night, which was not a good idea. He bit down on his lip and tasted blood. Her hands performed magic tricks, but when he went to help her, she shifted his hand and placed it at her entry.

He groaned, entered her wetness and stroked, hanging his head, the sweet fragrance of woman and sex rising to engulf his senses. His endurance was about to snap like a guitar string at the end of its life.

At the slight tap on his hand, he drowsily opened his eyes, sinking into her pools of desire. Coated in delicious stickiness, he grabbed either side of her hips when she raised them in readiness, and entered easily. He was home, thank God, and ready to push himself to the furthest point her body would allow.

She moaned and rubbed her hands along the length of his back, pressing her fingers into him. She kneaded his skin and moulded her body against his and joined their mouths again. Her tongue inside his mouth left him floundering. He let his body take over, and with each thrust, with each pull, she tightened her muscles that held him inside. She tightened and released, tightened and released, then began to shudder and shatter against his body. It took him over the edge and he joined her, emptying his seed inside.

He revelled in the spasms that continued to reverberate through his body. As they receded, they washed away the tension. Splayed over her, and as his heart rate slowly returned to normal, he left a trail of soft, gentle kisses along her neck. Her fingers twisted in his dark hair and massaged his scalp. He could easily be lulled into sleep.

But before he could, he rose and made his way to the bathroom. When he returned, she lay on her side. The urge to fold himself around her was strong. He laid his length along hers and, pulling her closer, rested a hand on her breast. She placed a hand over his and sleep came instantly for her.

He soaked up the calming sound of her breathing and absorbed as much of her as he could. Sleep wouldn't be far off for him either, but he wanted the chance to savour their first time. Tonight had been incredible, but a tiny part of him still worried about the impending meeting with Ella's father. He might be overreacting, and he hoped with every fibre of his being that he was, but this couldn't be their one and only experience. Surely this was the start of something great. A lifetime together.

He wriggled as close as their bodies allowed. For a few minutes, he damned his background in policing and investigative work. Why couldn't he relax and enjoy the moment? Why did every bad luck story he'd ever encountered in his working life rear its ugly head now?

Go to sleep, mate.

He tried to put his faith in a good place and believe everything would turn out okay tomorrow.

The thought of losing this woman, when they'd only just connected, tightened his chest in fear. This wariness was so unlike his usual way of barrelling through life and hoping for the best. He smiled against her hair. It was an attitude that had got him through life so far—even if luck had played a big part. Not anymore. He wasn't taking any chances or risks. He held a precious gift in his arms and no longer would he take anything for granted.

Satisfied he'd calmed his inner detective, he rallied for a good outcome tomorrow. With that thought, his body relaxed further and took his mind with it.

✦

Ella woke, drowsy but sated when Zane moved beside her. The sweet memories of earlier cloaked her like a jacket and she snuggled closer to Zane's side, reliving the heady moments of it.

"Hey, princess, are you awake?" he whispered in the dim light.

She smiled and turned to face him. Neither had turned the lamp off, so she looked into his sleepy, smiling face.

He rubbed her arm and took her hand, moving it downwards. When it connected with his hardness, she chuckled.

"I'm sorry to wake you, but you wouldn't happen to have some free time?" Zane asked.

He reached for a second condom and slipped it on before she could even wipe the sleep from her eyes. But she had all the time in the world, and wetness still coated the tops of her inner thighs, so she stretched her legs and rolled on top. He entered her and thrust with such force, she yelped.

"Sorry." He visibly reined in his strength and withdrew a little. "I'll slow down."

She sucked in a breath. "No, don't," she begged and raked her fingers down his sides.

He didn't.

They reached their climaxes so fast she thought it was a dream. Except when he stretched beside her to sleep, she noticed the time was two a.m. and his hand was nestled comfortably between her legs.

Chapter 18

It was mid-morning before they left their room the following day. When Zane unearthed another condom, Ella had nodded enthusiastically. Life was good. No, life was great. She hugged the thought as, with Zane by her side, she strode down the street full of confidence. Her father's building was within walking distance, and they dodged others where they could, but Zane's laughter rang out when she refused to part with his hand, forcing a suited man, obviously in a hurry, to rush around them.

She clutched Zane's hand with fierceness, wanting to declare to the world that this man belonged to her. To prove it, she stopped mid-stride and pulled back.

"Hey, what's wrong?"

"Nothing." She wrapped her arms around his neck and drew his face closer. "I just want to remind you how much I love you." She found his mouth and kissed him with careless abandon, playing games with her tongue. She ended it with a resounding smack on the lips and didn't miss how he pressed her closer, so she could feel how affected he was.

They stood this way for some time, with his eyes shining and softening over. She brushed some lint off his royal-blue collared shirt, aware he hadn't moved back, that his bulge was growing stronger.

"Being on the street isn't the best place for me right now." Zane whispered close to her ear.

Ella grinned. "Aren't you satisfied yet?"

"What?" He gently massaged her lower back.

"Stop it," she hissed, laughter about to erupt at any moment. "Next you'll fling my clothes off and have me right here."

"Stop giving me ideas."

She burst out laughing, leaned in and touched her forehead to his. "Zane," she wailed, "I have to concentrate on meeting my father, not on what we've been doing for the past twelve hours."

She smiled at the memories of the marathon night they'd shared. His ability to keep her mind off the impending reunion had been a godsend. If she could keep her nerves at bay right up until the last moment, she would be ten steps ahead.

He moved back, groaned and clutched at his chest as though stabbed by a knife. "Harsh words, girl. I thought you said you loved me."

She giggled, grabbed hold of his hand and dragged him forward. He made her laugh, and she was carefree around him, but his words of warning continued to sit in a tiny spot in her head. Could this go badly? As she had no idea why her mother had left without a trace, she had to concede that yes, anything was possible.

But she refused to dwell on a bad outcome. She was strong and fierce when she put her mind to it. General managers of global civil engineering companies had shaken their heads at some of her suggestions over the years, but she always managed to convince them in the end. If her father needed the same sort of treatment, she would lay it on. This was her life and future, and she would fight for the childhood dream she'd carried for years.

Outside the building, Ella and Zane stood in its shade and craned their necks to look at the top. She blinked rapidly and scraped a hand through her loose hair before rubbing both down her cream linen pants. She closed her eyes and tried for a calming breath. Now was the time to gather her resolve in, but her nerves had arrived and were tackling her from all angles.

"So, here goes." The words tumbled out.

Zane's hands found hers and tightened around them. "I'm not going to ask you to reconsider."

They'd gone through it again over breakfast. She hadn't changed her mind and neither had Zane. The photo of their young smiling mothers was the only item she would show her father. She was hoping for any clue he might give her about Zane's mother.

"I am going to wish you luck, though. Lots of it." He leaned in and kissed her on the sensitive spot tucked in below her ear. Ella inhaled his woodsy scent, filling her lungs with it. She wanted his strength to help her get through the next hour. She almost reconsidered going alone. Almost.

You got this, girl.

When she released the lungful of air she'd drawn in, she said, "Okay, I'm ready." She gave Zane one last squeeze before turning and walking towards the imposing sliding glass doors.

It was time to find her father's office.

She pressed herself as far back as she could in the lift. Ella eyed the severe business suits the men wore and the classy outfits of the women. The top floor was where she was headed. Where else would his office be? He owned the goddamned building.

She still struggled to let that information sink in. Would it ever?

It was a long ride up, with many stops along the way. Were any of her fellow lift occupants related to her? This city was teeming with Van Der Meelikos, after all. She tried to inconspicuously check those around her for any similarities to herself.

No one took any notice of her as they greeted each other and chatted together. When new employees joined or exited the lift, many appeared to know each other. Some were juggling coffee cups, muffins or bagels, eating on the run and in a hurry to get somewhere.

Only one other person was left in the lift when they arrived at the top floor. As they exited, she tapped him on the shoulder. "Excuse me."

He halted mid-stride and turned back as the doors closed. "Yes?" His eyes swept over her.

She groaned inwardly. Why did some men feel they had an exclusive right to do that? She reined in her impatience and spoke in a sweet voice. "Ah ... could you direct me to Thomas Van Der Meeliko's office?"

He took a step back and crossed his arms. "Now what would a pretty little thing like you want with Mr Van Der Meeliko?"

Do you want to throw in any more twang? she wanted to ask when he dragged his words out.

He let his gaze take a second sweep over her, from head to toe, and drew it out with a long, low whistle. "Mr Van Der Meeliko, hey?"

His drawl was beginning to grate, and her patience snapped. She used every reserve she had to remain calm. How else had she survived in a male dominated world? She slowed her speech and bit each word out with effort. "His secretary would be a great help, if you could show me the way."

That's all I'm bloody asking, you idiot. She clenched her hands by her side. Heck, she was barely metres from the elevators.

No way was she leaving this floor without meeting her father. She was willing to do whatever was necessary to make it happen, but first she had to get past the likes of this man.

Only, what if her father flat-out refused to see her?

Then she'd throw herself onto him.

Except, what if he wasn't there?

Ugh. Don't go there, girl, and don't blow your only chance.

She had to control her jittery nerves, knowing they might loosen her tongue. She took a steadying breath and smiled at the man again. His dark pinstriped suit draped his tall, arrogant frame, while his eyes looked calculating and lecherous.

God help me. The worst type of man. Just my luck.

"I'm family, visiting from overseas. He's expecting me. I've just never been to his office before."

A little white lie can't hurt, can it?

His demeanour changed. Gone was the arrogance, along with the smirk and the openly creepy stance. He pointed towards a desk, where an elegantly coiffured lady worked, and said, "Sorry, I can't be of any further help. I'm late for a meeting."

Behind her, the lift door opened. A woman exited and turned right towards a narrow hallway that Ella hadn't seen earlier. To her surprise, the man backtracked to the elevator, re-entered, and the door closed after him.

Holy crap. Is that all I need to do? Tell them I'm related to Thomas Van Der Meeliko and they'll be running scared? She smiled, adjusted her soft lemon blouse, then squared her shoulders. *Easy as. Wait till they hear I'm his daughter.* At this, she chuckled and made her way to the desk.

Once past the hall of elevators, Ella could see there was only one secretary on this floor, so in hindsight, she hadn't needed any assistance.

She took in the opulence of the decor. Ultra-modern. Made up of lots of glass and chrome, and with pots of greenery dotting the layout, the office looked recently renovated by someone for whom money was no issue. The secretary was busy typing, her attention on her work.

Ella took a moment to steel her nerves. *Here goes.* She had to somehow convince this person to let her in to the only office she could see. The door was closed, of course, but if the office covered the remainder of the floor, its expansive size could easily fit homes for twenty underprivileged families.

She shook her head at the direction her thoughts were taking. *Forget it. He's still your father.* She inhaled a deep breath and approached the desk.

"Um ... excuse me."

The secretary's face snapped up. "Oh, sorry. I didn't hear you come in."

She seemed friendly enough, which was a relief. She looked middle-aged, but it was hard to tell because of how well she was dressed.

"I'd like to see Mr Thomas Van Der Meeliko. Would that be possible?"

"Do you have an appointment?" She turned back to her screen, probably to check his appointment book.

Damn. The dreaded question. "Um ... not exactly."

The secretary stopped what she was doing and stared hard. "I'm sorry, but appointments have to be made in advance and approved by Mr Van Der Meeliko."

Ella's shoulders slumped. *Shit, shit, shit.*

She braced herself and racked her brain for the next sensible thing to say. She took a deep breath and said, "I understand this, except I've travelled a long way to be here. I leave Boston on Saturday and I'd appreciate you asking if it's possible to see him. I only need a few minutes."

"I'm sorry, er ..."

"Ella Harvey."

"I'm sorry, Ms Harvey. I must ask you to leave. If you'd like to make an appointment, let me know the reason and I'd be happy to start the booking procedure." She turned away and reached into a drawer, so only her softly knotted bun, with the occasional streak of grey, was visible. She pulled out a sheet of paper and handed it to Ella.

Ella refused to take it, frustration gathering like dark clouds. "You don't understand." She kept her voice calm and plastered a smile to her face. "I need to see Mr Van Der Meeliko today. As I told you, I leave on Saturday."

They faced each other, the slip of paper a Mount Everest between them, tension growing by the second.

Annoyance flashed across the secretary's face. She placed the sheet on the side of the desk closest to Ella, huffed and picked up the phone. Pressing one button, she spoke no words but hung up with a satisfied smile on her face.

What the?

Ella was left standing there, the secretary ignoring her while she continued with her work. The phone rang. The secretary answered the call and dealt with it.

Ella heard the ping of the elevator door. This was not going as planned. Should she run to the office door and try her luck? Open and enter and announce herself as his long-lost daughter? She had to think quickly and decide just as fast. How long could she stand here until the secretary grew impatient and called security in?

She jumped when a voice behind her said, "Excuse me, miss, I'm here to show you out."

She spun around and was confronted with a muscly security guard. Shiny chrome buttons on the huge expanse of his chest shone into her eyes and paralysed her for a moment. *What the hell? She* was being thrown out? Denied the opportunity to meet her father? *Shit*, she hadn't even been given a chance. *Not on!*

She stretched her neck, looking up into the severe lines of his face, and ground out her words. "I don't care what you're here to do. I need to see Mr Van Der Meeliko, *now*. I'm not leaving until I do."

He grabbed her by the arm. "I'm sorry, miss, but I need to escort you out."

She wrenched her arm free and made towards the office door she'd spotted earlier. He was by her side within seconds and grabbed hold of her, catching one of her arms. With the other still free, she banged on the office door, determined to make as much noise as possible before she was physically overpowered and silenced.

In the scuffle, the secretary gasped and muttered. When Ella twisted around, she saw the secretary standing by her desk with the phone to her ear.

As the security guard dragged her towards the lift, she shouted, "Stop! I need to see him. Don't you dare try to stop me." She bit into the guard's forearm until he yelped.

"Christ almighty!" he exclaimed, before a clear, authoritarian voice halted them all.

"Could someone *please* explain what's happening?"

The security guard stopped his progress towards the lift but retained his strong hold on Ella. She twisted around and eyed her father for the first time. Her heart raced out of control. She let her body go limp in the guard's stranglehold. Never once had she envisaged this scenario.

"Is the girl armed, Jacob?"

"I don't believe so, sir."

"Let her go for the moment."

Her father moved close enough for her to see his blue eyes. *They really are the same as mine.*

She untangled herself and smoothed down her clothes, then stood up straight and ran a hand through her hair.

He gasped. "Catherine ..."

Her breath caught in her throat. Not a single sound was uttered by anyone. When it occurred to Ella that her father was seeing her mother from all those years ago, she managed to say, "Er ... I'm Ella. Isabella."

She hadn't thought it possible, but his eyes widened further.

Chapter 19

"Helen, cancel the remainder of my appointments for today."

Ella's father stood at his office door, making the request to his secretary before clicking the door closed and turning to face Ella.

Now that she was in his office, she wanted to appear cool and confident, not flustered. With her hands behind her back, she squeezed her fingers together and forced the nerves to stop fluttering in her stomach.

He continued to stare. His mouth was a straight line and his hands were clenched tightly by his sides.

Was he in shock? *Of course, you dill. After all, he must believe his wife and child had died all those years ago.*

She was keen to learn why her mother had mysteriously disappeared, and though she would let her mother tell her own story when she returned home, for now, she would learn her father's side. She wasn't going to help him or offer any information. Calculated? Yes, but she didn't want her opinion to be biased. Though they were on opposite sides of the world, they were her parents. For better or worse. Whatever had happened between them was not her fault. She concentrated hard on staying calm but his next words threw her.

"So ... what makes you think I'm your father?"

Fair question, though she hadn't expected it up front, nor had she suggested he was her father—yet.

Ella unzipped her bag and delved inside for the photo. She stepped closer and handed it to him. "The woman on the left was your wife. She's also my mother."

He stared and stared at the photo. When she despaired that he'd never utter another word, he spoke, clearly lost in thought, with his gaze riveted to the photo.

"Catherine and her best friend. Mathilda Savro. I suspected she might've been involved but had nothing to go on. Married into that bastard Boston mafia family, *anything* was possible." Discovering snippets of what might've happened brought out the bitterness in his voice. No doubt he carried layer upon layer of sadness, guilt, anger, you name it. Over the years it may have dulled at the edges, but to be confronted with the ugly truth of what could've happened would bring it all back. The bitter taste of deception would never leave him—she could see it etched clearly on his face. Ella understood that much.

He slammed the photo on the corner of his desk and swore. "Why the hell didn't I dig further? I'd forbidden her from having anything to do with Mathilda, but I should've guessed she never would have severed the relationship. Damn."

He paced near his desk and to Ella it seemed as if he'd forgotten her. She took in every word he said, though. He wasn't aware of the importance of the information he was spilling. For Zane's benefit, it was vital that she pay attention.

He stopped and swung around, eyes gazing past her, not seeing. She had to give him time to get over the shock. It was no doubt the last thing he'd expected to deal with when he awoke this morning. She wanted him to talk freely, to give her clues about her mother's state of mind when she'd decided to disappear without a trace.

She took the chance to study him. His eyes she'd already noticed. His tall and willowy structure was not unlike her own, and his oval face was shaped like hers. His hair was dark brown and streaked with grey. She'd inherited her mother's thick and wavy honey-coloured hair.

He might've been a handsome man in his youth, but he'd aged greatly in the last few minutes. His shoulders slumped forward and the corners of his mouth turned down. Regardless of his wealth and comforts, he resembled a man in his sixties, despite being somewhere in his fifties. It was the sort of situation where she would normally feel compelled to reach over and wrap her arms around a person's shoulders. Assure him everything would be okay. But now, uncertain of what to do, she held back, her breath caught in her throat.

If she didn't say something soon, she feared he'd remain frozen indefinitely. Slight exaggeration, she conceded, but it looked as if she had to make the next move. "Ah ... Dad? It's ... it's great to meet you."

She stumbled on the word 'Dad'—the only dad she'd ever known was not this man. But that wasn't his fault—or was it?

He pulled his shoulders back and turned towards her. "Isabella ... um..." His jaw clenched and the corded muscles on his neck strained. He seemed to have some kind of wake-up call, because he was suddenly brought back to life.

"Excuse my rudeness." He stepped closer and, reaching for her hand, clasped it between his and pumped it up and down. "I can't believe you're *here* after all this time. You have no idea how many sleepless nights I suffered. When weeks and months went by with no word, it was assumed you were murdered. There was nothing the police could find."

Why had her mother left? Had he never considered that she'd chosen to disappear and start a new life somewhere else? Ella was doing her damnedest not to take sides, but her sympathy for her father was growing stronger with each word he spoke and with each emotion that engraved itself on his face.

"Sit down, sit down." He released her hand and pointed to the chair, then made his way to the other side of the desk and sat before rolling his chair forward. "Does your mother know you're here?"

"No, she doesn't." She kept her hands folded in her lap and resisted the temptation to knot her fingers together. Why had her mother lied all these years? Was Ella's now deceased stepdad involved in the disappearance or had her mother met him later?

Her father rested his elbows on his desk, and Ella imagined it wasn't something that someone in his position would ever do. *I suppose news of this kind can bring out the unusual in a person.*

"How did you find me?"

She tried to remain calm. "I used a private investigator." She refrained from mentioning how fate had intervened or how Zane had uncovered the truth. They were the sorts of things you only ever read about.

"How is your mother?"

Did he still care about her? "She's ... um ... she's fine."

"Did she ever mention me, my family, Boston?" he asked.

She shook her head. *How much detail do I give?*

"And you grew up where? I'm not quite familiar with the accent?"

"Australia."

"Ah." He nodded. "The last place I would've considered. Good choice, Catherine, good, good choice," he muttered, like he'd been trumped and knew it.

He was lost with his thoughts again. *Is he angry? Or anxious?*

While she was trying to decide, he asked, "What about you, Isabella, or ... or do you prefer Ella?"

"I was raised believing my name to be Ella. You can call me that."

He nodded, his head bobbing continuously, as though he were processing things, trying to catch up with twenty-something years of lost information. "Tell me something about yourself."

"I'm a civil engineer and have three half-siblings."

"Really? I have a daughter who's an engineer?"

"You sound surprised. Why?"

He chuckled wryly. "I'm surprised by how educated you are. I don't know why. There are lots of clever women in the world. It's just that I ... I struggle to get my adult children out of bed before lunch, let alone achieve something in their own right. When I was their age, I was already holding my own in the family business. They'll never achieve anything at the rate they're going."

"Oh." *A bit harsh.*

He waved her sympathy away. "All my own doing. When you do everything for them, they don't learn how to do anything for themselves."

She shrugged and said, "I'd be bored doing nothing all day or if I were stuck in a job going nowhere. It'd drive me crazy."

"Exactly," he exclaimed, sitting back in his chair and flinging his arms out wide.

Their eyes locked when they realised they had something in common, something they agreed on. Ella burst out laughing. It was all too weird, but at least she had one reason to believe they were connected by more than blood. Her father managed his first smile since learning of her existence.

"So," he said, mussing his hair, "if you have half-siblings, can I assume your mother is married?"

At the thought of her dad, her shoulders dropped. "She was. He died last year in a workplace accident. His death hit her hard. He was a good man."

His features hardened. "Was he a good father to you?"

She battled loyalties and her eyes watered. "He was the best father a child could ask for." She would never lie about that. He had to understand; while he was her biological father, circumstances she didn't comprehend had changed the course of her life. It'd brought her in contact with a man who had more than excelled in his role of father. "I had a great childhood."

He nodded again; apparently, it was his way of thinking things through. What was going through his head? Did he have regrets? Would he have done things differently if he'd had another chance? There must've been a good motive for her mother to leave. Not sure how to ask him, Ella let it rest for now. She had a lifetime to find out.

"Did you travel to Boston alone?"

"No. My boyfriend is waiting downstairs."

"Well, how would you like to have lunch together?"

She smiled and truly relaxed for the first time since deciding to come to Boston. "I'd like that, and I'm sure Zane won't mind either."

He pointed his finger at her and jokingly said, "As a father, I have the right to check this man out. If he doesn't pass the test, I might have to say something."

She grinned but hid that she now had a better understanding of the situation. Zane was the son of her father's nemesis. Her father's family was one of prestige and old money. Zane's was the polar opposite. One of tyranny, blood money and greed.

Her arms itched to give her father a hug. It was the first thing she'd envisaged doing in her fantasied vision of their first meeting. But it was too early for that, so she raised her hand in a quick wave instead and agreed to meet him in the foyer. She ignored the secretary as she made her way to the elevators. No love lost there.

She wondered how Zane would react when he learned the truth about his background? Would anger be his first response to the news? Ella hoped it'd be more along the lines of relief. It would make sense, at least, if his mother had fled because her husband was involved with the mafia. In comparison, there didn't seem to be a logical reason for why *her* mother had fled. Two friends disappearing at the same time was no coincidence. Ella had a feeling it had been a planned exit involving fraudulent birth certificates and passports. Had her mother provided the money, and Zane's the underworld connections?

Ella's mind swirled with possibilities, but she smiled as she made her way down. She'd met her father and had survived. All Zane's warnings had been in vain. Now the sleuth in her could join the dots. All she needed was to learn more from her father and have the chance to talk to her mother.

Bring it on!

Chapter 20

Unease settled in the pit of Zane's stomach, yet it had nothing to do with learning that his mother had once been connected to a powerful Boston mafia family. Now that he had a surname, he'd tapped the few letters into his laptop and the information had poured out faster than his mind could absorb. None of it answered who his father was, but he'd learned that the Savro family and their mafia connections were quite extensive in Boston.

No, the disquiet bothering him had to do with Ella's father.

In the back seat of the vehicle organised by Thomas to take them to Beacon Hill, Zane let his thigh touch Ella's. She stared out of the car window, taking in the views and no doubt absorbing all the new knowledge her father had shared with them over lunch yesterday.

He tightened his arm around her shoulder as the driver turned left at a sign indicating the way to Louisburg Square. They were leaving Boston tomorrow, but tonight they would dine at Thomas Van Der Meeliko's residence and meet Ella's half-siblings. All very cordial and proper. Zane couldn't fault Thomas on his acceptance of Ella, or his generosity towards them both, and he clearly didn't hold Ella responsible for her mother's decision. All Zane could surmise was that at some stage of their marriage Ella's mother had rejected everything Thomas and his family stood for.

Still, Zane couldn't pinpoint the exact reason why the nagging disquiet refused to go away.

He twirled strands of her hair around his finger. He had to let the concerns go and stop worrying for now. Again, he damned his years in policing and investigative work. It'd turned him into a suspicious bloke who saw past the veneer of a person. He had the ability, usually, to reach deep inside the mind of a person, unwrap layer upon layer, until he could identify the problem and deal with it. But Thomas left him feeling as if there were layers still to unravel; Zane hadn't gotten as close to the core as he'd hoped.

So what choice did he have? It was a patience game now. And how much damage could Thomas do from halfway around the world?

Relax, mate, and let it go.

His thoughts slipped back to how he and Ella had passed the time earlier. *Sweet Jesus*. How had he landed the girl of his dreams? There'd never be enough hours in the day to fill his need, especially once they returned to their everyday life. She was the oxygen his body craved; this week proved he was a goner. Yep, he may as well tell her. He was putty in her hands. She could snap her fingers and he would unashamedly oblige. Oh, yeah, at her beck and call. He smiled and didn't care that his thoughts meandered off track. He was quite enjoying himself, if his pulse thrumming underneath the top layer of his skin was anything to go by.

This afternoon, they shared another unforgettable coupling, one that had him stretching his groin in the confined space of his pants. He shifted forward on the seat and stretched his legs, finally understanding a tiny fraction of what an addict must deal with. He couldn't do without her, didn't want to do without her, and would rather not think about any other alternative.

He let his head fall back and sighed. It didn't take long for his worry to return and crowd the edges of his mind. What if this reunion did untold damage to Ella's relationship with her mother? Then what?

"What's up?"

He lifted his head and looked into her amazing blue depths. Already, she had an uncanny sense of his moods, but he couldn't tell her what was troubling him. Not yet. It had been barely twenty-four hours since she'd met her father for the first time. If he tried to take anything away from that, she would most likely accuse him of being jealous, or deliver some other accusation. She had every right to do so, except—and he wanted to thump his fist on his thigh—for the one line in the article he'd found in the files he'd trolled through. It kept running through his mind on repeat: 'unstable nature of his wife's health'.

He nuzzled her neck. "You know me. Would much rather be somewhere else doing delightful things with you. Food doesn't rate a mention in my books."

She chuckled and reached up to cup his cheek. "Just this once, I promise. When we return to the motel, I'm all yours."

"What ... what if I'm too tired?"

She scoffed, her cheeks glowing with humour. "I doubt that'll happen." She settled her face against his neck, her breath warm on his skin.

He pressed her closer and kept his thoughts to himself, but it still struck him as strange that every time Ella had asked her father a question about her mother, Thomas had deftly manoeuvred around it.

But Zane wouldn't press Ella again. When he'd brought it up last night, she'd shrugged and reminded him that she had the rest of her life to find out all the details of what happened. She added that knowing every detail now was never going to change why her mother left, so why worry?

She had a point, but he didn't quite see it that way. Thomas Van Der Meeliko was hiding something. Just like their mothers. There must've been a good reason for Ella's mother to leave. And something about her father's friendly behaviour didn't ring true. Zane could place a bet and win. He'd gamble that forgiving Catherine would happen over Thomas's dead body, and if that held true, then only one person would get hurt when this went wrong. Ella.

Zane could continue blaming his background in policing and investigations, but caution got under a man's skin. There was no avoiding it, and the alarm bells were deafening in his head.

As for his mother, he and Ella had agreed not to mention the connection to Thomas. They didn't want to risk damaging the fragile relationship they'd established with him. Complicate it and it could go up in flames. Zane would sort that matter out when he returned home. His mother no longer had a reason to lie. He'd discovered the truth, so now she could own up and tell him who his biological father was.

His feelings towards his dad would never change. Well, he hoped they wouldn't. His faith in his parents had only been strengthened with what he'd learned. Not for one minute had Zane doubted that his dad was in the dark. They wouldn't have the relationship they did with this huge secret hanging over them. For Zane, it would be enough to understand why his mother had fled Boston. Then he'd assess how brave or stupid he needed to be to jump in boots and all and confront his Boston family.

His mother's mysterious escape from such a family at least made sense.

❦

The driver veered to the right of the circular drive; the fountain at its centre sprayed water two metres high. The falling droplets were mesmerising as they danced in the lights of the car and floated on the water's surface. Pointed conifers lined the pond and the drive, their tall yet chunky trunks a testament to how many years they'd been planted. The front of the stately home boasted tall, rectangular windows, with lights shining from some. Ivy crept over the walls and covered most of the left half of the house. In the early twilight, the white-painted surface looked grey.

When the car stopped at the front porch Zane, not one to wait on ceremony, thrust open his door. Ella smiled at this and followed, alighting the car before the driver could get to their side to assist. She deeply inhaled the moist air surrounding the pond and looked up at the tall marbled columns providing structural support to the front of the building.

At the entrance, a manservant waited. He smiled a welcome before indicating they should follow.

Ella shivered as her shoes clacked on the black-and-white chequered marble floor. The same thoughts from earlier swirled around her head. *This could've been my childhood home.* It was so surreal she had to hold back from laughing out loud. What sort of person would she have been if her mother hadn't whisked her away?

They were shown into a room filled with soft mahogany lounge suites and the walls lined with books bound in dark colours. They oozed age and nobility, and Ella couldn't imagine a single romance or chick lit novel existing in the room.

Her father greeted her with a firm handshake. "Would you like a glass of wine before dinner?"

Ella followed him towards a bar and cabinet tucked in the corner and nodded. "I can get it if you like." She smiled before adding, "There's no need to stand on ceremony for us. We're used to taking care of ourselves."

Thomas raised an eyebrow. "So, I have an independent daughter." He chuckled and added, "Hmm ... can't be all bad."

Ella laughed and opened the door of the bar fridge. She took a moment to read the labels of the dozen or so bottles and found a sweet white she didn't mind the look of. She lifted it out and showed it to Zane. "Would you like to try this?"

He nodded and she poured them each a glass.

She turned when Thomas announced, "I'd like to make a toast." He raised his glass and Ella and Zane followed suit.

"Here's to discovering my lost daughter and to many, many years of friendship in the future."

When Ella took a sip of her wine, her father's eyes hardened. For a split second, they glazed over with what looked like fury but then softened. She dismissed it, thinking she must've misinterpreted what she'd seen. With a gentler emotion now visible on his face, he looked at her. "It saddens me that I missed your formative years. I want to make up for it."

He made no mention of her mother's involvement. Did she exist in his mind anymore? Zane's earlier warning beat against her chest, but she pushed it aside. This was her chance to connect with her father. What happened in the past had broken this family. She couldn't change those chain of events, but she wanted to understand why they'd occurred. In time, the truth would be uncovered. For now, it was her turn to share her father's affections. He'd missed out on a lot too.

They all turned at the scuffle at the door.

"I'll be damned if I'm forced to spend more than five minutes with the old bastard."

A young man entered. There was no disguising the tall, willowy frame and blue eyes he'd inherited from Ella's father. *Hmm. My half-brother?*

"Patrick." Her father's stern voice silenced everyone in an instant.

Patrick was unsteady on his feet. Either he'd been drinking heavily or he'd taken something else that was spacing him out.

"You wanted to see us, Father?" A young woman stepped out from behind Patrick. In her late teens or early twenties, she carried a defiant look and slammed the door behind her. The house should've rattled, but it was solidly built and had probably dealt with slammed doors in the past.

Slowly and deliberately, Thomas moved towards them. His intimidating behaviour had Ella's heart hammering. The cords on his neck stretched his skin, and anger burst out of every visible pore. Nobody could miss the God-like effort he made to rein in his fury.

He bared his teeth and clipped each word. "Patrick, Melita, I'd like you to meet your half-sister, Ella."

Silence deafened Ella's senses as her shocked half-siblings took a few moments longer to react.

Melita's hand flew up and her mouth fell open. "Jeez, Father, is she after our money?"

Patrick jerked his head back. He grabbed the back of his neck and squeezed hard. He laughed. The sound was bitter and could easily have been mistaken for a bark. "Let me guess, was she spawned by the first unfortunate bitch?"

Ella gasped, confusion causing her to reel at his rudeness. Nobody deserved to listen to this, least of all her. It wasn't her place to say anything, but if this was what life was like in this family and house, she owed her mother.

She felt a nudge and caught Zane's raised eyebrow, his cue to her to approach her half-siblings, no matter how hostile, and use some of her friendly Australian charm.

"Patrick, Melita, it's a pleasure to meet you both."

Melita was the closest, so Ella folded her arms around her shoulders and gave her a solid hug. Patrick was obviously not one to come forth, so she stretched a hand towards him, making it difficult for him to refuse a handshake. Her pleasantness might've shocked him for a moment because his hand came up to grip hers in what seemed to be a reflexive action.

"Are you staying for dinner?" Ella tried to make the question sound innocent, but even she could feel the threads of tension strung tightly between them. It saddened her that there didn't appear to be any sense of family in this household. "This is our last night in Boston. Tomorrow we fly back to Australia. I'd love an opportunity to get to know you both better before we leave."

Patrick took a step back, his black jeans and black dress shirt accentuating his pale, unhealthy pallor. "I don't give a damn who you are." He tore his gaze away from Ella and directed his intense stare at his father. "How many more of your bastards are going to turn up here?"

"Patrick!" There was bitter hatred in Thomas' voice when he spat out his son's name.

But Patrick didn't take any further notice of his father. He spun around, and when he left the room, the door took another hard slamming.

Chapter 21

Ella settled into her seat, relieved the last leg of their journey was about to start. The flight from Boston had taken them to Auckland for a two-hour stopover. With the plane now ready for take-off, a few hours would see them arriving in Brisbane.

They slept for some of it, but for Ella it was erratic and unsettling. Bone-tired and weary, she had a way to go before she could rest her exhausted head.

"Feel like talking?"

She whipped her head up. She and Zane had not broached the subject of her father and siblings since leaving their mansion. After Patrick's abrupt departure, they'd managed to continue with some semblance of normality.

Too tired to argue, she said, "I feel sorry for Melita. She might be pretty, but she seems lost. That's the best way to sum her up."

"Not to mention she has no direction in her life other than deciding which outfit to buy next, or which colour to paint her nails."

Ella agreed, resting against Zane's shoulder "Her features must favour her mother, because everything about her differs from me."

Zane nodded, "And no one mentioned her mother. Four years since she died and her name never came up once."

Ella rested her hand on Zane's thigh, his warmth radiating through her skin.

A lot about that night saddened her. Her father had spoken mostly of his family and how integral to Boston society they were. Disappointment had laced his voice when he implied neither of his children looked capable of continuing their family's legacy. He hadn't had any trouble speaking his thoughts in front of Melita. She'd maintained a bored look, but a small twitch at her temple had worried Ella. How damaged was she? Patrick looked broken too, and with no mother to soften the harsh blow of their father's words. Ella didn't doubt he spoke that way often *and* with the intention to hurt.

It unsettled her. How twisted could a family end up?

At the time, the thought had rocketed across her mind: *Hey, what about me? I could take on the family's legacy.* Except something about the lack of affection surrounding them and sadness at all that wasted emotion sent a shudder through her. Recalling the moment again caused a tremor to ricochet across her shoulders.

"Hey, you okay?"

In answer to Zane's question, she snuggled closer, but the aeroplane seats only allowed so much. "Just tired. I know we have to process everything, but can we do it after a good night's sleep?"

He reached for her hand and gave it a squeeze. "Of course. Try to get some sleep. It might help with the jetlag."

She nodded and closed her eyes, but instead mulled over the questions Melita had asked. She'd been curious enough and interested in where Ella had grown up and what sort of career she had. It struck Ella as unusual that it was normal for Melita to have nothing constructive to do each day. Had there been no plan for her after she finished school? Not even an administrative job in that high-rise? For all the wealth they appeared to have, it was evident no amount of money could cure a broken family. By all accounts, and with what she'd seen, damaged was the best to describe them. With all her heart she wanted to be close to her stepsiblings. It felt wrong to leave them behind. She wanted to fold her arms around them and take care of them. *For God's sake, they just need love.*

When she'd asked about Patrick's career an eerie silence had followed until Melita cleared her throat and said, "He's going through a rough patch at the moment. He'll be better soon."

Thomas's face had resembled a dark, brewing storm, and a streak of fear had touched Ella for a moment.

She reflected on this and scoffed as the plane lifted into the air. She barely knew him, but now that they'd met, she planned on staying in touch. While Melita came across as indifferent, it was probably because of her father's judgemental attitude towards her, or grief over her mother's death. Ella wished she could do something to help her.

She sighed and, with the security of Zane's hand touching hers, she made an effort to relax. She could face her mother now. The time for lies was over; the truth had to be told. She was confident everything would work out. She let her mind wander back over the amazing week she'd spent with Zane and couldn't wait to share him with her family. At least what was happening between them was perfectly right. With sweet memories of the moments they'd shared warming her from the inside out, she snuggled closer against Zane and let sleep take over.

* * *

As they waited at the luggage carousel, Zane wrapped his arm around Ella's shoulder. Passengers jostled for position; some manoeuvred trolleys in the limited space and others tried to control tired kids. All the while, the intensity of noise grew as more passengers arrived to claim their luggage.

"Glad to be home?"

She turned her tired but soft eyes up and he couldn't resist kissing her. It was what he needed to refresh his sluggish mind. Too many hours spent cooped up went against everything his body craved.

When he drew away, she said, "Hmm, don't stop yet. Your kisses are the yoga I've been missing. I could do this forever."

He chuckled and leaned down again, enjoying how she moaned in his mouth.

"You don't mind being in the middle of a noisy crowd, with everyone tired and cranky as they wait for their luggage?" Zane asked.

Her eyes opened wide as she feigned shock. "Can't hear a thing."

He laughed, loving the way the setting sun's rays shone through the glass windows and splashed over Ella's length, highlighting the natural colours in her hair. He swallowed, drawing her in and tucking her face beneath his chin. Should he detour to his place before he drove her home? Man, he needed her. He couldn't ignore the way his body reacted to having her pressed up against him.

She drew back and, angling her face, raised an eyebrow. "I had nothing to do with it."

He burst out laughing. "Nice try, but this doesn't happen when I hug a post." Her smile captured her entire face and grabbed hold of his throat, restricting his breathing.

Unaware of his reaction, she swung her backpack off and brought it to her front as Zane took a deep, steadying breath. He heard the grind of the carousel conveyor belt moving.

"I better find my phone and let mum know I'm back. I hope those Facebook posts about the great time I was having in Hawaii sounded convincing."

Zane grimaced. He hated how much lying they'd done this week. Hopefully, when they revealed their real destination and what they'd uncovered, both families would understand. Secretly, he crossed the fingers on his right hand, something he'd done since he was a kid.

As he kept an eye on the luggage travelling past, Ella's phone beeped rapidly with incoming messages, but when he spotted his suitcase, he left her side and grabbed it before it passed them. He wheeled it over to Ella, then when he saw hers approaching, he went to grab it, too.

"Shit, shit, shit."

He placed Ella's case beside his before putting an arm around her. "What's up?"

"I don't know. I've got a stream of messages from Luke and the girls. What—?" Her high-pitched yelp had him looking at her screen over her shoulder.

"What the hell? Your mother was arrested?"

She impatiently scrolled up and down. "This must be some sort of prank. What the heck are they trying to do? Give me a heart attack?"

"Let's get going. We'll be home in forty-five minutes." He'd left his car in short-term rental, and it'd take a few minutes to reach it. Taking both suitcases, he wheeled them purposefully towards the closest exit. "Have they said anything else?"

Ella shook her head. "To call when I arrive. I'll do it in the car. Let's make a run for it."

Precious seconds were wasted as they wheeled their luggage to the exit at the far end of the terminal. Once outside, the secured car park was only metres away.

An incoming call had Ella frantically swiping at her phone. "Luke, it's Ella. I've landed. Please tell me you're pulling a prank. Not a nice welcome home."

"What the hell did you do, Ella?" On speakerphone, Luke's voice carried to Zane as they reached the pavement leading to the secured car park.

"What do you mean? What's going on?" Frantic, she hunched over the phone.

A sick sensation swirled in Zane's lower belly, as if he'd just drunk sour milk and its stench had overtaken all his senses.

At the security gate, he pulled out his wallet and located his parking ticket. Once he activated it, he tugged on Ella's arm and pulled her along so she kept up with his extra-large steps.

With his car in sight, the weight of fear pinned him down as he clearly heard Luke's accusation.

"It's your fault, Ella. How could you have lied about what you were doing?"

"What's my fault?" she yelled back. "What have I done?"

"Shit, Ella, we know you didn't go to Hawaii. I've seen your itinerary. Going to Boston was a very bad idea. Mum's in custody because of you. Get here fast."

The phone fell from Ella's hand and landed on the concrete, the glass screen splintering. Zane only managed to catch her before she crumbled to the ground.

Hell.

When she got to her feet, he left the luggage and half-carried her the last thirty metres. He yanked the passenger side door open and strapped her in. Her voice was incoherent as tears tumbled down her cheek.

"Shh. We'll be home soon and they can explain everything."

He left her to run back for the luggage and her shattered phone, which he shoved in his pocket, then juggled their backpacks and hurriedly wheeled the suitcases to the car. He roughly threw them inside and slammed the rear door shut.

Luke's call must have something to do with Ella's father. All the distrust he'd harboured but had no answers for surged forth. Damn it, he should've acted on his instincts, argued longer before letting her meet him. *Is it my fault Ella's mother is in police custody?*

He shelved the voices in his head and argued that Ella had been unstoppable. With her mind made up she'd been hell-bent on approaching Thomas. Under any other circumstances he'd reassure himself with, *not your fault, mate.* But it was. It'd been his idea to go to Boston in the first place. If he'd been smarter and less impatient about finding any clues about his mother's past, he would've gone to her first.

His heart knotted as he hurriedly settled in the car. He'd never planned to risk his family just to uncover the truth. Now that he had, the cost to

Ella's mother was devastating. He'd played the fool by not heeding Mr Wilson's often repeated advice. His words ran riot in Zane's head. *When a person disappears without a trace, it's usually for a good reason.*

Shit, shit, shit.

He had to get Ella home, and fast.

Then find a way to deal with the mess they'd created.

Chapter 22

Zane broke every speed limit on the way to Ella's house, but nothing he said could console her, and she shied away from his touch. In her mind, she was the devil incarnate and deserved to be put on the fastest route to hell. Demons chased after each other in her head and fear grabbed hold of her chest, making it hard to breathe, especially as her eyes and nose were so clogged.

Pain throbbed at Ella's temples when she confronted her half-siblings. They were waiting on the driveway. Luke's face, drained of colour, reflected the harrowing twenty-four hours since their mother had been arrested. With moisture-filled eyes and in desperate need of a tissue, Ella tried to grasp everything Luke told her.

She couldn't. She collapsed to her knees, only vaguely aware that Zane lifted her into his arms and carried her inside the house. Luke's words ran around and around her head, not making sense.

She kidnapped you ...

... when you were a baby.

Your father sent the police here ...

... already has the paperwork to extradite her to America.

How could her father have done this? The same person who'd hugged her goodbye and claimed he wanted to keep in touch? How deceptive was he? Did he truly believe she would fall in line while her mother sat in jail?

His behaviour was foreign to her. It was so two-faced that the implications of being related to such a person made her skin crawl.

While she lay limp in Zane's arms, she doubted her tears would ever stop. Somewhere in the depths of her being, a tightly wound coil of anger twisted itself into a tighter spiral. It turned and wound, unyielding. Her tormented mind tried to justify her motives. Except, as the coil of anger grew stronger and stronger, she could find no reason to defend her actions. She'd wanted the fairytale ending to finding her father. Instead, she'd created a nightmare, and it didn't look like it'd end any time soon.

All the what-ifs inched closer and crowded her head. What if she'd never started the search for her father? What if she'd never met Zane? What if Zane wasn't so damn good at his job? What if she'd talked to her mother about the truth? What if Zane hadn't insisted they go to Boston? If, if, if circled her mind in torturous cycles and left her with only one option. It hurt like hell to suggest it, but she saw no other way.

She had to end it with Zane. She had to fix what she'd broken and focus on her mother. Nothing else mattered. Her impatience and recklessness had outdone itself this time, and she would regret it for the rest of her life if she didn't make amends. As much as she loved Zane, she had to let him go but wouldn't blame him. They'd argued long and hard over meeting her father, but she'd brushed his concerns aside, determined to do things her way. She'd been confident that the worst that could happen was that her father would disown her.

She grimaced, ashamed of how naïve she'd been. How could she ever look Zane in the eye again if her mother rotted away in jail? She doubted she could ever contemplate kissing him again, let alone lie with him. This was her punishment for having such a bloody fabulous week. God was peering down at her and having a good belly laugh.

She shrugged out of Zane's hold and he released her. She turned to face him. "I need to leave for Boston. Right now."

"I'll come with you."

She backed away on jittery knees and collided with Lily, who was sitting on the couch. "No, I don't want you to come. I want to go alone."

"Like hell you will." His chest puffed out and his hand ploughed through his hair. "You're not going alone."

She straightened her backbone. It was more symbolic than necessary, but she needed to appear strong and capable. She stared him down, determined to stop her lip from trembling. "Zane, I don't want *you* to come. What we had has to end now. I'm sorry, but it was all a mistake. We made a mistake. No—*I* made many mistakes, and now I have to fix them."

"Bullshit." Zane reached her in two strides and grabbed hold of her arms. "You're upset, you're angry. God help him, *I'm* so bloody angry I want to go back and wring his neck. But you're not going by yourself. He's a bully and he'll hurt you."

She wrenched herself free. Her determination grew stronger by the minute and her reasons for needing to do this alone made more and more sense. "No, you're wrong, Zane. I'm going to do this my way. I won't drag you through this. I'm not going to blame you, because this is all my fault, but you have to forget me. I'm sorry, but I want you to leave."

"Are you crazy?" he hissed, his lips drawn in a straight line. "You want me to forget everything we've done together? Just like that."

Her head wasn't functioning properly, but she didn't miss how his eyes glazed over with a crazed look, the stare of a desperate man.

Clearly on the verge of shouting, he added, "You think an 'I'm sorry' is all you need to say to make it okay?"

Something snapped. The earlier throbbing behind her eyes exploded. She couldn't hold the angst in any longer. "Yes," she cried, "an 'I'm sorry' will have to do. If we hadn't found my father, hadn't gone to Boston, my mother would still be here. She's being extradited to a foreign country, and now she has to fight for her freedom, all for taking care of her baby like any mother would." She sucked in a couple of hasty breaths, doing everything possible to hold her tears in. She needed to be strong.

She took a gulp and added, "Every time I look at you, I'll be reminded of what's happened to her. Of where she is, alone and away from her family, all because of what I decided to do behind her back."

Victoria came up beside her and wrapped her arms around her shoulders. "Ella, how about we sit down and talk it through first?"

But Ella's chest ached, so, so much. Talking was the sensible thing to do, but a shaft of anger so great, caused by her father, pierced the outer layers of her heart. This was her doing. It was wrong to blame Zane. She'd started the ball rolling and she alone would save her mother.

She shrugged out of Victoria's hold and shook her head. "No. He has to go, now. I'll explain everything, but I need to be on the next flight to Boston."

Ella managed to raise her eyes until her gaze clashed with Zane's. Turbulence spiralled in his, changing them from chestnut brown to a black abyss.

With his arms across his chest, his hands bit into the muscled flesh above his elbows. He clenched and unclenched his jaw, as though struggling to find his next words. When they came out, he spoke through gritted teeth with forced restraint, his facial muscles tightly wound up. "You do what you must, but this is not even close to over between us. You can fly to Boston alone if you want, but I'll be right behind, and don't you forget it. You're not doing this on your own."

He spun on his heel and stormed away. When the door slammed shut, she sank to the floor and curled into a foetal position. The time for tears was over.

Zane couldn't believe how tired he was as he scraped a hand over his face. He'd almost made it home. Had almost reached the sanctuary of his bed, where he planned to have a good bawl followed by a solid sleep.

Sadness warred with a deep anger. As he drove, his stomach muscles hardened each time he thought of Thomas Van Der Meeliko. If ever he'd thought himself capable of murder, it was now. What a bastard. He'd sucked up to both of them while knowing that when their plane lifted off the ground, he'd take care of a hidden agenda.

The tightness in his chest was close to blowing out, and when he was only a couple of streets away from his home, he fishtailed and turned his vehicle around. His good intentions had changed in an instant. There was only one person who *had* to help him now.

Heading in the direction of the freeway, he needed to hold his emotions in long enough to reach the Sunshine Coast, but hell, his head ached, the tension in his shoulders wouldn't ease and his chest burned with more pain than what he wanted to think about. There was no way he'd let Ella deal with this alone. They were in this together, and if he had to raise the Titanic to make her see sense, he would. Knowing that she could write off what they had was agonizing. As he drove the last stretch to his parents' home, he planned and strategised ways to convince her she was wrong.

It was only a mere couple of weeks ago that he had to find her father to win her trust. Now, to win her back, he had to rescue her mother. Surely with his contacts in both the police force and the private eye world, he'd be the best man for the job. But—he pinched his lips together—he knew better. They were dealing with laws in another country and a man with enough money to silence anyone, any time he pleased.

Fear for what Ella's father was capable of ricocheted through him. An extradition didn't happen within a couple of days without a lot of power behind it. Ella's mother was already on her way back to Boston; the full force of Thomas's influence was abundantly clear. They were going up against a man with millions of dollars, where it wasn't unheard of to buy favours at any price.

If the bastard hurts her, I'll hurt him back. Zane made the promise to himself as he blinked back the moisture beginning to build up. He could do this. He *would* do this. Ella was upset. He got that. She was angry. He got that. But how could she dismiss what they had? He *didn't* get that.

The thought of losing her wound him up. His hands clenched the wheel so tightly he struggled to turn corners, his movements jerky and dangerous. Heat flushed his body and he couldn't stop his muscles from quivering. It was time to confront his mother with the truth. He prayed fervently, like never before, that this wouldn't be the end of his family as he knew it.

He slowed down once he reached his parents' street and eased the car into their driveway. With the car lights shining at the windows, his parents would know a visitor had arrived.

Zane swallowed, trying to slow down his pounding heartbeat. He feared everything would irrevocably change the minute he stepped out of the car. He dreaded needing to do this, but his feelings for Ella overrode everything. With his shoulders curled forward he shifted on his seat, pulled the handbrake and closed the windows.

His father opened the front door, shadowed by his mother. Both wore worried frowns. He grimaced. Their night was about to get a whole lot worse.

With difficulty and a weighted chest, he opened the door and forced his tired body from the car.

"Zane, darling, we weren't expecting you." His mother—always concerned, always caring. He hadn't phoned to let them know he'd arrived back in Australia.

"Son, is everything okay?" His dad—the very rock of his existence.

"Mum, Dad ..." And he felt like an arsehole. A complete arsehole.

The ache in his throat got too much and made breathing difficult, which brought on a bout of dizziness. He took one step, then an unsteady one. His legs must've folded beneath him, because the next thing his brain computed was the touch of the soft grass cushioning his cheek and a shriek from his mother.

As he lay on the front lawn, his heart tore open and the tears finally came.

Hercules himself could not have stopped them.

Chapter 23

When Zane's mother thrust a sandwich under his nose, he forced it down. It was like trying to swallow sandpaper. Only the strong coffee brew that followed managed to help.

Fifteen minutes ago, he'd been sprawled on the lawn. Now, his parents flanked him at the kitchen table, the room suddenly small and suffocating. Neither said a word but constantly gave each other 'the look'. He had to get this food and drink down and explain—fast. He needed to be on the next flight to Boston.

It surprised him that he was feeling much better since breaking down on the lawn, though the nourishment might be helping. A man's body and brain didn't work well when the total number of hours since last eating ran into double figures.

Sliding his chair back, he went to sit on the other side of the small kitchen table so he could face his parents as he spoke. He took one of each of their hands and squeezed.

"I need to tell you both that I love you." He turned to his father first. The frown that burrowed deeper into his father's brow was definitely his doing. "Dad, I know you're not my biological father but—"

His mother gasped and shoved her chair back. In her haste it toppled over and the metal rim vibrated on the tiled floor. "Zane, what are you talking about?"

He turned to face his distraught mother. "I want to make it clear that Dad will always be my father." When he faced his father again, he added, "I need you in my life, Dad. I always will."

Instead of getting angry at her denial, instead of flaring up, Zane was at peace. She didn't need to lie anymore and it was okay that she had. Whatever reasons she had for leaving Boston, he was an adult now and could take care of himself from here on in. He needed them to understand he wanted nothing to change between them *or* to jeopardise their relationship.

"Mum, sit, please."

She sighed and righted her chair. When she sat down, Zane reached for both her hands and clasped them firmly in his. "I didn't go to Hawaii. I lied to you and I'm sorry. I went to Boston with my girlfriend, Ella."

Her eyes widened at his words and her fingers pinched his.

"The photo you have in the china cabinet. That's you and Ella's mother. She never did die in a car accident, did she?"

His mother shook her head as tears spilled over their hands. "What have you done, Zane? Oh, my God, did you go to Boston to find Ella's father?"

Not daring to break eye contact, he nodded. "Yes," he whispered, "and it was a mistake."

"Why? What did the bastard do?"

His father slid his chair closer to his mother's side and strung an arm around her shoulder, gently kneading her muscles.

"We arrived back this afternoon to learn that Catherine, or Cate as we know her, was arrested. There's only one person who would've alerted the police to her whereabouts."

"Oh, my poor Catherine. She'll always be Catherine to me." She rested her hand against her breast while gazing into the distance.

Zane held his breath, waiting for her to say something. Within seconds, her face snapped back in his direction, her trance broken.

"She would've had no idea how he found her. Does she know?"

He let out the breath he was holding, relieved she hadn't fainted. "Yes. One of Ella's sisters had suspected Ella was lying about going to Hawaii and made Ella promise to leave a copy of her travel plans in a sealed envelope in case of an emergency. When the police arrived for a Catherine Van Der Meeliko, Ella's step-siblings discovered the truth of where we'd been. It wasn't too hard to figure out who to blame for Catherine's arrest."

His mother rose and walked to the kitchen sink, leaned against it and stared out into the dark night.

"Mum?"

She didn't move or turn around.

"I also know you were once married to someone in the Savro family, and that they're Boston's version of the mafia."

She wrapped her hands around her waist, as though warding off a chill. Without turning, she said, "Your grandfather and father are both dead. I thank God for that every day."

Dead? Okay, I'll deal with that later.

"Mum, I need to leave for Boston straight away. Ella is being her usual stubborn self and is insisting she go alone. She ended our relationship tonight, well, at least tried to, but I have every intention of following her. I don't want her confronting her father alone. He's a dangerous man."

She turned. "My God, Zane, he's evil, but then so was your father."

She pushed away from the sink, came back to the table and gripped the back of her chair, her knuckles white in the fluorescent light. "I have a lot to explain, don't I?"

Zane rested his elbow on the table and cushioned his chin in his palm. "The only thing I want to know is if Dad has always known the truth?"

She wrapped her arms around his dad's neck and placed a kiss on his cheek. At the same time his father lifted a hand to cradle his mother's cheek. "Yes. He was my saviour all those years ago, my soul mate. I have no regrets about what I did."

His father twisted in his chair and smiled at Zane's mother. It pushed the ache in his chest up his throat. They had that special connection. He wanted it too and would do anything to make things right so Ella would take him back.

"Now, since I have plenty of explaining to do, I'm coming with you. We'll have enough time on the flight to talk."

His father jumped up out of his chair and faced his wife. "Are you sure? Is it safe?"

She took a deep breath, reached for his hands and took them in her own. "It's time Zane met his grandmother. She's still alive and the only person I regret leaving. She had a difficult life with a vicious and dangerous man. The day he was shot in a drive-by shooting was one of her happiest. She might have shown respectful mourning to the rest of the family, but she'd made it obvious to me, as only a battered wife could, how relieved she was. My life with her only son was no better."

How had his father died? There were hundreds of questions he wanted to ask, but his priority was to book another flight. He'd started thinking of all the things he needed to do, including getting a good night's sleep, when his father spoke.

"Well, I'm coming too. I'm not letting my family loose in some mafia-run city."

Zane smiled for the first time in many hours. He tried to remember when he'd smiled last and was instantly transported back to the airport, when he'd kissed Ella as they waited for their luggage.

A kiss that had happened a lifetime ago.

***

Ella's alarm sounded in the early morning as darkness shrouded the house. She stumbled out of bed and landed on her knees with a thump when her leg caught in the sheet. If anyone wanted to see evidence of how well she'd slept that night all they needed to do was look at the tangled mess of sheets on her bed. She'd tossed and turned relentlessly but must've eventually dozed off because when the alarm had beeped, she'd been sound asleep.

She rose from the floor, rubbed her right knee and made her way to her mother's room. Luke had volunteered to drive her to the airport to make the four thirty a.m. flight, but she wasn't going anywhere without a good luck talisman. Weirdly, with her thoughts stewing all night, she had dreamed of carrying the little blue box with her to Boston for good luck. Yep, it made no sense now that she was awake, but she couldn't rid the idea. She needed all the luck she could get.

With Luke and her sisters upset and angry, she had to fix this any way she could. She had no clue what to do, but her mother needed to know she was there and close. There was no way she would leave Boston without her. She would never be able to face her family again if her mother remained behind bars. As for Zane, well ... she wasn't going there. It would be better if he moved on. She didn't doubt this whole process of saving her mother would be messy and draining, and she needed every ounce of courage she could gather to make it through each day. God alone knew how many days it would entail. She had no family to call on for support in Boston, except for her biological father, and she would rather stab him to death.

Now, with the aid of a chair, she reached into the same wardrobe she'd cleaned all those months ago. She quickly removed the blankets and assortment of things her mother kept up high. Each item landed with a loud thud, the noise resounding through the quiet house. It would wake her sisters, but too bad. She needed some semblance of a goodbye or hug from them before she left—anything to sustain her on the return journey to Boston and everything that waited for her.

Luck would then play a big part in what happened after that.

Within seconds she held the cardboard box. She carried it to her mother's bed, switched on the lamp and dumped the contents of the box on the new quilt. She grabbed the blue box and clutched it to her chest, then switching off the lamp, she left to dress and maybe run a brush through her hair. Her luggage, still packed, would return to Boston with her. She didn't care what she looked like when she arrived.

It frightened her the way her thoughts had turned. She'd never considered herself a violent person or questioned what she'd do in a situation where saving her own life might mean taking someone else's. But the anger which coursed through her organs gave off severe warnings. She didn't question the need to hurt her biological father. The urge to hurt him ran hot in her blood. She'd already imagined winding her hands around his neck and tightening her grip until he relented and squashed the stupid charge he'd concocted all those years ago. Anyone who knew her mother would never doubt she was of sound mind. It was laughable to even say it.

Ella now had a better understanding of her mother's motives from twenty-five years ago. All that would've mattered to her mother was her and her child's safety. How could anyone punish her for that?

Ella had plans. Oh God, how she had plans.

But, first, she had to get there.

Chapter 24

Ella rubbed her tired eyes and settled in a grubby seat on the Commuter Rail that left Boston. It was headed for the Norfolk Centre. She let her head fall back and tried not to think of all the germs touching her skin and clothing. With way too little sleep, the wires in her brain were severely skewed. For now, she took no responsibility for how her mind worked.

When she'd arrived in Boston last night, she'd booked the same accommodation as the week before as a start. She had no idea how long she'd be here. Luke had given her the latest information on their mother's whereabouts, including details of the Lotusville Correctional Centre, only thirty-six miles southwest of Boston. *Miles.* It confused her that such a modern country had never made the move into the metric era. Strange that Australia had made the change back in 1966. She smiled fleetingly as she recalled her stepfather bragging about how special his birth year was. For her it was an easy milestone to remember.

She still missed him so much, especially now. Clamping down on her teeth, she wrestled tears desperate for release. She'd fought them the entire flight, letting anger take over instead. What would he think of all this? How distressed would he be, with his wife dragged away and shipped to another country, a wanted criminal? Had he known about her history? Had she committed bigamy? Ella couldn't imagine being in a relationship with such dark secrets. She had to believe her stepfather had known. If not, everything she'd ever believed about her parents' marriage would be tainted.

She rolled her shoulders as the train rattled along the tracks. She was one step closer to finding out how much her stepfather had known. *If* her mother told her the truth.

Having arrived at her destination, she hailed a taxi for the short four-mile trip to the correctional facility. Her heart beat extra hard for the entire distance, her mind only half on the conversation the taxi driver was trying to strike up. He sounded friendly, with the few snippets she let infiltrate, and his wide smile helped her to relax. At least a little.

"Here you go, miss."

She stared at the building through the window, confused. With the door open and one foot out, she asked, "Are you sure?"

He chuckled. "Sure am. It's not your usual prison with chains and locks. Minimum-security prisoners and those to be released soon are sent here."

"Oh." She wasn't sure if it was relief pouring through her limbs as she stretched her legs and exited the cab, but she managed a smile, handed enough cash for the ride, plus a tip, through his open window and said, "Thank you."

"No worries. You got a friend in there?"

Her frown tightened across her brow. "No, my mum."

She turned to face the three-storey building. Its façade consisted of many square windows, and half a dozen steps flanked by chrome handrails that led up to a sliding glass entry door. She took a deep breath and forced her legs to move.

She reached the top of the steps and knotted her hands. A light breeze lifted tendrils of hair falling out of her loose bun. She hesitated for a moment and reined in her roller-coaster emotions. How did others deal with visiting family in prison?

She took another couple of steps forward and the glass doors slid apart, revealing an open foyer. The immediate change of temperature in the air-conditioned room sent a shiver across her chest. Involuntarily she wrapped her arms around herself and her fingers bit into the soft flesh of her arms. The waiting room consisted of six padded chairs covered in brown fabric, more comfortable-looking than she'd expected. A brochure stand stood forlornly between two of them; it was filled with untidily stacked pamphlets advertising services available to the families of incarcerated persons.

"Can I help you?"

Ella turned around. The person's voice had come over a speaker.

A reflective glass security wall was positioned on the opposite side of the room. She didn't realise people were working behind it. It was clearly a two-way mirror, where only those on the other side could see through.

On closer inspection, she noticed a sign stating that persons seeking assistance were to move closer to the window, press the red button and speak. Strips of clear glass allowed her a partial view beyond the security wall. Three women sat working at desks; one portly lady waved her hand at the red button where the microphone was located and indicated Ella should talk.

She pressed the button, holding it as advised. "I wish to see my mother, Cate ... ah, Catherine Van Der ... ah, Meeliko."

Shit. She had to remember that over here—her mother was no longer Cate Harvey.

A prompt reply came. "Take a seat and we'll advise you of the procedure."

Forty-five minutes later, Ella's number was called and she jumped in a fit of shivers. A range of emotions passed through her. Nerves assailed her; tiredness and hunger not helping. Compounding her nerves was the fear that her mother would reject her. What if she wanted nothing to do with her? Refused to see her?

Guilt followed. If her mother spent years behind bars, how could Ella face the rest of the family? The questions kept circling around her head. Every new question opened a host of fresh doubts. This was new territory.

Her engineering background did little to help her with the complexities of criminal law in the USA. She needed expert support and advice and wouldn't think twice about using every cent of her savings to get it.

As for Zane, how was he taking it? He'd followed through on his threat to follow her there. Her shattered phone still worked, and the number of messages she'd received from him since waking was testament to his stubborn nature. But she wasn't playing games. When she'd told him it was over, she'd meant it.

She followed a security guard away from the foyer and was told there were security checks to complete. Her handbag was taken from her, as well as her phone, and both would be returned after the visit. A security gate, similar to those she'd seen in airports, set off a beep when she walked through it and she was told to empty her pockets. But the only item she carried was the little blue box—the metal bracelet was the culprit.

A female security guard instructed Ella to remove her jacket, then unobtrusively carried out a physical check of her body.

All this activity had taken Ella's mind off the impending meeting, but when she realised she'd be sitting opposite her mother in only minutes, her heart raced all over again.

"You can come this way now." The security guard motioned towards a heavy stainless-steel door.

Ella's limbs refused to move easily; she had to concentrate on lifting her feet, one at a time, to take the steps needed to reach the door. He unlocked it using a numbered keypad and indicated for her to follow him inside. Ella swallowed, unsure of what she would find.

The narrow room was split in half with a thick pane of glass, and individual cubicles were partitioned either side of it. Bright, midmorning light shone through the many square windows. The sun's rays danced across her vision, its refection splayed on the glass partition. The airy open feel of the room gave her the false impression that she could take her mother's hand and lead her outside. Do some shopping or have lunch together. Her fingers clenched tighter against her palms. She itched to get out when she remembered the place wasn't a shopping centre but a jail.

Reality made her chest jolt. Would her mother be waiting? Other visitors occupied seats and were speaking with prisoners, distinguishable by their bright orange overalls, on the other side of the glass.

Nausea rattled her stomach and she rested her hands on it in an attempt to halt the queasiness. The guard led her to the far end of the room, where an orange-clad woman sat with her head hanging low, matted brown hair covering her face.

"Mum!" Ella exclaimed, no longer able to hold back. She collapsed onto the stiff plastic chair in front of the viewing glass and her tears finally found their way out.

Her mother's face shot up. Dark rings circled her eyes; her skin was pale and ghostly.

"Ella," she whispered, her voice sounding broken. "I thought it was the legal aid lawyer coming back again. I can't remember if they told me who was visiting."

The partitions allowed some privacy, and the viewing glass had a hole cut out so they could hear each other. There was also a slit at the bottom that enabled them to hold hands.

Tears streamed down Ella's face at the realisation of what she'd done to her mother. "I'm so sorry, Mum." The horror of what she'd instigated bore down on her. "I'm so, so sorry." This nightmare was not going anywhere.

"Shh ..." her mother soothed as she clasped Ella's hands tightly.

Ella tried to halt her tears, but the build up to this moment had been growing for many hours. They dripped down her hands and mingled with their fingers. She was nowhere close to being able to talk yet.

With no tissues, Ella slid her hands back and used her sleeve to wipe her face. She needed to find some strength and find it fast. Her visit was timed and she had already wasted precious minutes. She reached across for her mother's hands again and clung to them.

"Mum, I'm going to do everything possible to get you out of here."

Her mother's fingers pressed firmly against hers. "Ella, don't do anything. Listen to me."

Ella tried to look at her mother, but she couldn't do it. Her head fell forward.

"Ella," her mother begged, and reluctantly Ella lifted her face. She nodded, her teeth clamped on her bottom lip, determined not to waste any more time.

"I don't regret a single thing I did. I repeated the same prayer to God for years. All I wanted was to remain undiscovered until you turned eighteen. Look how many extra years I received."

"But," Ella spluttered, "you're in jail because of me. Why didn't you tell me about your past? I would've kept your secret."

Her mother shook her head, tears now escaping and trailing down her cheeks. "I couldn't go back on a promise. But you're right. If I had explained everything to you, I might've saved us all this hassle. I guess I worried about how you would take the news. What if you thought you were living a lie? I wouldn't blame you for telling someone. And you had every right to seek your father."

"What about Dad? Did he know the truth?" It was the question that really mattered, though she couldn't understand why. The answer wouldn't change the facts. Her stepfather had been the best father a child could've hoped for. However her mother answered, Ella's memories of him would never be tarnished.

Her mother withdrew a soiled hanky from a pocket on her overalls and blew her nose. She nodded as she dabbed at her eyes. "Yes, he did. I had no choice but to tell him. We only married when we learned your biological father had remarried. At least then I knew he'd done all the legal stuff to clear the way." Her face fell and tears dropped on the small ledge holding the glass pane. "Oh, Ella, he was such a good man—a decent, loving, kind soul." Her shoulders shook. "God, I miss him so much."

That was all Ella needed to hear. Never again would she doubt the depth of her mother's love. Never!

"Mum, Mum, shh, please don't cry." Ella knew the promise her mother had spoken of must have something to do with Zane's mother. If she admitted already knowing it then Ella would have to explain about Zane. But this meeting wasn't about her. It was about her mother and how to free her.

Her mother's hands reached through the gap for hers and squeezed them tight. "I was always too scared to tell you, and your father backed me all the way. In his opinion there was no harm in you never finding out. I can't promise that we were ever going to tell you."

"I'm still going to pay the best lawyer to get you out."

"Don't." Her mother swiped her eyes with her long orange sleeve and straightened in her chair. "Thomas's wealth will swallow us both. His influence and power will squash us. You'll end up with nothing and I'll still be sitting here. No. Go home and take care of the others. Victoria, especially, needs you. They all need you. I've already had a session with the legal aid team and if I'm lucky I'll get no more than a couple of years. Then I'll be free to do what I want. I can live my life free of the fear I've learned to deal with. Thomas can't hurt me after that."

Ella's chest constricted. "But I can't let you do that, Mum. I can't." The coil of anger twisted again, tightened, built up to a rage she'd never fathomed could lay dormant inside of her. "Is that why you left Boston?"

"You've met him. Look how he turned on you."

Ella nodded. Acid burned her throat, and his betrayal sliced her into quarters.

"The last straw, after he'd secured a court order declaring me unstable, was overhearing a phone conversation where he discussed a plan to kill his nephew. I knew that if I didn't get out, I'd be next. There were a couple of times where I woke up after being knocked unconscious ... I wasn't sure I'd survive. My survival and yours were the only things sustaining me through those dark days."

"Oh, Mum." Ella's heart thumped against her chest. The gift of a wonderful life was not to be taken for granted. The fear her mother had carried until they were both safe would've been mammoth.

"After I heard his nephew was dead, a friend of mine helped me leave. We organised fake birth certificates and passports and fled to Greece for a year before settling in Australia. Thomas killed that man, and all these years the guilt has lain here"—she rested her hand on her chest and sniffled—"because I should've informed the police. But I couldn't do it, Ella. I couldn't bring myself to do it. Our safety was more important."

She clutched at her mother's hands and thought of all the pain her mother had endured, the huge sacrifice she'd made so they could have a better life.

"You at least are safe, Ella. That was all I ever wanted, and I got more than what I prayed for. I made a pact with my friend, and I haven't seen her since the day we arrived in Australia. I owe her so much."

Ella lifted her moisture-filled eyes and looked into her mother's beautiful face. She didn't see the stark orange outfit or the dark rings around her eyes. Neither did she see her grubby hair, long overdue for a wash. Instead, she saw a woman of strength and love; she wanted to be just like her.

"How did you find Thomas?"

Startled by the question, Ella stiffened. "I found a small box in your wardrobe when I was cleaning. A private investigator identified you from a photo in a missing persons file. The baby bracelet came from a Tiffany store, so he knew to look at America, and the newspaper write-up on the back of the photo narrowed his search to Boston."

It was all the truth, except she didn't mention Zane. Not yet. What was the point? There was no future for them while her mother sat in jail, which hurt—badly. The pain in her chest contracted and depression settled over her, like a thick, heavy blanket suffocating her. She sighed deeply, wanting to stay underneath it, curl up into a tight ball and never have to get up again. Except she wanted Zane's strong arms around her, right this minute.

She wanted him to kiss her favourite spot below her ear. She wanted her mother to be safe at home. She wanted too, too much.

A chasm opened down the centre of her body—a large, lonely gaping hole—and she had no chance of ever filling it again with love and all things family.

Ella looked up to find her mother's face had fallen. A slow trail of tears slid down her cheeks.

"I always knew holding on to those keepsakes was a mistake." She grimaced and added, "Not once did I think those few items could give away so much information."

"Mum, I'm so sorry. I wish I could take back the last week." But as she spoke, Zane's face popped up, muddying her thoughts. To erase the last week meant swiping clean the precious moments she'd shared with him.

The best and worst week of my life.

Ella struggled with the weight of misery cloaking her weary body. She squeezed her eyes shut for a few moments and willed strength to seep into her bones. She had to get Zane off her mind. Now.

She took a deep breath and ventured with, "Mum, did you know I have a half-brother and sister?"

Her mother nodded. "I've been keeping tabs on Thomas for years. His second wife committed suicide."

"Oh, Mum. Was he really that bad?"

Her mother's posture stiffened, the muscles around her jaw tightening. "Ella, stay away from him. Don't let him intimidate you and don't accept anything from him. You're over eighteen, so he has no hold over you."

"But—"

"No buts, Ella."

The coil of anger tightening in the pit of Ella's gut contracted with another twist. Oh, she was going to pay him one last visit. He deserved that much. Her mother didn't need to know. She was certainly his daughter—she could be a bastard too. There was no way she was going to leave this town until she had her say. Face to face.

"Ella, are you listening to me?"

A timer buzzed, fringing the edges of Ella's mind. Her time with her mother had come to an end, but she would be back tomorrow and the next day.

"How do I get hold of the legal aid people taking care of you?"

Her mother pushed herself up against the glass, her hands reaching out as far as possible. Ella rose and moved away.

"Ella, did you hear me?"

"Madam, it's time for you to leave." A security guard had walked up to Ella's chair.

"Sure. Thanks for everything." She turned back to her mother and said, "I'll ask at the office about teeing up a meeting with the legal aid team. I'll be back tomorrow."

"Ella," her mother hissed.

But Ella didn't reply. A guard on the other side of the glass instructed her mother to leave, and her parting glare screamed at Ella not to do anything stupid.

But Ella had no intention of heeding her advice. Not yet.

Chapter 25

Pissed off. That was the best way to describe how he was feeling. Ella hadn't returned a single message, but he knew exactly what flight she'd arrived on and where she was staying. It annoyed the hell out of him that she was keeping her distance. She was shouldering all the blame, but heck, it'd been his idea to go to Boston. He didn't doubt that his arguments against rushing in to meet her father would be doing the rounds of her head, tampering with her sanity. God almighty. He wanted her in his arms so he could comfort her. This situation was his doing too. She needed all the assurance she could get and a whole lot extra.

If she was hurting, so was he. And there wasn't a single soul in Boston they could call upon for moral support. Her new stepsiblings wouldn't be much use, and if Thomas so much as laid one finger on her, Zane wouldn't be able to hold himself back. He'd do whatever it took to protect her.

Unable to leave Brisbane until the morning, Zane had gone back to Ella's to explain the situation to her family. Luke had returned from taking Ella to the airport and wasn't thrilled to see him. While Ella's sisters were pleased he was going to Boston, Luke wasn't. He was angry about the stupid things they'd done, and Zane, as the professional investigator, should've known better.

Nothing Zane said had pacified Luke.

When Luke demanded Zane stay away from his sister, Victoria had relented and promised to keep Zane up to date with information as it happened. He hadn't expected such strong opposition from Ella's brother, but he accepted it and was prepared to wear it.

Zane was only five hours behind Ella in arriving in Boston and had managed to get a half-decent night's sleep. His parents were awake; he could hear them talking in the small kitchenette. He kicked off the blanket and read the latest message on his phone. Victoria had sent him details of the correctional centre where Catherine was being held. Not the message he wanted, but his mother was keen to visit that morning.

He needed a couple more hours of sleep and closed his eyes. If only his body and mind weren't so wound up. A small throb hovered at the fringes of his temple. If he didn't control his anger, it'd explode into a full-blown headache, which was the last thing he needed. He wanted to be in a good frame of mind when he confronted Ella. He had to convince her that breaking up wasn't going to help either of them. Fighting her father as a team was the better plan.

He rolled to his side and groaned. He knew how her stubborn mind worked, so nothing would go his way. Why did she have to be such a bloody independent woman? When the phone slipped from his fingers, he rolled onto his stomach and pressed his face into the pillow. *But I want her just the way she is.*

He turned over and picked up his phone again. Another check didn't reveal any new messages. *Damn.* He needed to see Ella today, more than he wanted to meet Catherine or his grandmother for the first time. His mother planned on visiting both.

He gave up on sleep and rose from the bed. There was too much in his head. His mother had talked nonstop on the flight, and his mind was now filled with images of his murderous father. The final straw, she told him, was learning through a friend that her husband had killed Thomas Van Der Meeliko's nephew. He hadn't gone to jail for it, and his mother never learned what had eventually put him behind bars, only that he'd received what he justly deserved when a fellow prisoner bludgeoned him to death.

Nice way to go.

Was it wrong that Zane had no desire to learn more about the man who was his biological father, or that he couldn't conjure up any feelings for him?

Numb.

That was the best way to describe how the truth had him feeling. His mother's recount of her previous life sounded like a movie. Never would he have imagined being connected to anyone who'd lived that sort of life. It was so distanced from how he'd been raised that it was hard for him to grapple with. What was more frightening was that it might have been his normal.

He found a change of clothes and made his way to the bathroom. A shower might wake him up.

His mother had told him she owed Catherine her life and, throughout the years, had never forgotten it. Hence, that was the reason she didn't hesitate to fly to Boston when Zane had broken down with the news. Without Catherine's assistance, she would never have escaped. They'd pledged to keep their secret once they'd gone their separate ways in Australia, but his mother had taken a huge risk when she'd told his dad the truth.

Neither of his parents, though, had banked on providence stepping in and bringing Ella and Zane together in one almighty twist of fate.

⁓

"So, we're going to turn up on her doorstep after twenty-five years?"

His mother turned his way and nodded, not looking the least bit worried.

Zane clamped his jaw. They'd delayed their visit to Catherine until after lunch and had instead hailed a taxi to take them to his grandmother's home.

"How do you know she's at the same place? She could be dead after all this time."

"She's not."

He didn't want to be there and couldn't hide the irritation in his voice. "She could be the type of person waiting with a gun pointed at us."

In the back seat of the taxi, his mother sat between him and his dad and chuckled. She was obviously refusing to be daunted by his snarly mood. Instead, she took hold of his hand.

"Zane, I promise that she'll do nothing of the sort. I know I didn't paint the best picture of your father, but your grandmother, like me, never belonged in that family. The only difference was I escaped."

He'd let it go for now. If his mother wanted to reconnect with her mother-in-law, who was he to argue? In his mind, his grandmother was a connection to the monster that was his father, who now took up space in his head.

It didn't surprise him when the taxi drove through a suburb of Boston not far from where the Van Der Meelikos resided, but the house they stopped in front of surprised him. It wasn't pretentious like the Van Der Meeliko home; in a lot of ways it looked neglected. The garden was nothing to write home about.

Zane swung his door open and hopped out while his dad paid the fare. The house didn't sit too far back from the street, and the stark grey door looked as inviting as a winter storm. He squared his shoulders, ready to do battle, and tested the ornate two-metre high gate. When he found it unlocked, he wondered if it was a sign. What kind, he had no idea. Shit, an unlocked gate could mean anything.

He shook his head. This was crazy. All he wanted to do was fight his battle with Ella. Why wouldn't she return his messages? He reached into the pocket of his coat for another glance of his phone, hoping for something. Nope. Nothing. *Great.*

When the massive grey door opened, revealing a tiny, wrinkled maid, his mother screeched.

"Zhia, oh my God, Zhia! You're still here."

The woman's kindly eyes widened and her mouth fell open. Zhia didn't get a chance to utter anything before Zane's mum wrapped her in her arms. It was close to a suffocation job. As tears fell freely down their faces, Zane's father put his arms around them both to lend some comfort.

Zhia pulled back first. "Mathilda, my dear precious Mathilda, is it really you?"

His mother nodded as his father shoved a tissue into her hand.

"Come, come in. Rosetta will be beside herself. Your return is long overdue."

They waited in the family room where heavy dark blue drapes were partially opened. Zane shivered in the badly lit space and moved closer to the floor-to-ceiling windows to pull the curtains apart. Light struck the other side of the room, the many photos that adorned the opposite wall now clearly visible.

Zane swallowed and made his way towards them. He wasn't so sure he wanted confirmation that he resembled his father. His mother's words. He stopped at the first photo of his father and something tugged at the strings that connected his heart to everything. Could this man have been so evil? A murderer? He stared at the framed image in which his father was the centre of attention, surrounded by friends. They all wore the same college jerseys, displayed comfortable smiles and reflected comradery. He looked to be in his early twenties and had a confident smile. What had gone wrong? What had turned him into the person he'd become?

"Mathilda? Mathilda, is it true? Have you finally come back?"

Zane turned around to find his mother in the arms of his grandmother, who was the picture of health; in her sixties, by his calculations. They clung together, with tears falling again. This time his mother's shoulders shook.

Zane glanced across at his dad, who beckoned, and so Zane walked towards the pair of women. He'd learned only yesterday that his mother's real name wasn't Tilly.

"Let me look at you, Mathilda."

Rosetta stepped back and held his mother's face in her hands, then she leaned forward and kissed both her cheeks. "You broke my heart when you left. I understood why you did it, but I hated you for taking Zachary away."

Zane's mother turned to glance at him. Rosetta did too, and Zane knew the instant his grandmother made the connection. Her hands dropped from his mother's face and she reached for him, yearning etched her face, a feeling that had probably never left her all these years.

"Zachary?" she whispered.

"Rosetta, I changed his name to Zane. He only learned yesterday that his birth name was Zachary."

"My dear God, where did you take him?"

"To Australia." His mother reached for his father's hand and tugged him closer. "I married this man, Rosetta. Jonathan was a good father to Zane. He made us both very happy."

But Rosetta didn't shift her gaze from Zane. Her body shook as she mimed holding a baby against her chest, her tears still falling. "There were so many nights I wanted to hold his tiny body against my own and sing him to sleep, to shower him with all my love."

A lump formed in Zane's throat. It wasn't meant to feel like this. This woman was the mother of a monster. What right did she have to feel this way?

Except her pain was visible, and it hurt him, too. He took a step closer and towered over her. Wrapping his arms around her, he gave her the comfort she'd been denied for so many years as her tears soaked through his shirt.

When Zhia wheeled in a rattling trolley, Rosetta took a step back. "Look at me. Important guests and I cry the whole time." She pulled out a hanky and dabbed at her face. "Let's sit and have morning tea."

She took hold of Zane's hand and refused to let it go, even when they sat side by side on the settee.

"Thank you, Zhia," Rosetta said. "Would you like to join us this morning?"

The tiny maid's smile spread across her face. She sat beside his mother and took hold of her hand. It was unlikely she'd get her hand back any time soon.

Heroically, Jonathan stepped in. "Allow me."

He waved them all away, insisting they stay seated. "I've been trained to do this." With a smile he took control of the tea trolley and did the honours of pouring tea and passing the sweets.

"Well, Mathilda"—Rosetta sniffled one last time into her tissue—"I know we have a lot to catch up on, and you have no idea how timely your return is." In an instant, his grandmother's tears vanished and she wore a smug look.

To Zane's surprise, his mother chuckled. "You haven't changed at all. I'm glad you haven't lost your sense of humour. So, pray tell, who's been taking advantage of you this time?"

Rosetta let go of Zane's hand and accepted a cup and saucer from Jonathan. After taking a sip, she said, "For years, they've been trying to pension me off into a smaller apartment and take whatever money I still have." She chuckled and placed her tea on a side table. "The only good thing your 'I hope you're in hell' father-in-law did was never change his will before he died. Everything was left to me. After his death I was hell-bent on retaining everything. Of course, I was keeping it for Mario, but after he died, I had every family member by my side. Vultures, the lot of them. Trust me, anything they could legally get they already have."

"The good old family. Always reliable, hey, Rosetta?"

Zane's eyes widened as he took a big slug of tea. It was too hot and burned his mouth. He coughed to cover his discomfort. He wasn't surprised that his grandmother didn't get teary and emotional when she mentioned her deceased husband and son, or how she and his mother seemed to have a secret language between them.

His grandmother nibbled on a biscuit. She picked a crumb off her teal skirt and placed it on her saucer. Grey hair rested against her neck, with short tendrils and curls taking whatever direction they wanted. Noticing

Zane looking at her, she fingered the fine gold cross necklace that adorned her long, graceful neck. For a fleeting moment she looked sad.

"You can't imagine how relieved I am to know you've both lived a decent life, away from this destructive lot. I'm so proud of you Mathilda, and I thank God every day that my grandson will never know what his destiny might've been if his grandfather and father were still alive."

"So, I didn't fool you? You didn't think our disappearance was a result of murder?"

Rosetta shook her head. "Never. Not once."

When silence filled the room after his grandmother's declaration, Zane mulled over the conversation. If he'd been raised in Boston, he might've been cast in the same role as his father. If he'd had the Savro surname, people would have assumed things of him, a lifestyle it seemed that was second nature to this family.

He let out the deep breath he'd been holding and looked at his mother in awe. He remembered her words to him the day he'd returned home after the bike accident. *A mother would easily give up her life for her child*. She'd done just that, and he owed her everything for giving him a normal and fulfilling life. Never would he doubt her love for him, though he'd never done so in the past.

"Healthwise, how have you been?" His mother broke the silence.

"Oh, Mathilda, I've always been blessed with good health. Of course, as the old and senile great aunt, I'm treated like I have dementia." Her fingers laced together on her lap, and a smile spread across her face. "I never shied away from the job I had to do, and that was to pray for you every day. I had to believe you were living a better life and bringing up my grandson like I'd hoped to once."

The first frown graced her face. "I wasn't sure if I'd ever see you again, but I didn't blame you. Hate was a harsh thing to feel but it was still there." With her laced fingers knotting, her happy-go-lucky demeanour vanished to reveal sadness and pain. Zane could see she'd held onto it for many years.

When her jaw tightened, Zane knew she was working hard to push the pain away.

"It hasn't been all bad," she said. "Lately I've begun taking small trips. I've joined groups and taken tours with old and senile people like me." She chuckled and added, "It must be time for a longer holiday. I've always wanted to see Australia. The time is now ripe."

"We would have you in an instant. Yes, you must come."

"I will soon. Now I can sleep at night knowing I have purpose again and a rightful heir to my wealth."

"Rosetta, we didn't come here for money." Zane's mother ran a hand through her hair, showing signs of agitation.

"Why did you come back?"

His mother's hand dropped to her lap. "It's a long story, but I'll tell you."

"Your secret is safe with me. I will never reveal your whereabouts and no one will ever know you came here. You can trust me. As for my wealth, it *will* be yours one day. I promise. Now, no arguing. Allow an old lady to indulge her family.

Can you not picture the faces of all the scavengers in this family who pretend to care about me when they realise all my wealth is gone when I die? I always planned to give it away before I died, and now, I have even greater cause to do so. Darn, I'm tempted to sell this house and migrate to Australia without a trace." Her laughter tinkled around the room. "I think your visit will add ten years to my life."

Zane's head was swamped with information overload. Did he want blood money on his conscience? He sat back and, like his dad, listened to his grandmother and mother recount the past twenty-five years and the reasons they were in Boston.

After another hour of talking, and two cups of tea later, he was tempted to reach for his phone and check for messages. His snuck his hand into his coat pocket, when he was startled by his grandmother's voice.

"Zane, I have something for you."

He sat up straighter, not sure what to say. Bloody hell, he didn't want a wad of cash handed over.

"Zhia, you know the box I keep on my dresser, with Zachary's name on it?"

Zhia nodded and rose, her tiny feet whizzing across the room in an instant. Everyone rose from their seats and promised to come again before they left. His dad pulled out his wallet and a business card and, taking a pen from Zane's mother, wrote down phone numbers.

Zhia reappeared with a small padlocked wooden box. His grandmother took it from her and passed it to Zane. "This belonged to your father. It was returned to me after his death. Wrapped in brown paper, it had 'For my son, Zachary' written on it." She turned to Zane's mother and said, "He must've believed you weren't dead either. It saddened me when I realised he'd obviously known you'd left him and had taken his son. Who knows, maybe he had regrets."

Rosetta turned back to Zane. "I've never opened the box and have no idea what it contains. I hope it reveals the spirit your father had before he turned on society."

With heaviness, Zane took the box. There was so much he didn't want to deal with. How much strength did he have left? Wasn't it enough that Ella's mother was in jail and he was partly to blame?

Chapter 26

Ella drained her strong coffee and flung the takeaway cup in the bin to her left. She drew in a lungful of air. This was it. Her hands were balled into tight fists, and her nails dug deep into her palms. She doubted she would ever know the joy of relaxing again. All her pent-up anger since learning of her father's betrayal led her to this moment. She was on fire. Blood boiled in every vein across the length and breadth of her body. Nothing was sacred anymore. Nothing else mattered.

She angled her neck and glanced at the top floor of the imposing high-rise. Fury continued to bubble in her veins, which was hot and ready to burst.

After leaving her mother, she'd arranged a meeting with the legal aid team before returning to her hotel room, where she'd steadfastly refused to reply to any of Zane's messages. Instead, she'd showered, changed into a navy-blue pantsuit and reapplied her make-up as if it were war paint.

If Thomas was out, she would wait. There was no turning back now and no giving in. Ever.

She squared her shoulders and approached the building. At the bank of elevators, she caught one before its doors closed and made her way towards the back. With many suited men and well-dressed women entering and exiting the ascending lift, she gritted her teeth and did everything possible to keep her anger alive. She fought her nerves, pushing them away with iron will. Better to keep them away from her heart and head. She didn't have time to reason with either.

When she reached the top floor, she was the last occupant in the lift. She stepped out and the doors slid closed behind her. Taking a deep breath, she purposefully walked towards her father's office. She'd made it to within a couple of steps of the door when someone gasped behind her.

"Excuse me, you can't go in there."

Ella neither halted her footsteps nor turned around. Banking on the door being unlocked, she almost buckled at the knees when she turned the handle and the door opened. As an afterthought, she turned towards the rapidly approaching secretary and glared at her.

"Watch me."

Barely in the room, she slammed the door shut and locked it.

She spun around. The table she remembered from her first visit was surrounded with people, every chair filled with dark-suited men—a meeting of sorts. Her father sat at the head.

"Ella." He rose from his seat, the muscles on his face taut. "You can't come barging in here."

Some men rose, as though about to leave. Clearly, they realised this was a private matter.

Don't let him win. The mantra ran around her head and spurred her into action. A few steps had her by the table. She didn't want anyone to leave. Her first task was to calm them with her unexpected arrival.

"Please remain seated, all of you." She let her gaze settle on each of the seven faces; God alone knew what they saw reflected back.

Ella couldn't describe what now unravelled inside her. She had no idea what to say. Aborting her planned speech, she ran on adrenalin alone. God help her.

"I'd like you all to bear witness to what I'm about to say. After all," she paused, "if you hear of my death in the papers tomorrow, the death of Thomas Van Der Meeliko's daughter, I'd like to hope you'd have the courage to contact the police and tell them it had been orchestrated by my father."

Mouths dropped and eyes widened.

"Yes," she grimaced dryly, "I'm the long-lost daughter of Thomas Van Der Meeliko. A few days ago, he saw me for the first time in twenty-five years. Pretended he was pleased to see me and made huge promises of keeping in touch and connecting again as father and daughter should."

She sauntered to her father's side, but how she'd coaxed her stiff legs to move, she would never know. It'd just happened.

"My plane had barely lifted from the ground before his true colours were exposed."

He stood upright with tension oozing from his rigid shoulders. She let the full impact of her glare settle on his face, then returned her attention to the men around the table.

"I was born to this man's first wife. She disappeared without a trace. Smart lady. Bashed too many times by her loving husband and left to die on numerous occasions. He used his power and money to bring a court order against her and claimed she was mentally unstable. Really?"

She waved her hands, questioning, asking these men for answers as to why someone would do that.

"My mother is the most grounded and sensible person on this earth. His claim was so far removed from the truth, he obviously didn't know his own spouse."

"That's enough, Ella."

"What's enough, *Daddy*?" She gestured again to encompass the men. "Don't you want all your friends here to know what a great husband you were? How your first wife left before you could kill her, how your second wife committed suicide because she couldn't stand your company, or how none of your children love you?" She poked her fingers into his chest and added, "Me included."

Papers shuffled and someone coughed.

Her father was close; only a handspan separated them. She brought her face even closer to his and hissed, "Drop the charges, you bastard."

She looked into black pools, his anger matching hers. She didn't give a damn.

Loud enough for everyone in the room to hear, she spat, "To stop me, *Daddy*, you'll have to kill me. I'll keep talking until the day I die. This story will be sold to the highest bidder at every opportunity. I'll use social media like you never imagined. Trust me, everyone in Boston and the entire United States of America will know who the *real* Thomas Van Der Meeliko is if it's the last thing I do."

He grabbed her upper arm and tried to drag her from the room. She dug her heels in, and only then did she hear loud knocking on the office door.

Behind her, someone said, "Don't, Thomas."

With those two words, her fear disappeared and her confidence returned.

When he dropped his hand, she laughed, sounding deranged and hysterical. Yep, that was the best way to describe it.

She took a step back and spread her arms wide. She forced a smile to stretch across her face. "Guess what, everyone? My mother sacrificed everything when she left. But I thank God I was raised in an amazing and normal family environment, with a loving and caring stepfather who treated me like his own. The only unstable part of my mother's life was living with the fear of discovery."

Ella took in her audience. Having them boosted her confidence—or her stupidity. She would dwell on it in the aftermath. For now, she had to keep going while the words churned out. Except the bile trying to rise up her throat had other ideas. She coughed to avoid gagging and pushed on.

"Three days ago, my *father*"—she pointed in his direction—"learned of my mother's whereabouts." She paused to get enough air in her lungs as they constricted. "And now she sits in jail. Hard to believe, isn't it? Why, you may ask? For protecting herself and her child from this monster. This man, who has a shitload of money, had the power to do this. He brought back into force a quarter of a century old court order, wrongfully executed in the first place, and accused her of kidnapping."

The loud knocking on the door escalated to bashing before the door swung open and slammed against the wall, surprising everyone.

The same muscly security guard Ella had encountered only days earlier stormed in and confronted the room full of people. The secretary hid behind his bulk as he raised his gun.

Chairs scraped back and men scampered behind them with fear etched on their faces. Could their day get any worse?

"Put the gun down!" someone yelled.

The security guard carefully lowered his arm and replaced the pistol in the holster. He turned to Thomas, obviously seeking further instructions. Her father's shoulders squared, the shock of this confrontation quickly wearing off. He stood to his full regal height.

"Everyone out," he shouted, "now." His steely voice cut through the tense silence. It motivated the men into action, including the security guard.

Ella didn't move. She wasn't finished yet.

"Except you." His mouth twisted into an ugly sneer.

"Oh, trust me, *Daddy*. I'm not going anywhere." She turned when someone tapped her shoulder.

One of the suited men had stopped short of leaving the room. "Would you like me to stay?"

A lump formed in her throat. This unexpected show of kindness was the last thing she'd expected. "Thank you, but I'll be fine. Like I said, he'll need to kill me if he wants to silence me. I hope someone is strong enough to tell police the truth if that happens."

He pulled a business card out of his pocket and slipped it into her hand. "Call me tomorrow."

So, her father had enemies. A small smile played on her lips as the room emptied. Why did that not surprise her? How many more would be willing to help her knock that vile smug smile he'd maintained on her first visit? Oh, how she remembered it well, and how it now made her insides twist with revulsion.

With her back to her father, she noted the worried glance the secretary gave him before closing the door with a loud thud, leaving them alone. That woman was loyal to only one person—and it wasn't Ella.

Let the games begin. She chuckled and spun around to face him. Strangely, her anger dissipated. Venting in front of his business colleagues had satisfied every bitchy cell in her body. Her actions would have consequences, but instead of fearing the unknown, determination dripped off her—it could no doubt fill buckets galore—because she was prepared to die for her mother. The thought had only burst through her brain during her earlier tirade. If he didn't agree to drop all the idiotic charges he'd trumped up, she would die exacting all the revenge she could.

Thank God she'd had the foresight to end things with Zane. He didn't need to be part of this, dragged into this horrendous debacle with her newly discovered dysfunctional family. This situation was so far removed from her and Zane's everyday life, she could've scripted it and sold it to the highest bidder in Hollywood.

Her father moved slowly and deliberately towards her. His towering presence was meant to intimidate. It didn't.

With hands on hips, her chest puffed out, ready to butt against his.

"I promise, you'll regret what you did today." He stared her down, clearly trying to frighten her.

"You don't scare me. Like I said, I'm prepared to die for my mother. I bet not one soul in this whole world would do the same for you." Silenced thickened the space where they stood, and the cords of his neck protruded on either side. "And after the world knows the truth about your skills as a husband, they'll learn that you killed your nephew."

A frown dug into his brow. "What?" he spat. "What the hell are you talking about?"

"DNA, *Daddy*. Once I inform the police about the murder, they'll do the DNA check. You're going down, and it'll be my absolute pleasure to take you there. Unless—"

"Over my dead body." His sneer turned ugly. "You are one stupid girl if you think I will let you and your mother get away with this."

"Oh, poor Daddy. No one loves you. You must feel so special."

"I have two other children."

"You have a very bored daughter who can't decide what to do each day. And you have a son, so high on drugs he doesn't know what day of the week it is. Trust me, I'll be doing everything possible to take them back to Australia with me, so they can sort out their lives. They won't need your money for that. I'll take care of them. You see, I was raised by a loving and caring man who taught me values. One of them being that money doesn't buy you happiness. Something you should've realised years ago."

He snatched her arm and pulled it behind her back. With his mouth near her ear, he hissed, "If you know what's good for you, you'll leave here and return home immediately."

Ella wrenched at her arm. "Get your hands off me."

Her father's hold tightened. He twisted her arm further and pain sliced across her back. "So," he drawled, "you're prepared to die for that lying bitch?"

Ella bit her tongue, not wanting to make a single sound but unsure how much longer she could hold out. Her eyes bored into his, and she hoped they torched his soul. This man, her father, was evil.

Fear pressed against her chest when he twisted her arm tighter.

Certain it would snap off, she spat in his face. "Go ahead. This'll be your last day as a free man, you bullying bastard. I better thank you for providing an excellent audience for my appearance today. Probably the only thing you've done right in your entire, miserable life."

His reaction to her words was to tighten his hold further. Seconds stretched into eternity, giving her enough time to replay her life, projector-style, in her mind. The room spun and she gasped for air, but none made it to her lungs.

Chapter 27

Zane sat to the side, unnoticed, and allowed his mother and Catherine to reunite. Catherine's shock, when his mother approached the partitioned glass, had been understandable.

Annoyed that Ella wasn't returning his messages, Zane didn't have to ask Catherine whether she'd been that morning to visit. She had. Of this, Zane had no doubt. She'd probably sat in the same chair his mother did now. If he was deluded enough, he'd surely smell eucalyptus in the room. But he wasn't stupid. Just madly in love with a woman who was driving him crazy.

In the waiting room earlier, he'd sat on something sharp, which had pinched his lower back. On closer inspection, he'd found that Ella's little blue box had slipped between the cushions. Inside was the bracelet with the inscription he knew by heart. When he showed the find to his parents and had explained who it belonged to, he was stunned to learn it had been a gift his mother had given Ella on her christening day.

The entire situation was becoming weirder.

What worried him was how all this newfound knowledge would alter his perspective on life. Would it change the man he was? His usual style was to run head-on through life, collecting damaged bits of life along the way and tossing them over a fence. Hell, he'd never been this in love before, and with everything changing so fast, he couldn't use his usual tricks for getting through each day. He was being forced to slow down and consider each move. Very unlike him.

The first blow had come when he'd inspected his birth certificate. Then, in the short space of a few days, he'd learned the truth about his real father and grandfather and about the violence both his mother and grandmother has suffered. Dark secrets his mother had kept from him.

Not knowing the reasons for his biological father's actions hurt the most. Not able to get closure would leave a gaping hole somewhere in his heart. No matter how important his stepdad was to him, he was still connected to an unknown man who'd died as he'd lived. Cloaked in violence.

His grandmother's desire to leave him her fortune didn't sit well with him either. It wasn't the sort of money he could spend without it niggling at his conscience. But she'd been insistent, and that's when the idea had come to him. Maybe it was his destiny. He could put the money towards a women's shelter that provided protection from domestic violence. It often coincided with drug and alcohol abuse; he could set up education programs, bringing awareness to teenagers so they'd avoid entering or continuing the vicious cycle.

Changes had come about in society in stranger ways.

When he switched his attention back to his mother and Catherine, his breath hitched in his throat. Tears poured down both their faces. The hardships these two women had dealt with in their lifetimes were more than any one person should endure.

He turned away for an instant, missing the connection and comfort the little blue box had given him. Damn it, what he'd do for the feel of Ella's hand in his. Hell. He missed everything about her, and she could deny it all she wanted, but something deep in his subconscious told him they belonged together.

They'd arrived at the Lotusville Correctional Centre directly from his grandmother's home. With a maximum of two persons allowed to visit, his father was in the waiting room. Zane had entrusted the little blue box to his father and dwelled on how he'd return it to Ella. He wasn't about to just hand it over. That would be too straightforward.

In an attempt to drag his mind off Ella, he focused on their mothers' conversation and heard a lot of apologies coming from his mother. She would have to learn to accept that no one was at fault. He'd seen worse when it came to reunions. Unfortunately, guilt had a way of choking a person. If they'd done things differently in the past, could it have changed the course of their lives? Those sorts of questions would haunt them forever.

Once her initial flood of tears had abated, Catherine swiped her face, leaving moisture smeared across her cheeks and wet patches on the bright orange sleeve of her prison overalls. Her eyes widened with surprise when Zane scraped his chair closer to the partition. "This ... this can't be ..." She swung back to face his mother. "Tilly, is ... is this ...?"

He moved closer until he was sitting in front of Catherine. "Yes, I'm Zane. There's a lot we need to discuss. Firstly, I want you to know that I love your daughter and I'm going to help her fix the mess we made."

"What? You're in love?" Catherine shrieked. "Ella was here only a little while ago. How come I know nothing about this?" She twisted to look at his mother and asked, "Tilly, did you know anything?"

So, Ella didn't mention me.

"He told me everything on the flight over." His mother reached for Catherine's hand and squeezed it. "Zane does part-time investigative work and the photo of us you kept hidden alerted him to our connection. I kept the same photo all these years and he recognised it immediately."

Catherine slumped against her chair. "So, *you* found Ella's father?"

He knew she hadn't meant to accuse him, but it didn't stop him from leaning forward and massaging his temple. "I had no idea what kind of monster he was. All I knew was that my mother never told us the truth about what happened to her friend in the photo. I also never once suspected my dad wasn't my biological father. Initially, I didn't tell Ella any of this. I wanted to find out what I could first, but not even that went to plan."

Zane recounted the events leading up to Ella discovering the replica photo in his mother's cabinet and how all hell had broken loose between them. He explained how he'd accessed cold case files and discovered a grainy photograph of her, allowing him to learn the identity of Ella's father. It had been his idea to come to Boston—a purely selfish decision because he couldn't find anything on *his* mother. He didn't know about the link between them and hadn't been prepared to ask his mother yet.

When he finished telling her about his and Ella's week in Boston and of meeting Ella's father and half-siblings, he reclined. "She's being pretty stubborn about not wanting any help, but it's my fault too, so I need to fix it."

Catherine grimaced. "I'm sorry, Zane. She *was* acting strange in the weeks before she went—well, I *thought* she was going to Hawaii. Then one day she demanded to know who Isabella was. My God, I was so close to telling her everything. I guessed she'd found the hidden box in my wardrobe, but I never imagined she'd progressed further. I promised I'd make myself tell her the truth, terrified as I was, once we wrapped up Victoria's treatment."

She shook her head and fought more tears. "Damn," she swore, "I can't believe I didn't pick up on her lies. Thank God Victoria did. She knew something was amiss but didn't ask any questions. She insisted Ella leave details of her itinerary in case of an emergency and was beside herself when the police turned up. She had no idea about my past. That's when I explained everything."

"How did the pair of you manage to change your accents so soundly? I've never been able to detect anything?" Zane asked.

Tilly grimaced beside him. "A lot of hard work and total commitment to erase any hint of our past."

A timer buzzed somewhere nearby.

On the other side of the glass partition, Catherine panicked. "Zane, you have to get to her, fast." She stumbled out of her chair, the sight of the security guard coming her way putting fear in her face. "I begged her not to have anything to do with her father. Told her to take nothing from him and not to go anywhere near him. But ..."

A chill swept its way along the back of his neck. *Damn it. She'd do this.*

He rushed to his feet and swore when the chair fell back. A security guard approached at the same time as a shadow lengthened across the room, the sudden disappearance of the sunlight sending a bad premonition Zane's way.

"Zane," Catherine talked over her shoulder, her voice shaky as the guard led her away. "I know the look she gave me. I know she's gone to him. She'll be planning all sorts of revenge. But he'll squash her and suck every bit of life from her." Her last words were shouted over the partitioned glass, desperation lacing her voice. "Go, Zane! Please. Please, save my baby."

He righted his chair and could hear Catherine sobbing as the guard led her through a security door. He put his arm around his mother, who was just as distraught. "Come on, Mum, we need to hurry. You heard her."

⁂

Zane tapped his thigh. The taxi couldn't get to the centre of Boston fast enough. It was bad enough that the rail service out of Norfolk had been delayed due to an electrical problem.

His head throbbed, threatening to burst if he didn't calm down. *Calm down, my arse. When I get to her, she'll know all about it.*

He yanked his phone out of his pocket and sent a hurried message to Ella, saying that he knew what she was up to and that she should stop. Backtrack. Get the hell out of her father's building.

But he knew. Bloody hell, did he ever. His senses were on full alert and he knew exactly where she'd be. He was one hundred percent certain of it. *Damn her stupidity and stubbornness.*

After handing money over to the cab driver, he'd flung himself out before the vehicle had a chance to stop, and ran towards the familiar high-rise. He sprinted to the elevator bank and swore impatiently as he waited for one to arrive.

Finally, he was in. The numbers rose with agonising slowness as the lift made stops along the way. He gripped the chrome rail and ignored the strange looks he was getting when people entered and left. His face would be sporting the world's biggest scowl, but he didn't care. He wasn't there to make friends.

As impatience threatened to strangle the hold he had on his emotions, the doors slid apart and relief spread across his flushed skin when he realised he'd arrived at the top floor.

Once past the elevators, he saw only one other person. She stood beside a desk fanning herself with a magazine, her back to Zane. Ella had told him there was only one secretary on the floor and Thomas's office.

This must be the secretary.

"Excuse me, is Ella Harvey with Mr Van Der Meeliko?" Zane said, rushing up behind her.

She gasped and, turning around, dropped the magazine.

He didn't have time for this. "Please, tell me, or I'll head straight in myself."

The secretary crumpled to her seat, with hair coming out of her bun. "Oh, do what you want. What do I care? Who else wants to barge their way in today?"

On closer inspection, Zane thought she looked about ready to pass out. "If Ella Harvey is the same person who only a few days ago claimed to be Mr Van Der Meeliko's daughter, then yes, she's in there." She waved him in the direction of the office. "Go. Make my day. Take her away, she's nothing but trouble."

He ran. The office was only metres away, but his legs couldn't go fast enough. As he reached the door, he pushed its handle down before swinging it open, leaving it to slam against the wall.

He gasped. Thomas had Ella's arm locked behind her back in a tight grip. When he saw Zane, he froze for an instant before releasing Ella.

Ella twisted around, and when she cried out Zane's name in anguish, it tore at his insides.

"Get your hands off her." With a flurry of movement, Zane had a fistful of Thomas's shirt. Every muscle on Zane's face twitched with fury as he shoved Thomas back and threw a punch.

Thomas stumbled before righting himself, and at the same time the security guard stormed into the room.

"Mr Van Der Meeliko." The security guard rushed towards Thomas' side, but Thomas shooed him back.

After a quick touch to his face, and clearly finding no blood on his hand, Thomas let his arm drop and stood tall. Then his posture stiffened and his mouth gaped open.

"Oh, my God. Oh, my holy flaming God. How did I not pick it up the last time I saw you? Christ, you're a Savro, aren't you? I can see it in your face. You're Mathilda's kid. You bastards are still mixed up with my family. When will you leave us alone?"

Before Zane had a chance to draw breath, Ella shot a smart-mouthed comment back—and he could have strangled her for it. "You don't have a family. At least not one to be proud of. Anyway, he's not my boyfriend anymore, so you can leave him alone."

Zane grabbed her arm, his hand shaking as he moved towards the door. "Let's go, Ella." He didn't like anything about this entire affair.

His grip tightened as her final words sunk in and belted him across the chest. *What the hell was that supposed to mean?*

"I'm not finished with either of you yet," her father yelled after them.

Zane barely registered Thomas's threat. Because his biggest threat was right beside him, trying to free her arm.

Chapter 28

"Ouch. Let go of my arm," Ella spluttered, but Zane's grip was firm. Reluctantly, Ella let him drag her along with his long strides, until they stood at the elevators. With his free hand, Zane slapped the lift recall button, refusing to speak to her or release her.

"For God's sake, Zane, let me go. You're hurting me," she hissed.

This seemed to galvanise him into action. He dropped her arm and spun around to face her. "What the hell was that all about?" He glared at her as his voice reverberated off the walls. A vein twitched on his temple and his nostrils flared. "You couldn't reply to a single message of mine? What about your mother? She told you not to come here, didn't she?"

What? How does he know?

"And what the hell was that bullshit about me not being your boyfriend?"

Ella swallowed and tried to hide her pain. She had to do this, to protect him from her father's wrath. Because she planned to goad her father to breaking point. He'd shown what he could do when pushed past his limit, and she couldn't afford to have Zane caught up in this. She wouldn't stop. Never. Not while her mother sat in jail.

She took a deep breath and stood her ground. "You heard me. I told you in Brisbane." She dug her fingernails deeper into the soft skin of her palm and pinched herself. "Go home, Zane. I don't need you here."

"Bullshit!" he roared.

"Does someone need to be escorted away?"

They both spun to face the security guard, who'd approached silently.

"No," they barked at the same time.

The guard took a step back at their raised voices as a lift opened behind them. None too gently, Zane grabbed her arm again and pulled her inside.

Alone in the elevator, Zane wrapped her in a hug. "You told me you loved me." Her heart thumped against his chest. "In this very city, barely a week ago. Did it mean nothing to you?"

She bit her bottom lip to stop it from quivering and stepped back. She stumbled when the lift stopped and the doors opened to allow others in. But that didn't stop Zane.

"What about the times we shared in bed? What? Still means nothing?" He'd raised his eyebrows, but his eyes were cold and hard, his anguish reflected in their depths.

Ella pressed her hands together behind her back. She kept her shoulders straight and tried to appear unaffected. But his words cut through her.

Someone coughed. Zane's tirade was making others uncomfortable, but he didn't seem to care. His gaze continued to bore right through her. "I warned you there were risks in searching for your father. You told me you could handle it, that no matter what happened you wanted me by your side." He shook his head. "Shit, barely five minutes had passed after you got bad news and you told me to go. What the hell came over you? I know you're scared, I get that, but did you really think I was in this just for the ride? You don't think this affects me too?"

She swayed when the lift halted at another floor, the small space filling up fast.

But no crowds or strangers were going to stop Zane. "That bastard up there is going to squash you, and those were your mother's words, just so you know."

She stifled her gasp. *He's been to see Mum? Shit, Luke and the girls must be keeping him updated. How the heck am I going to shake him off if my family keep interfering?*

The lift stopped on the ground floor and the occupants filed out. She couldn't drag her gaze away from Zane's. Hypnotically, she looked into his dark pools. *Stop!* A person's eyes held the truth, and there was no way Ella could hide her feelings. She loved this man—he was everything she'd ever wanted. But she had a mission to accomplish—a man to squash beneath her heel. A wrong to make right so her mother could live the rest of her life without fear. Her mother who'd risked everything so her child could live a happy and carefree life without the constant threat of fear and violence. Ella had been gifted that life and lived it—now she was prepared to give it up for her mother. She wasn't risking anyone else's life. Just her own.

Resolutely making a decision, she squared her shoulders and bit down on her tongue to harden her resolve. "I said go home, Zane. I don't want you here."

"And I say bullshit." His voice rose an octave. "You're not facing your father alone again."

"Excuse me, is everything okay?"

"Yes," they both shouted as they turned towards the man holding the lift door open.

Ella groaned inwardly. It was the same pinstriped suited, arrogant man she'd encountered only days earlier. He looked directly at her, his gaze just as calculated and lecherous as the first time they'd met.

She huffed and stormed out of the lift. If she could get to her hotel a few blocks away, she would lock herself in her room and instruct reception to turn visitors away. Zane would eventually take the hint and leave—where he'd be out of harm's way.

Zane followed her when she left the building. The afternoon sun hid behind the high-rise and cast a shadow over them. "Don't walk away from me, Ella. I brought you here in the first place, dammit! Let me help you sort out this mess."

No! You're not to blame. Please don't say that.

She came to an abrupt halt and spun around to face him. This had to end. Now. She had to get rid of Zane. God help her, she'd just witnessed the worst of her father. It was okay for her to die at his hands, but Zane didn't deserve that. He needed to be completely out of the picture before she carried out her social media attacks. Once started, there would be no stopping her.

She took a deep breath and searched for her inner strength. Damn it, where was that stupid pride and independence she bragged about to her colleagues? She could do this. It wasn't the first time she'd been challenged. But it *was* though the first time she would be braving it against someone with wealth and power—an entire city at his beck and call. While she'd never had *that* strength, there was no other option, even if it took every cent of her savings.

Only, dealing with Zane was different—heck, everything about Zane was, but the rules were the same. Be precise and clear—and don't back down.

She exhaled slowly and squared her shoulders. "It's over, Zane. I'm sorry, but everything has changed. You have to go."

Anger at herself, her father, the whole world in general was helping her keep up this charade. No way would she let her father think they were entangled. She'd die an ugly death at his hands, and strangely, she was okay with that. She'd lived a good life and was lucky enough to have experienced true love. Ella was free to die. Every passing minute convinced her of the reason she was put on this earth—her death would finally put her father where he belonged—behind bars. Of this, she was certain. If she died and justice wasn't served, she would haunt her father from the afterlife and make his life a living hell. She wouldn't back down—dead or alive.

She made ready to flee, to leave Zane behind. To banish from her mind the hurt written all over his face, not to mention the anger and disbelief.

Then she heard, "Zane? Ella?"

She whirled around.

"Mum? Dad?" Zane spluttered. "Weren't you going to the hotel?"

Zane's mother eyed Ella warily. She was certain her last words to Zane would've rung out loud and clear, and shame crept its way up her neck and flooded her face.

"We decided to come for a walk. See how you were going," Jonathan explained.

Tilly took a step closer and the expression on her face changed to concern. "Ella, my darling"—she opened her arms wide—"come here."

Ella couldn't move. Tilly did, and enfolded Ella against her chest and spoke softly. "Oh, Ella, it's been so long since I last held you. I missed you so much when your mother and I parted."

Hold it in. Hold it in. For goodness' sake, don't let them see how you're hurting.

But she couldn't. She burst out a quick apology before she turned and ran.

Chapter 29

Ella rubbed her brow, trying to ease her tiredness. She prayed her mother's case would make headway. Except she didn't believe that was ever going to happen. Her luck had run out. Probably at the same time the little blue box had gone missing. Baffled, she'd retraced her steps, but to no avail. It had vanished at some stage between the time it was returned to her after the first visit with her mother at the correctional facility and when she'd organised the meeting with her mother's legal aid team. Numerous search attempts since then had revealed nothing. She vividly remembered the dream she'd had on the night she'd left Australia; she knew that without the box, things wouldn't go her way. Stupid, but the brain had a strange way of resolving things and putting everything into perspective.

No little blue box, no mother out of jail. Simple, really.

She tried to make sense of what was being said without sighing. "Albert, what do you mean my father didn't kill his nephew?"

Albert slumped over his desk.

He'd helped Ella in every possible way, ever since the day he'd handed her his business card nearly six weeks ago in her father's office.

"Someone else came forward recently and made a statement. They did a DNA check and it's come up positive."

She sat back, causing her chair to wheel away from Albert's desk. "Who the hell would've decided to do that after twenty-something years? Why didn't they do it years ago?"

Ella buried her head in her hands. She was close to losing it. Thank goodness she had Albert's support and her newly discovered aunt and her family. Albert Jenkins was a lawyer and an occasional business associate of her father's. He told her he'd always suspected Thomas of cruelty to his wives, especially after his second wife committed suicide. He'd been good friends with Ella's mother and had put Ella in contact with her mother's only sister.

She'd been stunned at first. In all her years of wanting to find her father, she'd never stopped to consider whether she might have family on her mother's side that she didn't know about. As well as her aunt and uncle, she discovered three new cousins, all of a similar age. They filled the empty spaces she'd carried around for years. But, as that ache in her chest flared up again, she acknowledged that they couldn't fill the one spot that would remain empty and soulless forever.

Don't think his name. It'll only make it worse.

She lifted her chin and clenched her jaw. "Do we know who killed his nephew?"

She hated to even think her father's name. The trial was due to start in a few days and there was still so much work to be done. Thomas's guilt of the crime of his nephew's murder was supposed to be the crown jewel of their case. Now that it had been thwarted, her father still had his billions to back him. Her mother had been right—he had the capacity and financial power to squash her. Smother her until she was left without air. It was his way of killing her, and he was a day closer to achieving it.

"I do." Albert replied.

"And?"

Albert shuffled in his seat. He looked away to avoid eye contact.

"Albert?" she demanded. "Who did it?"

He turned his gaze back to her. Ella didn't miss the apology in his face. She could see he'd do anything to avoid telling her if it would lessen the pain. He'd been nothing but kind to her, and if she broke down, it wouldn't be the first time he'd shouldered her tears.

"Mario Savro killed him. Zane's father." Albert's features remained frozen, giving her time to absorb the news. She sat transfixed, not believing it. "You didn't want to hear that, did you?"

She shook her head. Tears burst through her barriers and trickled down her face. *Of course, I don't want to hear it.* It was hard enough, in the dead of night, knowing she couldn't touch Zane and hold him close. It had been heartbreaking to count each day of the past six weeks since she'd fled from him. She wanted Zane to bully his way back to her side. Who else would take control and sort out the mess they'd created together? He had all the expertise and experience in doing just that; except he was doing exactly as she'd asked. *Leave me alone. Go away. Go back home. Forget all about me.* She had her own stupid pride to blame for pushing him away. Had she learned nothing? Would she ever rein in her stubbornness, or learn to control it? It had never served her well in the past, why would it now?

The pain of admitting he might've erased her from his mind and accepted her ultimatum hurt like crazy. She wasn't close to doing the same. He *must've* dismissed her, because not once in the weeks she'd been in Boston had he tried to make contact with her. That was not the Zane she'd fallen in love with. Nothing would've stopped him. Nothing would've kept him from her—but not a single call or message had come her way. Some days she was constantly checking her phone to be sure.

When she was able to talk about him, she'd confessed the truth to her mother. Her mother had known most of the details and told her that Zane and his parents had remained in Boston for a couple of days before returning to Australia. Her mother also advised her to be patient. Ella had scoffed at the time. She didn't understand how to be patient, and her stubbornness had already caused the injury—a life-altering one. It was another moment she wasn't proud of. How many pages of her life story would she fill with those sorts of moments? In this instance, it was too late for damage control. It was clear that Zane had moved on.

The realisation hurt because *she* could never have changed her feelings so fast. Zane moving on was what she deserved, although knowing that didn't stop her from beating herself up night after night.

And now she had to contend with Zane's mother revealing her secret and shoving *her* mother's chances back to square one. Why couldn't it have been her father who'd done the killing? Because it would've been too good to be true. Too easy. The bastard was fighting back with everything her legal team threw at him only to land safely on his feet.

"Ella, we'll leave it in the hands of our team now. They're experienced, and we're lucky the public is a lot more sympathetic now towards wives who suffer domestic violence. As unjust as it is, they'll be hard-pressed to find jury members who haven't read something on social media. I know you've been hard at it, but it's time to let it rest." He offered her a box of tissues. "I love the law, Ella. Let's hope the truth prevails."

Ella considered it wrong that her mother had spent any time at all in jail, and she had already spent six weeks there when she should've been with Victoria and the others. They were all suffering as a result of the destruction to the secure bubble of their family.

Ella wasn't certain if sending her Boston half-siblings to Australia had been a smart idea. Luke was still angry with her; however, she sensed a change in his attitude after he'd met Patrick and Melita. It hadn't happened overnight, but she'd picked up the subtle signs as the number of weeks she'd spent in Boston with her mother stretched alarmingly close to double figures. His attitude during their phone conversations convinced her he'd matured a great deal since learning of their mother's secret. Taking Victoria and Lily, and her Boston half-siblings under his wing, as though he were man of the house, proved it. She loved him more for it and wouldn't forget the sacrifices he was making because of her stupidity.

She rose from her chair and hugged Albert goodbye. "Thanks Albert. I don't know what I'd do without you."

He squeezed her in return. "I cared about your mother once." He raised a hand to calm her. "It's not what you're thinking, we were just close friends. Once she married your father, I sensed changes in her that weren't right. When she disappeared, I speculated but had no evidence. I never pretended to like your father, but sometimes, in business, I couldn't avoid him. Helping you is my way of making up for not taking better care of your mother when I suspected she needed it. I might've prevented a lot of pain for everyone if I'd acted years ago."

Ella pulled another tissue from the box and lifted her handbag to her shoulder. "Don't feel bad. I was lucky. And I wouldn't give up anything for the childhood I had in Australia. Even Patrick has settled into the outback rehabilitation clinic I asked Luke to send him to. The sooner his body is cleansed of the drugs and toxins he was taking the better." She dabbed at her eyes and added, "I spoke to him last night and he told me he'd fallen off a horse. Said he landed a few good bruises but it hadn't stopped him from getting back on. I told him we'd make a jackaroo of him yet."

Albert laughed. "You're the best thing to happen to him and he knows it."

Suddenly lightheaded, she chuckled. "I told him to learn the ropes and buy himself a cattle station. A week ago, he quoted me a rough figure of how much money he had in his own right and I nearly fell off my stool."

Albert continued to chuckle. "So, he has enough to buy a cattle station?"

"Yes, more than enough."

"What about Melita? What's she up to?"

Ella leaned her hip against Albert's desk. "I instructed her to take care of Victoria. From what I hear, Luke is teaching her to drive. Details are sketchy, but so far, there have been no accidents. She has her learner's permit and they're going on long trips to work up the hours required to get her licence." She shuffled away from Albert's desk and added, "They're always together."

"Is something happening between Luke and Melita?"

"Don't have a clue." *Who am I to obstruct the course of love?* "On her good days, Victoria is teaching Melita to cook. By all accounts Melita has talent. The other day, Victoria told her she had to get out of the house, so she applied for a working visa and picked up a couple of days' of work at an exclusive clothing boutique and loves it. I think for once she feels useful and wanted."

"Let me guess, you told her to learn everything so one day she can buy her own boutique."

Ella burst out laughing, surprising herself. It'd been a long time since she'd done so. "Not yet, but thanks for the great idea." She scrunched the tissue in her hand and landed it in the waste bin. "I'll give her more time with the family first, then hit her with it."

Ella left Albert's office with every intention of visiting her mother—she hadn't missed a single day. With thoughts of Patrick and Melita on her mind, nothing had given her greater satisfaction than when they'd both agreed to leave Boston and visit her family in Australia. Having them on her side satisfied every revenge-filled cell in her body. Like another blunt knife in her father's back. It was what he deserved. Under Thomas's guidance, her half-siblings had done a great job of screwing up their lives. They'd had no direction and no hope.

Had she saved them in time? Ella hoped so. She wanted them to experience how normal people lived. In Boston, they'd been so far removed from the real world and had no skills to cope in it. Thomas only cared about appearances. She couldn't imagine he was the kind of father who'd give them a hug or take them fishing. Was he so caught up in his own self-importance that he never saw what he was lacking? His absence of love? He'd let money and power overrule common sense, so he deserved to lose his children. Ella wasn't going to encourage them to go back any time soon.

She had a need to hurt her father, because he sure as hell was trying to hurt her.

Chapter 30

Zane lifted his glass of beer and drank. Luke, across from him, did the same. They were at the Port Office Hotel in Edward Street, where a Sunday afternoon session of Jack Johnson played in the background. They sat away from the cover band to hear each other better.

"I'm sorry about how I treated you, mate. It was uncalled for." Luke admitted.

Zane shrugged. He'd left Boston angry and hurt. Knowing that Ella could dismiss everything between them left him aching and bewildered. Knowing she didn't want his professional help baffled him. She wasn't the only one hauling around a suitcase full of guilt.

Luke had been unrelenting at the time. He'd reminded Zane to leave Ella alone. For the two days he'd remained in Boston with his parents, only Victoria had taken pity on him. Eventually she'd suggested he return home and forget about Ella; at least she'd sounded apologetic and remorseful about the rift.

Luke's anger had struck a chord. The enormity of what he and Ella had done was frightening and something he had to live with every day—a family had been torn apart and would probably remain that way for many years. After Ella had run off, Zane's repeated attempts to contact her had fallen on deaf ears. He was barred from entering her hotel and the last thing he needed was the threat of deportation if he continued to harass Ella. He'd never had an altercation with the law before, and the realisation of what the Boston police were threatening him with made him take a reality check.

"How is she, Luke?"

Luke lowered his glass and raised an eyebrow. "Mum or Ella?"

Zane grimaced. Luke knew exactly who he was talking about. Six weeks was a long time and his patience was close to running out. He tore open a packet of crisps and offered them to Luke. A peace offering for all the anguish he'd caused their family.

They both helped themselves to the snack for a few moments. The crunching sounds blended in with the music and background chatter. Zane took another swig of his beer and looked away from Luke's probing glance.

"Do you want to be in Boston for the trial?" Luke asked.

Zane met Luke's gaze once more and nodded.

"You've got three days to get there."

Zane slid his half-empty glass to his left. "How did she take the news that my father killed their only hope of getting your mother released?"

Luke made a face even though Zane intended no pun. "Ella is hurting. She was in tears last night." He paused for a moment before taking another mouthful of beer. When he put his glass down, he added. "Look, mate, I'm sorry I've kept you away from her. She'll need you after the trial."

Zane spoke with hesitation. "Any likelihood your mother will get off?"

Luke followed a pattern on the tablecloth with his finger. He didn't look up when he said, "Probably not, but the good news is the legal team don't expect she'll have to serve more than two years." When his hand halted mid-pattern, he looked up. "Thomas is being a real bastard. He has all the big guns lined up and is paying them a fortune. With his sort of money, he doesn't have to spare any expense. He's unearthing witnesses prepared to testify against Mum. She's never heard of half of them."

Zane's stomach clenched when he asked the next question. "Has Ella received any more death threats?"

"No, just the two, but the police aren't taking any chances. They're watching Thomas like a hawk, and she has security around her twenty-four seven. Seems Thomas is pissed off his kids are in Australia against his wishes."

Damn you, Ella. It hadn't taken him long to gather why she'd dumped him. He'd been following her social media campaign, and she'd done nothing but blacken the Van Der Meeliko name. Death threats were a given. If someone hadn't shot her by the time the trial finished it'd be a miracle. She knew that, so she'd wanted him out of the way.

"Have you spoken to Patrick lately?"

Luke leaned back in his chair. "Most days I give him a quick call, but I have to go through the supervisor. He's been fantastic and has encouraged regular phone calls." He reached for his glass again. "It might only be my imagination, but I'm sure Patrick enjoys our chats. It's like he's starved of family attention. Or any attention since his mother died. He told me he's keen to learn to drive one day, if I have spare time." Luke chuckled, "I reckon I detected some sibling rivalry when I told him I was teaching Melita."

"Melita's a good soul," Zane confirmed, which caused Luke to nod.

It was no surprise to Zane that something might be happening between Luke and Melita.

The muscles in his stomach clenched again. He knew that feeling. Had experienced it fully with Ella, and damn it, he wanted it back. He wasn't giving up yet.

The lack of Ella's presence left him in a constant state of nausea with no appetite. He'd lost weight, along with the energy needed to wake up each morning. He struggled more with each passing day.

They finished their drinks and Luke rose. "I promised Melita I'd pick her up from the boutique. I'm taking her to the beach for the afternoon."

Zane scraped his chair back. Getting up, he sighed heavily as he slid his chair in towards the table.

"You okay, mate?" Luke asked.

Luke's concern touched a nerve. Zane knew he'd eventually lose this friendship if Ella never changed her mind about them being together. The coming trial loomed; so much hinged on it. He would never get another chance if Catherine remained in jail for years to come. As certain as the sun rose each day, Ella would not leave Boston while her mother remained locked up. And he would continue to blame himself for putting her there.

"You enjoy the afternoon, mate. I'll be right." Zane answered.

Luke angled his face, doubt written all over it. "Do you want me to talk to Ella? Tell her it was my fault you didn't contact her?"

He shook his head. "I'll see her in a few days. I'll talk to her then if she lets me."

Luke clapped him on the shoulder. "She'll come around. You wait and see."

He *had* waited ... and waited. He'd played by her stubborn rules. Had let her have her way. He'd spent the past six weeks devising plan A and plan B. Each one included Ella. There was little chance he would give up completely. Though he'd backed down and returned home, there was still a lot of rant and rave left in him. He'd already debated whether he should've fought longer and harder, should have forced Ella to come around. She would've eventually seen reason when common sense penetrated her shocked state of mind.

Instead, he'd let her have her way.

He worried that she was feeling lost and alone. Not to mention anxious and nervous about the trial. She would be constantly berating herself for breaking her family apart and would not rest easy until her mother was back within their fold. That strong and principled woman was the Ella he loved. He wanted her back.

His family had been brought closer. When the truth was revealed to his younger brothers, it'd changed nothing between them. Their mother had plenty to say and a thousand reasons for keeping the secret, but the bottom line was that there wasn't a single day during which she'd regretted her decision. She vowed to go to her grave without ever revealing her new identity to anyone in Boston.

Zane sympathised with Ella and her family. For him, the outcome had been a good one. Theirs hadn't. But it irked him that she'd kept her distance. It made no sense that she hadn't come around sooner and contacted him.

He waved goodbye to Luke and reminded himself that he hadn't tried to contact Ella, either. Regardless of Luke's earlier ultimatum, nothing should've stopped Zane from fighting for her. The more he thought about it, the more he was sure Ella would've wanted him to.

Zane slung his backpack over his shoulder and walked towards Brisbane's Botanical Gardens, which were at the end of Edward Street and only a block away. It was hard to forget the memories he and Ella had created during their mad lunch-time dashes to their special alcove.

Relief coursed through him when he found their spot empty. It was the first time he'd built enough courage to come alone. *I'm not entirely alone.* Each time he took out his father's diary to read over his entries, he felt a presence by his side. A disturbing but comforting presence he couldn't shake.

The diary was the only item he'd found in the locked box his grandmother had given him. Two photographs had been stapled on the last page. One was of his father holding him aloft as a baby. The joy and happiness on his father's face was obvious, which restored Zane's faith that his father hadn't been a complete monster.

The other photo he kept in his wallet. It was of his mother and Catherine, and their two babies lying face up on a picnic rug. The grass was greener than ever, the sky clear and blue. His mother and Catherine both laughed and each held the hand of their baby.

Him and Ella.

The shock of seeing the photo had punched him in the guts. It'd floored him and left him gasping for air. It was the last thing he'd expected to find.

He also hadn't expected to learn the truth about his father. His candid words revealed the feelings of a man who'd been forced into a life he detested.

Bullied, threatened and made to follow in his father's footsteps.

The two years he'd spent in jail were a godsend for him. No longer accessible to the mafia heads of the family, his only goal had been to die before he was released. Either way, he'd understood the rules. You broke the code of silence, you were a dead man when you returned to the outside world.

Zane had marked a few pages and shared them with his mother—including the page where his father admitted killing a Van Der Meeliko. Despite hurting Catherine's chances of being released, his mother had been morally bound to inform the Boston police. For Zane, revealing the truth created another blow. He couldn't live without Ella but nor could he live with his mother not telling the truth. It was a no-win situation that continued to gnaw at his insides.

Now, as a cooling breeze rustled the leaves surrounding the alcove, he flicked past that page and instead found the one entry that still had the ability to leave his heart in his mouth. Blood stained the page and his father's handwriting appeared shaky.

Hello Zachary,

Firstly, my son, I don't believe that you or your mother are dead. I wouldn't have survived this long if I'd believed otherwise. Knowing how clever your mother is, I believe she's taken you to a safer life. God bless her.

I had never thought of God before in my life, but in this place, he found me.

Please believe me when I tell you that I loved your mother. She stole my breath every time she smiled. Tell her I'm sorry. Tell her that she deserved more than me. Tell her I thank God every day that she had the strength to leave when she did. With the drugs I was taking, who knew where we might've ended up. Most likely your mother would be dead, or both of you, by my own hand. Not something I'm proud to admit. But drugs were the only way I could escape the inescapable. The family. The code. I hated it Zachary, and I hated the man who fathered me.

Please never do drugs, Son. They made me mean, kept me angry and got me through jobs ordered by the family. I hope they all rot in hell.

In this place I do everything possible to cause trouble in the hopes that it will release me from this life. I'm never leaving here. I'm never going to see your smile again or hold your chubby fingers. Today I received only a small bashing. It left my fingers swollen and bloodied, but I have so much time on my hands, I had to write to you.

There's so much to say and too little time. I have a lifetime of regrets and enough fatherly advice to write a book. My greatest fear is that your true identity will be revealed. Hide from the Savro name. Never claim it. If your mother has changed your surname, embrace it.

Also, if you find your soulmate, never let her go. Do the right thing by her and shower her with all the love you can. I missed my chance. I missed it all, and only God knows how broken I am because of it. I fill my dreams at night with memories of the days after you were born. How happy and connected we were. I never found that kind of joy again. It was a once in a lifetime opportunity and I blew it.

Remember, Son, I love you. Papa.

Zane rolled the stiffness out of his shoulders and leaned back. His father finished every entry with the same line. *Remember, Son, I love you. Papa.* He'd read the entry a few times, and each time it tugged at his heartstrings. It made him think of Ella and how connected they were. Was it a family trait that he should be left broken too? Was it in his genes to never find that special connection again?

He refused to believe it, but the words had a habit of continually whirling around in his head. He shoved the diary in his backpack and groaned inwardly. Anger got him to his feet. *Stop this bullshit moping. Get the hell over there and do something about it.*

The trial was on. *Hip hip hooray.* He'd waited so bloody long for this moment. He had his excuse to return to Boston. Time to tell Ella, face to face, that she was wrong to go it alone. It was time to start their life together.

As he strode towards the entrance, he tried to shove aside the tiny sliver of doubt that hovered at the back of his mind. Would going to Boston make any difference? It'd be an expensive waste of time if she refused to see him. His mother was on standby to come too. She kept in touch with Catherine, lending a hand from Australia. Everyone was helping out where they could, talking things through and throwing ideas into the mix.

The only breakdown in communication was between him and Ella.

Chapter 31

Ella muttered and swore under her breath as she entered her father's high-rise. It was the day before the trial, and it was no different to every day she'd spent in Boston during the past weeks. She shared every frustrated and aggravated step with her mother, starting with the initial court appearance where her mother had pleaded not guilty.

Ella stormed her way into an open lift, reached over someone's arm to jab the top floor button, then stared straight ahead. Rude, but she couldn't help it. She'd lumped her father's employees into the same basket as him and couldn't get past what this building and everyone in it represented.

She held copies of the death threats she'd received. Yep, she planned on delivering them back to her father personally, despite being advised against having any contact with him. She wanted to make the bastard squirm. Make sure he understood she wasn't one bit afraid of him. Not even of dying.

Her mother's attorney had the original copies of the threats. Ella had found each of them slipped under the door of her apartment. Not a single fingerprint had been found. *Grrr.* This was her reaction at the time. She'd wanted to howl like a hyena and scratch her father's eyes out.

Who'd done his dirty work?

Arriving at the top floor, she was the last to leave the elevator. She didn't waste any time walking past the secretary towards her father's office.

"Excuse me?" Helen asked.

Ella raised her eyebrows without breaking her stride.

"Oh, it's you," Helen muttered behind her back.

Before Ella pushed through her father's office door, she had her scowl in place as she gripped the handle. *You'd think with all the commotion I created only weeks ago he'd be smart enough to keep it locked.*

Having money didn't mean you had common sense.

When she slammed the door shut, her father looked up. He sat at his desk and she didn't miss that his sharp look of surprise disappeared as fast as it appeared.

"You're not supposed to be here. What do you want?" He had long since given up the niceties they'd shared during her first visit.

"Why, Father, it's a pleasure to see you, too." Sarcasm was becoming her thing. "You'd think tomorrow would be soon enough for us to see each other again, wouldn't you?"

He pushed his chair back and rose. Anger clouded his face as his hands clenched by his sides.

"Oh, please, don't answer. I bet you can't believe I'm not teetering on the edge of insanity, scared shitless of you. Too afraid to open my mouth." She took a step closer to his desk and thrust the death threats onto its corner. Levelling her gaze with his, she added, "I wanted to personally hand-deliver these beautifully prepared notes you were kind enough to organise for me, and to make sure you knew they were well-received. Didn't want you thinking it had all been a waste of your time."

A frown marred his brow and he dropped his gaze to the copies. "What the hell are you talking about?" He snatched them from under her hand.

"Oh, nice try, *Daddy*. Trust me the police have you in their sights."

He shook his hand in her direction. "Get out, girl. Don't you dare bring your lies to me."

She stood her ground and met his daggered glare. "You don't scare me. You never will." She turned on her heel and marched towards the door.

She was holding up better than she thought, but her control slipped. As she opened the door, the constant anger battling inside her subsided for a

second and the words she *never* would've dreamed of saying spilled out.
"We could've made such a great team."

Thomas shuddered when the door slammed. He couldn't move. The
muscles in his legs and back contracted for an instant and he froze. He
couldn't force his neck to twist. Left or right would do. Hells damnation,
he wanted to turn away from the image of Ella striding out of his office.
No one would ever tell her what to do.

He'd struck fear in everyday people for many years. They trembled
when he raised his voice, bowed down to his every command and never
made the same mistake twice. Ella had just reminded him that she wasn't
an everyday person.

*She's my daughter. My God, she's everything I ever dreamed of in a
child. She's intelligent, brave, sassy and incredibly stubborn. No different to
someone else I know.*

His left knee buckled and he shot out his hand in time to grab the edge
of the desk. He stumbled back and fell into his chair, overcome by his
disorientation.

Death threats? Which bastard is playing tricks with me? Confused, his
head started to ache. He reached for the copies and scanned the wording.
Who's messing with my daughter?

He had no answers, just plenty of enemies.

To compound the problem, Ella had made no secret of her presence in
Boston or her reasons for being here. She'd appeared on television shows
and local radio stations, and had saturated social media with her posts. As
usual, the Van Der Meeliko name was in the news, but this time for all
the wrong reasons. The mysterious disappearance of a prominent citizen
over twenty years ago piqued everyone's interest. The reasons Catherine

left with her baby struck a chord with the media. Thomas had bitten his tongue and refrained from making any comment. All he could do was bide his time and bring the wrath of his wealth down on their pretty little heads during the trial.

Except ... the way Ella had gone about her attack left him reeling. He'd never been this afraid or ... *proud* before. He let his face fall into his hands and considered the word. It wasn't appropriate with the trial beginning tomorrow, but it struck him as the only way to describe the weird sensation churning inside him. Ella had the guts and stamina he strove to find in employees, the kind he'd hoped to instil in Patrick and Melita.

Her parting words scrambled his insides. Would the invisible strings tying him to his daughter be enough to stop this hatred and the need for revenge?

The fight in him had built to a crescendo over the past weeks—he was primed and prepared for the trial. His money was his power broker and he'd never been ashamed to use it before. From the beginning, he'd believed his case was no different to any other time someone had tried to blacken the Van Der Meeliko name. The notion that it *was* hadn't occurred to him until ...

He scrunched the death threats then pressed the intercom button. "Helen, hold all phone calls and cancel my appointments for the afternoon. I don't want to be disturbed."

Thomas tossed the ball of paper into his bin and rose wearily. His shoulders were hunched like those of an old man, his feet not quite lifting off the floor when he walked to the window. He leaned against the wide pane of glass and looked down onto Boston Central. His hip slid down until he perched on the ledge. A sigh escaped.

He stared out at the view that had always enthralled him. For once, he didn't see it as he usually did. His own son was in a foreign country a damn long way from Boston, by all accounts, living on an outback station riding horses, for God's sake. Why hadn't *he* ever done anything so adventurous?

Maybe there was more to life than this view he'd always cherished. Revenge and hate could hurt you in places you never thought possible.

He was far from perfect and had a multitude of sins that needed forgiving. But at the end of the day, how could you expect anyone to love you if you didn't love yourself?

Crumpled against the large pane of glass, with the sun partially hidden behind the clouds, he admitted his shortcomings to himself. He'd been born to rule, control and threaten at will. But none of that meant he was happy.

He loosened his tie. He could do with a stiff drink but he didn't have the energy to get up. Instead, he ran a hand through his hair, tugged on its ends and lost track of time.

He remained hunched this way, a weary vulture come home to roost for the last time. Battle scars and all. For all his successes, he was a lonely old man living in any empty mansion, cut off from his family. Had he really failed as a husband and father? *His* father had been a better man. He clearly remembered how his father had made time for his nine children, despite the many hours he'd worked. His mother may have died young, but she'd been cherished by her husband. Maybe it was his father dying of a broken heart a few years later that had sealed his own fate as an emotionless wreck. Funny how he'd let those memories slide to the very back of his mind. His bull-headedness, combined with his passion to survive and uphold the family company, had always been his mainstay. To veer off course was to fail, and anyone who attempted to drive him off his path was met with anger. Arrogance had granted him his position at the top, a place where he could navigate his way above any of his siblings. But that had made him untouchable ... and now, when he least expected it, he craved the proximity of his family. Except no one wanted to be anywhere close to within touching distance.

For the first time, he wasn't proud of his reputation. It had taken his estranged daughter to show him that.

There was a lot to sift through for a man of his bearing. All the while, the sun began its descent for another day, reminding him of how insignificant he really was.

Chapter 32

The trial was never going to be a quiet affair. Extra police and security stood guard outside the building. Ella craned her neck. The large room, with brown timber panelling, was filling fast. The media section took up a major portion of the courtroom and reporters still jostled for space.

Her mother's defence attorney and representatives sat ready. The prosecution lawyers made their way in, talking and comparing notes. Some spoke on their phones.

Ella sat in the public gallery only a couple of metres away from where her mother would soon sit. She knotted her fingers in her lap. She'd barely managed half an hour of sleep last night, so she was fighting fatigue and an ongoing stint of depression. It was no surprise she wasn't at her best.

She'd gone to Lotusville after barging into her father's office and had spent the entire time crying. Her tears had started before she'd arrived, so there was little her mother could do to console her. Her parting words to her father, the man she'd grown to despise, had more than shocked her, but they'd stemmed from years of childhood dreams. Plenty of scenarios had passed through her imagination over the years, including their fairytale reunion.

But not even that had gone as she'd wished.

Zane's absence compounded the problem. God, she needed him almost as much as she needed to breathe. But she couldn't bring herself to contact him. Every time she sat poised ready to call him, something held her back. Was she ashamed of how she'd behaved? Was it the lack of contact from him? Which hadn't been his fault, she could admit that much, but it was so out of character. The Zane she knew and loved would've barged his way into her hotel room and demanded answers, given reasons and asked plenty of questions.

While she tossed and turned the previous night, she'd made a promise. When all this was over, regardless of what happened to her mother, she would force herself to eat humble pie and contact Zane. He deserved an apology, if nothing else.

There was no hiding how much she needed him. She hoped she hadn't killed their relationship. If he'd moved on, her ensuing pain would be justifiable punishment. She deserved no less.

No one spoke about him. Not her mother, her brother or her sisters. It was as though he'd fallen off the face of the earth and nobody but she had noticed. She sighed and tried to smile when Albert turned around and whispered, "You okay?"

Ella shrugged. She wasn't, but now wasn't the time. In only minutes her mother would be brought in and her fate sealed. She had no idea how she'd react if it went badly. And she expected it to. *So much for confidence in the justice system.*

Ever since they'd learned Zane's father had committed the murder, the notion that they didn't have enough evidence to help their case lurked in the back of her mind. Regardless of how many years had passed since the court ruling had been imposed, it still stood, and her mother had broken it. Hers had been the desperate plight of a young mother utilising the only avenue she'd had to protect her child. Her father's attorney would hammer home that she had lied and deprived him of the opportunity to be a parent to Ella.

Too bad that Ella could've been dead before her second birthday if her mother *had* stayed in Boston.

Luke had called this morning. He'd put his phone on speaker, and Victoria and Lily had also been in the room. Lily had said very little, but Ella had clearly heard her crying in the background. It was a grim reminder of the terrible mistakes she'd made. Would the guilt ever leave her?

Ella searched for her aunt and uncle, who had promised to come for support. To know they were there would help her cope when the time came—she would need a shoulder to cry on—but the room was filling swiftly. If they didn't come soon, they would have no choice but to stand and wait on the street. Ella looked for a raised arm, or any hint in the throng of people, to signal their presence. When she glanced towards the far side of the room, her heart catapulted to one side of her chest and she gasped. Zane sat unsmiling beside his mother, with his gaze riveted on Ella.

Now frozen, Ella had no control over the slow trickle of tears sliding down her cheeks. There was little explanation for them, not counting the stresses of the past weeks. The guilt, depression, frustration, hopelessness, loneliness, the ... the ...

Shit. Who am I kidding?

She gripped the back of the chair and relaxed slightly. With superhuman effort, she twisted to face the front, wanting nothing more than to clamber over people and chairs, land in his lap and fling her arms around his neck.

She wanted to shout out to the world that he'd returned.

He hasn't forgotten me. It took a split-second to make that startling revelation.

She cried happy tears and chuckled out loud, except the presiding judge entered the room and the crowd was made to hush.

Not far behind him, the jury appeared and were shown to their seats. It was only a minute more and her mother, flanked by security guards, made her entrance.

Ella wanted to cry again, but for a different reason. The jade green suit Ella had purchased for her mother hung loosely on her shoulders. She looked haggard under Ella's scrutiny, but Ella had also organised a make-up artist and hair specialist, who she'd given strict instructions to bring her mother's hair back to its natural colour. The great hairdo and make-up hid a lot. She looked beautiful in a wistful and sad way; the past six weeks hadn't been kind. She'd been worried sick about Victoria's treatment and fretful over Lily and Luke—she was always in a state of agitation whenever they spoke of home. From what Ella could see, parenting was a thankless task that never left you.

Ella wiped away any evidence of tears and forced her mouth to slide into a smile. She had every intention of feigning cheerfulness.

When her mother made to sit down, she spotted Ella. She kissed her hand and placed it against her heart. It was her way of showing Ella, no matter what happened, her love for her would never waver. She'd told her so, over and over, during the past weeks. But Ella's heart had frozen over, and nothing seeped past the ice. She'd done her best to hold her emotions secure and had thought she'd succeeded until her confrontation with Thomas yesterday.

Her irresponsible actions still didn't kill her guilt. Did Zane still feel it too? Was that why he'd come back to Boston? Had he been in contact with Luke, or had he read enough on social media to know the trial was about to begin?

Nothing could force her to look back over her shoulder. Too rigid to move, she remained facing the front. Now, they waited only for Thomas's arrival for proceedings to begin.

Come on, you bastard. Where the hell are you?

Minutes ticked by until, finally, the presiding judge hushed the crowd with a strike of the gavel. At the prosecution's desk, Ella sensed urgency. An attorney frantically tapped a message into his phone. Another left the room to take a call.

"Is the prosecution ready to proceed?" The judge sounded impatient. Immediately a request was made by the prosecution to allow them a further few minutes. They all left the room in a hurry.

Albert whispered something in her mother's ear and turned to Ella. He shrugged, baffled like the rest of them.

After about five minutes had passed, the prosecution's team re-entered the courtroom and the crowd was made to hush again.

"Your Honour, the prosecution wishes to withdraw all charges and cease any further proceedings."

The whole room erupted.

"Quiet, please." The judge used his gavel to make his annoyance heard and turned towards his associate to confer.

When the room quietened again, the judge proceeded to talk. "Are you aware this is inappropriate at this late stage and that I will be forced to charge all costs to the prosecution?"

The attorney nodded in agreement. "Mr Van Der Meeliko is aware of this and apologises for the inconvenience. He instructed me to advise that all costs pertaining to today will be covered, with an additional fee paid for the unwarranted time today's proceedings incurred for you and your staff, Your Honour, as well as the jury."

The judge's shoulders drooped in acceptance. He looked disappointed, as though he'd been looking forward to presiding over this publicised case. He let the gavel fall towards his bench for the final time and turned towards the defence team.

"Catherine Van Der Meeliko, this is an unusual situation. I cannot compare these circumstances to any other case I've presided over in my long history as a judge. I will reprimand the prosecution and deal with them separately. This reluctance to proceed should've been dealt with long before the proceedings were due to begin today." He paused, gathered his papers and placed them in a folder before looking up again. "It appears you are free to go home."

The crowd behind Ella roared, and she joined in, stumbling from her chair and shoving those in front to reach her mother. Tears, lots of them, coursed down her face as she wrapped her arms around her mother's neck.

Her mother's shoulders shook and her tears mingled with her own. There was no way Ella was letting go of her in a hurry. She didn't care if the media wanted to talk to them. They could wait.

It was Albert who prised her from her mother. "Ella, I need you to step back for a few moments."

Without hesitating, she did so and turned to find Zane. The world fell out from under her—the spot where he'd sat was empty, though Tilly remained seated and dabbed at the tears coursing down her face. Ella looked around frantically, desperate to find him. She needed to apologise. Was anxious to tell him she loved him. Maybe he was on his way to her.

In a daze, she haphazardly dodged cameras, journalists, chairs and people. She had to find him. Nothing else mattered now that her mother was safe. She was puffing badly, like she'd run a full marathon, when she staggered the last metre. "Tilly, where is he?"

Tilly was on her feet and doing her own scouting. "I honestly don't know. He was here one second, gone the next. He didn't say anything."

"What do you mean, gone?" she yelled over the noise.

"I don't know where he went. I sent a message, but he hasn't replied." She lifted her phone to check again. "Oh, wait, he says he'll explain later. Huh?"

This should've been the happiest moment of Ella's life. Instead, a dark cloud appeared. Why would he disappear? Had he thought she'd only seek him out if her mother were freed? She got that he might've doubted her loyalty to him if the outcome had been different, but to disappear at such a crucial time?

Her legs buckled and she crumpled to the floor. This all seemed so unfair. She'd only been able to spread herself so far over the past few months. The anxious waiting had taken its toll.

Tilly was beside her in an instant, shouting for someone to lend a hand. Someone did, and Ella was made to sit up. Suddenly claustrophobic with the crowd around her, she struggled to breathe. Anger choked her senses. Why had he bothered coming all this way, only to leave when she really needed him?

Ella struggled for calm and made a Herculean attempt to control her breathing. She did her best to push the angry demons away and give Zane a chance to explain. She didn't want the attributes she hated most about herself to show up today. She'd never been proud of her quick temper, stubbornness and lack of patience. But why, with all her chips falling, were they winning? Her body weakened as she tried vainly for patience. It was a losing battle and she knew it.

"Could someone call an ambulance, please?" she heard as blackness descended.

Chapter 33

"I think I'll still go for that one."

Zane leaned against the glass jewellery cabinet and handled the small square case holding the diamond solitaire.

The helpful sales assistant smiled. Dressed in a navy-blue skirt and coat, she resembled a flight attendant. "She's a lucky girl."

He smiled back, and she blushed. *If only you knew.*

News of the trial had saturated the local media in Boston for weeks. No one with the Van Der Meeliko name would ever fly under the radar again. Ella had been cunning in her campaign. Being beautiful, smart and Australian had helped her win the sympathy vote. He'd kept track of the news from Brisbane, so it hadn't surprised him when the first newspaper he picked up after arriving in Boston had featured a full-page photo of Ella on the front cover. If he told the sales attendant the truth about who he was, she would never believe him.

He was in the same Tiffany store from which his mother had purchased Ella's baby bracelet. 'Copley Place Mall, Boston', the small hidden label beneath the satin cushion in the little blue box had read. He had a rough idea of Ella's ring size, and this ring fit snugly on his little finger.

He'd rushed out of the courtroom in the middle of the upheaval to make it to his appointment. When scheduling it the day before, he'd honestly believed the hearing would still be in its early stages, and he'd clean forgotten to say anything to his mother. His mind was on a hundred other things—and doing this had been at the forefront.

With the trial over before it had begun, he wanted to give Ella the ring, tell her how much he loved her and ask her to marry him. His life had changed drastically when he'd met Ella. He might've sailed along for years, living comfortably in the bubble of his serene life, and his mother would've taken her secret to the grave if he hadn't uncovered the truth. But he was relieved he knew it now. It filled the gaps that had hovered subconsciously in his mind. It answered the questions he'd never been able to ask. He felt complete. More importantly, it taught him the strength of forgiveness. His mother should've told him years ago. Had he reacted differently, it could've fractured their relationship. Instead, it made him stronger and more resilient. It was the reason he'd backed off and given Ella time and space to deal with the court case.

If he'd learned anything during this entire experience, it was that every person had a story. His father was the perfect example. It'd been gratifying to learn he wasn't the monster his mother believed him to be. Zane had learned a lot from his father's diary entries, and they'd helped his mother heal too. Now he only wished for calm, so their lives could return to some normality and so he could convince Ella that they were meant to be together.

He wished himself luck as he grimaced.

Zane sent a hasty message to his mother in reply to hers before turning off his phone. He wanted to concentrate on the job at hand. His decision, he hoped, would prove to be a positive step forward for him and Ella. They needed this after the traumatic turn of events these past months.

"Sir, can I show you this range?"

Zane chuckled and accepted her willingness to give him her attention for the full allotted hour. She tucked a stray strand of hair coming out of her neatly fashioned hairstyle as she waited for his reply.

Why not?

He nodded, humouring her. He wanted the diamond solitaire ring. Its raised single diamond signified for Zane that Ella was the *single* most important person to him. He didn't want a cluster of small diamonds. It didn't fit.

When he passed over the entire range but still pointed to the ring of choice sitting on the glass counter, the attendant conceded defeat and chuckled.

"Mr Peden, I see you're determined. I won't try to change your mind with any more selections."

"Thank you. Your service has been excellent."

Again, a slight blush touched her cheeks. He guessed the girl was only a few years out of school.

"She'll love it, Mr Peden."

Funny that. Not once had Zane considered what he'd do if Ella refused. He'd spent most of the flight over thinking about buying the ring and how he'd propose to her. He bypassed plan A and had gone straight to plan B. In order for it to go smoothly though, they had to be on speaking terms. Or at least not yelling at each other.

He clamped down on his jaw, hoping she would at least give him a chance. Surely, with her mother free to return home, nothing should stand in their way. Right?

As he watched the attendant return the jewellery to the secure glass cabinets, he considered the possibility of Ella saying no. Fear clutched at his chest for a few beats. He grunted before dismissing those thoughts to the back of his mind. Zane didn't doubt that once the stress Ella had endured subsided, she would see reason and listen to him. Zane loved her, what else mattered? He'd given her space and had understood her reasons for needing it. The media campaign had made no secret of what she thought about her father. Surely, if she'd wanted Zane away from the turmoil, it meant her feelings hadn't changed. That she cared. Why bother protecting him if they had?

He looked at his watch. His hour-long appointment was drawing to a close, and he itched to return the courtroom. He'd heard the exciting news as he'd sped out of there. It was the best possible outcome, but God help him, why had the bastard dragged them all through weeks of headaches only to change his mind? Zane shook his head. And at what cost? The tally included legal fees and living away from home costs—not to mention the mental and physical wellbeing of both Ella and her mother. He couldn't wait to wrap Ella tightly in his arms. It was an astonishing result, and he would do everything possible to ease Ella back into her normal everyday life.

As he drew out his wallet, he eyed the new little blue box he was about to receive. Not much had changed about its design, except this one would be tied with a white ribbon. If there'd ever been a ribbon tied around the box resting in the zipped pocket of his jacket, then it had disappeared.

Nerves suddenly burst from his chest. First fear, now nerves. What the hell was going on? He truly believed Ella was the only one for him, his soul mate—he was prepared to stake his life on it. And what other use would he have for a rejected solitaire diamond ring?

With the transaction complete, Zane left the plush store and walked outside. He took a deep breath and tucked the new box in beside the old one. *Well, you've gone and done it now. Let's hope she bloody well loves you.* He curved his lips up as a ray of sunlight, jostling between a pair of dark clouds, streamed over the street. It was time to ring his mother. She wouldn't leave the courtroom unless Catherine knew she was there and ready to assist in any way—of that he was certain—so she would know where to find Catherine and Ella.

The familiar sound of incoming messages beeped when he switched on his phone. His mother had sent three, and he counted a couple of missed calls, too.

A frown etched his brow when he read the first one.

Ella has fainted and is on her way to hospital. Call me.

"What the hell?" He swiped the screen. In another message, his mother instructed him to take a cab to the hospital, and the address was provided in message number three.

He ran erratically, constantly on the lookout for an available cab as his heart continued to thump heavily. It didn't take long to wave one down.

Forty-five minutes? Damn, why did I switch off my phone? That was when the messages had started. Forty-five minutes ago! *Shit, shit, shit. I could've left town for all anyone knows.*

For the entire twenty-minute ride to the hospital, he couldn't come up with any excuse for disappearing without a trace. *Damn.* He thumped his thigh hard enough to make it bruise. Sometimes *nothing* went to plan.

He thrust money at the taxi driver and flung himself out of the cab, yelling a 'thank you' over his shoulder. Inside the hospital, he raced to the administration desk and asked for directions.

"Tenth floor, sir. The nursing staff can help you once you get there."

Frustration clawed at him when he arrived at the bank of elevators. Every time he needed to ride in an elevator in this city, there was always pressure for it to arrive quickly, and even more pressure for him to get to the required floor. He was sure that these elevators were moving in slow motion—he groaned loud enough that other visitors turned his way.

When he finally arrived on the tenth floor and the doors opened, he sped out and heard Ella's sweet voice. He came to an abrupt halt, metres away from the nurses' station.

None too politely, she stood ramrod straight, her shoulders tensed to capacity. "There's nothing wrong with me, and no, you *do not* need to jab that needle into my arm. I'm discharging myself, so stop badgering me."

Zane didn't catch what the nurse said, but he clearly heard Ella's reply. "Send the account to my father, Thomas Van Der Meeliko."

His mother stood by Ella's side, though Catherine was nowhere to be seen. Ella and his mother turned to leave and both came to a sudden stop after almost colliding with him.

"Zane?" his mother questioned, her relief evident.

At the same time, Ella spoke his name, but it came out reproachful, her expression angry and hurt.

"Thank goodness you made it." His mother's worry lines disappeared from her forehead as she reached up to pat Ella's arm.

"Why did you bother coming?" Ella retorted, her jaw straining so that every muscle on her face looked stretched and taut, as if ready to snap. She disengaged her arm from his mother's touch and stormed off, striding past him towards the lifts.

Zane grabbed her upper arm and placed himself in front of her, their noses almost touching. "Oh, no, you don't."

She wasn't going anywhere. Not until she explained. He wasn't letting her temper get in the way of his plans.

No bloody fear.

Dark rings circled her eyes and her face was pinched with fatigue, but she wouldn't meet his direct gaze. He'd be a stupid man to try to kiss her right now.

But that's exactly what he wanted to do.

Chapter 34

Oh God. His woodsy scent would be her undoing.

"Leave me alone, Zane."

He relaxed his grip on her arm enough for her to shrug out of it and continue towards the elevators—but he remained one step behind.

"No way, Ella. Not this time. I'm not going anywhere. Not until you explain what the hell you mean. You don't think your comment is a bit rich coming from you, seeing as *you* told me to leave when I was last here?"

As providence would have it, an elevator opened, though it was full of people. Zane and Ella both stepped inside, but his mother was left behind. They were jostled against each other as the lift made its way down and stopped at various floors.

Ella refused to look at him. "You're too late."

Zane turned to face her and she winced when his shoulder butted against a middle-aged man. "What the hell do you mean, I'm too late? For God's sake, your mother's free to go home. *You're* free to go home. Isn't it time to sort this out?"

She should've felt intimidated or embarrassed by the scene they were creating, but she didn't care anymore. "I said it's too late. When I needed you in the court room, you weren't there. Was it too much to hang around for a few more minutes?"

She knew she sounded immature, but his disappearance rankled. There she had been, desperately missing him, and he'd gone AWOL, right when she'd needed him. Maybe she didn't want to be strong and independent all the time. A shoulder to cry on wouldn't go astray occasionally. What was wrong with being an ordinary girl and wanting an ordinary boy to love her? She was tired of all that free-thinking stuff where you had to stand on your own two feet. Be your own person. Couldn't she still be that person *and* lean on the man she loved sometimes?

His scornful chuckle dragged her back to the present and the overcrowded lift. It jerked to a stop at ground level, and she rushed out onto the street, trying to keep one step ahead.

"Ella, damn it, will you stop for one second and listen to yourself."

She came to a halt and transformed into that independent and headstrong person again. Probably from sheer habit. One she should've stuck to instead of turning weepy over the past weeks.

She rounded on him, "I didn't ask you to come to the trial. But, damn it, there you were, and you *still* didn't stick around. Go away. I don't need you. I've managed okay on my own."

Everything inside her head and heart hurt so, so much.

She couldn't look him in the eye. Instead, she turned away. Her resolve to remain strong kept her buoyed and ensured her legs didn't buckle when she walked off.

Zane's voice boomed out and hit her square in the back. "Ella Harvey, I love you. I can't do this on my own. If you walk away, how can I ask you to marry me?"

Only then did her legs wobble and her steps begin to falter. With heat racing up her neck, her movement tapered off until she stood hesitantly. People on the sidewalk stopped and smiled.

"Go on, dear, didn't you hear the man say he loves you?"

"I'll marry him if you don't want to." Another woman threw in.

"Make love not war." A long-haired teenager jostled past holding a skateboard under his arm.

The comments continued; everyone had something to say. She stood speechless and uncertain of her next move, her back still facing Zane. His few words had destabilised her world. She didn't think it was possible that he still wanted her. She'd been the worst to him, even during the past ten minutes. Why wasn't he walking away?

Oh, Zane. Am I good enough for you?

Whether from the reaction of the expectant crowd hovering around, or his overpowering aura reaching out to surround her, she sensed his approach and knew when he was only inches away. She sighed when his hand touched her shoulder. The magic between them was still unbelievably strong.

"Ella, please turn around."

The pedestrians standing close by nudged shoulders with one another. Words were spoken and passed around.

"I think he wants to ask her to marry him."

"He says he loves her."

Ella lifted her chin and turned to face him, her eyes finally meeting his. Worry weaved around each of his irises, and red lines crisscrossed the tired whites of his eyes.

"Make way, make way, excuse me. Is there a problem here? What's all the commotion?"

Ella turned at the commanding voice and thought she could see a police officer winding his way through the throng of people surrounding her and Zane.

"Aren't you the one from the newspaper? Involved in the Meeliko or whatever trial going on?" a forty-something suited man queried over everyone's heads.

A softly spoken homely old lady, who stood only inches from Ella's elbow, said, "Shush, you. The man wants to marry her. Give them space." Her small elfin face had a huge smile plastered on it.

By this stage, the police officer had wrangled his way through the crowd and now stood in front of Ella. Her pulse rapidly increased as the onlookers' words bombarded her from all directions. This was a scene by anyone's standards.

The police officer addressed her, though he spread his arms out wide, forcing everyone to take a step back. "Excuse me, miss, are you being harassed?"

She caught her quivering bottom lip between her teeth. The emotions spiralling through her were not normal. Ella was a woman in control most days, so why not now? Shaking her head, she bit down harder, forcing her tears away. She didn't need to show weakness. She'd survived the past seven weeks and had won. What was there to cry about? Zane didn't need to see the sad, weepy excuse for a woman she'd turned into in Boston.

But she wanted to cry—one last time. Not happy tears. Not sad tears, but tears of relief.

After treating him so badly, Zane still loved her, though she didn't deserve it. Who knew why he persisted? But persist he had, and here they were, standing together on a street in central Boston, a throng of eager people surrounding them, strangers all, but nonetheless looking for a happy ending.

Zane's actions forestalled any further words from the police officer. He dropped to one knee, and the crowd sighed as he did. A dozen phones recorded the moment.

When he took her hands in his, he squeezed them hard until she looked at him. A sense of excitement filled the space around them as the small crowd jostled for a better look. Even the police officer had a smile on his face.

But her attention was jerked back to Zane when he tugged on her hands. "Ella, I love you. Will you marry me?"

She didn't have to think about her answer. It lay in the electric currents connecting them, in the unexpected hush of the crowd as they waited for her response, and in the love that shone directly at her from Zane.

She nodded, incapable of uttering a single word.

Zane stood and wrapped his arms around her waist. She circled hers around his neck and buried her face against his neck.

The crowd cheered as one before the effects of love and happiness had them surging closer, everyone wanting to offer their congratulations.

When Zane took a step back, the elfin-faced old lady placed a flower, which she'd probably plucked from a nearby garden bed, in Ella's hand. Weepy-eyed, she smiled.

Zane's hand went to the inside pocket of his coat, and Ella gasped when he pulled out two little blue boxes.

"How did—?"

He leaned forward and kissed her wet cheek. First, he handed over the older of the two boxes. "I believe this belongs to you."

She rested it on her palm and removed the lid. Inside, nestled comfortably on its bed of satin, was her baby bracelet.

She looked up into his smiling eyes, and her voice stuck in her throat. "Where ... what ... how ...?"

He took the box back and kissed her favourite spot below her ear. "I'll explain everything later. I have something else for you."

The sight of the new little blue box sent a hundred messages to Ella's heart, though the white ribbon was her undoing. Zane opened the box.

The sun, on its descent, slanted across them as if on cue and picked out the cut and clarity of the solitaire diamond. A hundred pulse points over Ella's body began a rapid beating, every nerve ending alive as Zane removed the ring and placed the box back in his coat pocket. He took her left hand and gently slid the band onto her ring finger. The lump in her throat made it difficult to swallow.

A phone was thrust near her face, and Ella could no longer hold her emotions in. She flung her arms around his neck and squeezed for all her love was worth.

"I love you, Zane. I'm so, so sorry for hurting you. I can't believe you still love me. My feelings for you never changed." She had to shout close to his ear, the noise of the onlookers too loud for ordinary conversation. "Thank you for coming back. Thank you so much."

He forced her back a fraction and gave the policeman a meaningful look. The policeman scattered the mob away, then Zane turned and pinned his gaze on Ella, his face serious again.

"I've thought of you every day, and damned you every other. I understand why you needed to get rid of me. At times, I wished you weren't always so headstrong and independent." He paused and his glare softened. "But that's the woman I fell in love with and I'm proud of what you achieved here. I bet it was your influence that changed your father's conscience."

"Really? But I was so nasty to him. Why do you think he changed his mind?"

"Because, for the first time in his life, he acted like a father should."

Ella dropped her forehead against Zane's. She savoured the moment and reflected on her father's change of heart. Now she was all mixed up, but her feelings towards her father were a big hurdle to overcome. She'd been through too much to forgive him. Not today, anyway.

She remembered Zane's words from earlier and pushed all thoughts of her father away. When she raised her face, she saw a different Zane. No longer did he look drawn, tired or serious. He now wore a lazy grin and she hungrily accepted it, devouring every morsel she'd missed about him.

And there were seven long weeks of memories to catch up on.

"Did you mean it when you said you didn't want to do this alone?"

Zane gathered her back in his arms. "What don't you get about happily ever after?"

She laughed, but only for as long as it took for his mouth to find hers—after that, nothing mattered.

EPILOGUE

On the couch, Ella snuggled into Zane's arms. She could finally relax.

Zane had insisted she celebrate her birthday in style, so she'd suggested a small family affair—except her family was no longer small. They'd all overindulged with a big lunch, then everyone had lounged around like lazy lizards. Now, the afternoon—she took a glimpse outside—was slowly moving into dusk.

Tilly and Jonathan, who'd made the drive down from the Sunshine Coast, sat across from Zane and Ella, and talked to her mother. Zane's two brothers were outside on the patio, drinking beer and playing cards with Luke and Lily. Melita wandered inside, though her eyes were always on Luke, and flopped down on a beanbag.

Patrick reclined across from Ella with his arms behind his head and his eyes shut. His skin glowed with good health. Ella's heart swelled each time she had a moment to watch him. He'd come a long way since their first meeting. For once he was enjoying life, had purpose, and was living it to the fullest. He'd grown up and matured. Already there was talk of a sun-bronzed Aussie jillaroo chick. When he spoke about her, with his American accent, it made it all the harder for Ella to keep a straight face.

"Hmm, how about that siesta you wanted?" Zane whispered.

Oh, God, how the blood rushed uncontrollably around her body at his closeness and everything he suggested.

"We'll wake Victoria," she whispered back. "You're always so noisy."

Now in remission, Victoria was recovering slowly. She tired easily, so no one questioned it when she'd disappeared for a nap.

He harrumphed. "Not my fault I talk in my sleep."

Ella giggled while trying to project a frown. "That's not what I meant and you know it." He did talk in his sleep, and strangely enough, it was a comfort when it woke her.

His hand crept over her hip and rested below her breast. He nudged it gently and groaned quietly behind her. She closed her eyes and squeezed his thigh.

Her engagement to Zane still felt surreal. The photo of their reconciliation had been plastered over the Boston papers for days. She'd hated it. The publicity had been fine when it was centred on her mother's trial, but she wanted to keep her personal life private. She'd knocked back interviews on midday TV shows and radio, insisting her private life was her own. She couldn't get out of the place fast enough.

That was four months ago, and sometimes she needed to take a few moments to sift through the ordeal and learn from it.

Back in Brisbane, she'd returned to work without fanfare. Very few had made the connection between her and the Van Der Meeliko name. *Thank God*. But there had been other changes. Zane had a new employer, one that suited his degree, which was only weeks away from completion.

"Hey, Ella?"

Lazily, she opened her eyes when Patrick spoke. "Yeah?"

He straightened his recliner and rested his hands on his thighs. "I've been meaning to say this all day, but ashamedly, I've been putting it off."

Relaxed, she asked, "What? Is everything okay?"

He smiled, reassuringly. "Um, I hope so. It's just that ... um, Dad wants you to know he would be honoured to walk you down the aisle."

Ella jerked to attention. "What the—? When did he tell you this?"

Patrick knotted his fingers together. "He was passing the station and dropped in."

"He what? He's in Australia?"

Patrick attempted a lop-sided smile. "How do you Aussie's say it? He's gone walkabout. Took a year off work after throwing the reins over to one of my cousins. Told him to prove himself."

Ella sat transfixed. Her father, who she was determined to hate forever, had done something so drastic and out of character?

Suspiciously, all the conversation in the room had gone deathly quiet. Her gaze darted from Patrick to Melita, then to her mother and Tilly. She flicked a glance back at Zane. "Am I the only one who didn't know about this?"

Zane's awkward shuffle behind her was the dead giveaway.

"Mum," she wailed, "you knew?"

Her mother paused for too long. "He phoned me."

"He what? You didn't hang up?" Her voice was beginning to rise.

Her mother winced and her hands fluttered nervously in her lap. "Ella, he rang to apologise for a lot of things. I was happy to take the call."

"Jeez." Ella turned and read Zane's guilty expression.

He raised his hands in defence. "I was sworn to secrecy. I didn't like it, but Patrick wanted to be the one to tell you. If you want to blame anyone"—half-heartedly he pointed across the room—"he's your man."

She slumped back. Zane took the opportunity to wrap his arms around her and kiss her temple. Subconsciously, she'd pictured Luke walking her down the aisle in three months' time. Now she had this dilemma to contend with. It should've been cut and dry—she'd vowed to hate her father forever—but her heart had taken a detour. Something had changed within her since her father's backflip in Boston. She could see the glimpse of a man who was trying to make things better.

The media had gone ballistic after the courtroom antics. The Van Der Meeliko name had remained in the news headlines for another few weeks.

"What do you think?" Patrick asked.

"Where is he now?" she demanded to know.

Oh, God, she wasn't finished with him yet, but she so badly wanted to be. If he wanted to walk her down the aisle, she'd make him grovel for the right, insist he help a charity or two in Brisbane. Something to make her feel good, just because.

"Somewhere in the Northern Territory, roughing it, sleeping under the stars. You know, that sort of thing."

She gawked. "Are you serious?"

"Well, he *did* buy himself a top of the range 4WD utility for the experience. It might be a slight exaggeration to say he's roughing it."

She'd let the idea of her father walking beside her on her wedding day invade her thoughts when Patrick added, "He also wants you to know that he never sent those death threats, and if he ever finds out who did, there'll be hell to pay. In his words, no one messes with his girl."

"He said that?"

His girl? Like he was claiming rights to her after the shoddy way he'd treated her and her mother? *Over my dead body.*

Patrick nodded at the same time her mother spoke.

"He's very proud of you, Ella. He can't believe what a gutsy and brave daughter you are, strong enough to headbutt him without an ounce of fear. Anyone else would've cowered. It was your actions that made him take a look at his life and reassess."

"Mum, you can't be serious?"

"In his own words, you being taken away from him was meant to be. Your return has finally put him on the road to salvation. He has a lot to repair."

This was too much to take. She *so* wanted to hate him. Her anger could burn for years, but her father had found his humanity, which made it almost impossible to maintain her rage.

"I think Ella needs time to think this over." Zane extricated his legs from behind her and rose. "Come."

She took his hand and they left the room. She would've smiled at his duplicity, because it was what he'd wanted all along, except she was dizzy with all the thoughts running rampant in her head—the foremost one being, what the heck did she do about her father's wish to walk her down the aisle?

In her room, Zane dropped onto the bed and stretched his arms out in invitation. Without hesitating she fell against him. He pressed her close and kissed her with wild abandon. It never changed; each time was like their first kiss.

He pulled back and his warm breath brushed her skin. "I love you, Ella. Whatever you decide is okay with me."

She nodded, tears quickly building. Love and weddings weren't supposed to create so many hard decisions. While this one sounded like an easy one to make, it wasn't.

"You don't hate him?" she asked.

He shrugged and traced circles near her temple with his thumb. "I've had a few days to mellow."

As her lip trembled, she lowered her face and rested it on his chest. Comforted by the beat of his heart against her own, she let it lull her so she could think.

To concede to her father's wishes went against every principle she believed in. What would it say about her? Should she put aside her concerns and relent? She'd matured a lot in the past year after being forced to see and do things differently. It might only be a result of growing up, but she wanted to believe she was maturing into a better person. She was working hard to leave behind her quick temper and strong-willed ways and to accept that some things couldn't be changed. She had Zane to thank. While he had a tendency to barrel his way through life, his other side was calm and soothing—the perfect balm to her sometimes irrational and impulsive ways. No longer did she want to be boss all the time. She smiled, certain she'd found her match. He rarely gave in to her my-way-or-the-highway attitude—and she was okay with that.

"Hey, Ella?"

She moved away, allowing him to pull his wallet from his back pocket.

"I have something to show you."

She glimpsed the photo he'd kept of the two of them as babies. It'd rocked her very existence the first time she'd seen it. She couldn't believe how fate had meant for them to be together from the very beginning.

He pulled out a folded piece of paper and handed it to her. "Have a read."

"What is it?"

"You'll see."

Warily, she unfolded the sheet. It was a colour photograph of a beautiful little chapel sitting right by the ocean.

St Mary's by the Sea. Port Douglas, Queensland.

Idyllic location, perfect for weddings.

Make your special day another day in paradise.

Zane tucked her hair behind her ears. "Want to invite the family up north for a wedding?"

He'd remembered.

For a moment she was dumbstruck. Her hand had frozen, and the sheet of paper slipped and dropped to the floor. Had fate intervened again? She tried to close her gaping mouth.

It only took a split second, but then *everything* slotted into place. She no longer had a decision to make. This was the nudge she'd needed.

Finding movement possible again, she closed her mouth, snuggled up to the man she loved and tucked her face against his. She reached up and wrapped her arms around his neck. Contentment spread through her as she tangled her feet with his.

When she lifted her face and rested it on his chest, she smiled. "I'd be honoured to have my father walk me down the aisle. And I don't doubt he'll also be more than happy to cover the expense of relocating the family north." She chuckled. "I have a feeling he'll be desperate that I accept his apology. This way he can earn it."

Her terms were mean-spirited, yes, but it was impossible to completely lay to rest the turmoil her father had put her through. She might forgive him one day, but it wouldn't happen overnight. She'd seen him at his worst and now he had to work hard to show his better side, in much the same way that she had to change her impulsive and impatient ways. If she could one day accept her father with all his faults, then she would know she'd done her best.

If there was anything to be learned from her stay in Boston, it was that being angry hurt all the time. She'd suffered from the constant tug of anger and hate, and had finally dealt with it by pushing it aside. The alternative had been to risk damaging her life. That sort of hate created a domino effect—it touched everyone around her. By managing it, she was succeeding in keeping those she loved close, and she desperately wanted to keep Zane close, for a very long time.

Zane's eyebrows rose, probably at her audacity, before he succumbed to a fit of laughter loud enough to wake Victoria next door.

Ella joined in, and it wasn't long before Zane nudged his hands underneath her shirt and started doing what he'd intended all along, noise and all.

THANKS FOR READING

Thank you for reading Little Blue Box. I hope you enjoyed it and continue reading the stories of Ella's step siblings. Set in Queensland, you'll recognise town names and places, along with our dusty outback and our refreshing rainforest.

Readers often ask me where my ideas come from. Sometimes it's a thought that germinates into some much bigger. In this case, the idea of a mother disappearing with her baby and changing her identity, and then being discovered many years later, was an actual news item I heard on the news one night. The reason for the mother leaving I can't quite remember, but that doesn't matter because as a fiction writer, this is where the fun begins. A story such as this can make for quite a complicated family, but it gives a writer a smorgasbord of characters to write about.

The Australian at Heart series does just that. First Ella, who was born in Boston but raised in Australia. Then Ella's newly discovered step siblings. I drag them out of Boston and weave a story for them in an Australian setting. These stories are heart-warming, emotional, passionate, and come with a happy ending. It just may take some heartache to get there.

There are many people to thank along the way. Firstly, Alicia Hope Author, for making the suggestion at the very start to join Romance Writers of Australia. This one act put my writing career on the right path. Through their critique matching program, I was paired with fellow newbie member, Lisa Stanbridge Author and we clicked from the very first chapter we exchanged. To this day we continue to exchange chapters every week. It truly is a match made in writer's heaven.

My mum deserves a special mention. An avid reader herself, my love of reading and writing comes from her. She's waited patiently for this first published book, so here it is, Mum. Then there are my three daughters. Always supportive and never afraid to voice their opinion about something I've written. Bless you. To my other half. I know he wishes he had someone to talk to when I'm huddled in my corner doing my thing. It's a damn lonely life being married to a writer! But still, I'm grateful he doesn't care how little dust I clean off the furniture or how rushed dinner is.

And finally, a big thank you to you my readers. Thank you for supporting this Australian author.

ALSO BY FRANCES DALL'ALBA

The **Australian at Heart Series** tells the stories of four interconnected siblings.

<u>Little Blue Box – Book 1</u>

Regrets, lies, and earth-shattering secrets. When Ella learns the identity of her biological father, nothing will stand in her way. Not even his power. When things don't go to plan, can one little blue box put Ella and Zane back on the same path? This second chance contemporary romance is filled with suspense, emotion and a life-changing sizzling romance.

<u>The Stone In The Road – Book 2</u>

Emotional, passionate and heart-wrenching. This suspense-filled captivating romance will have you dancing in the rain and smiling through your tears. Set in tropical northern Australia, we don't always get to choose our path.

<u>**The Silk Scarf – Book 3**</u>

An unravelling silken scarf … mysterious gold … a breathtaking romance.
An emotional and unforgettable contemporary romance set in Australia.

<u>**Rustic Denim Love – Book 4**</u>

Forgotten secrets … blazing fires … burning love.
She's busy and diligent, doing the best she can to save her crumbling family.
He's funny and witty, with a solution for every problem.
This one may just beat him.

Link to read more and BUY.
https://francesdallalba.wixsite.com/francesdallalba/australianathe artseries

<u>**The Priceless Star – Book 4**</u>

Forgotten treasures … a perilous ransom … shattered hopes

She's chasing answers long buried since the war.

He's content with a steady working life. Until he's not...

Sent to Far North Queensland to research a wartime mystery, Lucia Levorico escapes her privileged life and finds unexpected passion with reserved local, Theo Mather, under an outback sky – until a sudden goodbye and a devastating worksite tragedy tear them apart. When a ruthless ransom plot targets Lucia's wealth, their only reprieve will come from sharing the unravelling of a wartime mystery and its priceless treasure. Unless they're willing to fight for what they have.

<u>Link to read more and BUY</u>.

https://francesdallalba.wixsite.com/francesdallalba/swayof the stars

Eight Seconds, is a standalone story inspired by Australia's first female open bullrider. She pushed past the barriers and succeeded in a male dominated sport, creating a new legend showcased in two Australian halls of fame.

Triumph, hardship, true grit ... and one crazy dream.
An inspirational story about one woman, with one dream, and one almighty driving passion.

Link to read more and BUY.
https://francesdallalba.wixsite.com/francesdalla lba/eightseconds

Jack& Eva, is a standalone contemporary romance set in tropical North Queensland. It showcases our unique and adorable Lumholtz tree kangaroo and the valuable work done by Dr Karen Coombes in her care and continued research of them.

Broody meets bubbly ... and a bunch of cuddly tree kangaroos.
When the tempest blows over, will Jack and Eva be able to find a way forward, or are they destined for a train wreck with a bunch of furry animals caught up in the middle?
Fall in love with our adorable tree kangaroo while reading an emotional and passionate contemporary romance set in Australia.
Link to read more and BUY.
https://francesdallalba.wixsite.com/francesdallalba/jackandeva

ABOUT THE AUTHOR

As a contemporary romance author, Frances loves nothing more than losing herself in a good romance. She's all about helping you forget the housework, or the bus to work you're going to miss, if you don't put the book down now!

She's devoted to giving her readers an emotional, passionate, possibly some ugly-cry, fairly steamy love story, that'll melt your heart and have you fighting for the happy ending right until the end.

Frances sets her books in North Queensland. She makes no excuses if some of her settings include amazing lakes and waterfalls, stunning views from tops of mountains, spectacular outback scenes, or crystal-clear creeks shadowed by tropical rainforest.

When she isn't writing, Frances is climbing mountains, searching for waterfalls and swimming across lakes. She loves to exercise, would prefer it if someone else cooked dinner every night, and never notices dust on the furniture.

She lives with her husband in tropical Far North Queensland, Australia, and uses her great baking skills to tempt her family to visit home often.

Say hello to Frances

Visit her website: https://francesdallalba.wixsite.com/francesdallalba and subscribe to her newsletter. It will keep you up-to-date with everything happening in her author world.

Follow Frances on Facebook, Instagram, Bookbub, TikTok, and Goodreads. To do so, click on this link: https://linktr.ee/francesdallalba

Still have a question?

Ask her at: https://francesdallalba.wixsite.com/francesdallalba/contact

<u>**Leave a Review**</u>

Did you enjoy this book? The best favour you can do for an author is to leave a **review**. If you'd like to leave a review, go to your place of on-line purchase of the book, or search for the book on **Goodreads** and leave a review. Thank you.